MALICE IN
WONDERLAND

Also by HP Mallory:

THE JOLIE WILKINS SERIES:

Fire Burn and Cauldron Bubble
Toil and Trouble
Be Witched (Novella)
Witchful Thinking
The Witch Is Back
Something Witchy This Way Comes

Stay Tuned For The Jolie Wilkins Spinoff Series!

THE DULCIE O'NEIL SERIES:

To Kill A Warlock
A Tale Of Two Goblins
Great Hexpectations
Wuthering Frights
Malice In Wonderland
For Whom The Spell Tolls

THE LILY HARPER SERIES:

Better Off Dead

MALICE IN WONDERLAND

Book 5 of the Dulcie O'Neil series

HP Mallory

MALICE IN WONDERLAND

by

H.P. Mallory

For Finn

Acknowledgements:

To my mother: Thank you for everything.

To my editor, Teri, at www.editingfairy.com:
Thank you for always doing such a great job!

To my husband:
I love you.

To my son, Finn: I am so proud to be your mama.

To all my beta readers, thank you so much for all
your help!

To the winner of my "become a character in my
next book" contest,
Erica Comacho: Congratulations and I hope you
enjoy your character!

To Lacie Soule:
Thank you so much for entering the contest to
name this book and thank you so much for coming
up with such a fantastic title!

ONE

There have only been a handful of moments in my life where I've been struck speechless.

And this was one of those moments. Why? Because Christina Sabbiondo, a woman who was involved in the illegal potions trade, had just informed me that she was also the head of The Resistance. As you can probably deduce from the group's title, The Resistance existed to do just that—resist potion trafficking from The Netherworld and, more pointedly, resist the tyranny of the Head of the Netherworld.

Coincidentally, the Head of the Netherworld also happens to be my father. Lucky me.

"What?" I managed to blurt out, shaking my head as I wondered if maybe I'd just hallucinated the last three hours of my life. I mean, in the past one hundred eighty minutes, I'd managed to foil my father's attempts to introduce an incredibly addictive and even more easily spread narcotic into my neighborhood, I'd nearly been raped by a Titan, only to watch my very recently ex-boyfriend put a bullet through said Titan's forehead. As romantic as that might sound, my ex-boyfriend then arrested me because I was working for my father; (I'm really not a bad person—I was forced into it); and after an exhaustive conversation where I tried to prove my innocence, and he tried to prove my guilt, I found myself behind bars. Then, just like that, Ms. Sabbiondo walked back into my life, professing my innocence, and now here I was.

Christina smiled broadly, her doe-like, brown eyes dancing with merriment—as if she'd been dying to tell me all along that she never really was one of the baddies—that she and I were playing on the same team. And I had to admit that somewhere inside myself, I was rejoicing. Why?

Because I'd always liked Christina. Not only was she a fellow Jeep owner, but she was also one of a select number of fairies (just like me), so how could I not like her?

"Dulcie, I'm on your side," she said, the smile dropping from her lips as she took my hand and faced me earnestly.

"But," I started, still not understanding how that could be, my brain not functioning on all eight cylinders. "But how did you ... You worked for my father for six years!"

She nodded. "Yes I did, but that isn't to say that I was happy working for him. The Resistance has been a long time coming, Dulcie. It just took a while for people to realize we couldn't continue living under your father's iron rule. It took us five years to develop The Resistance, to organize ourselves and devise a way out of everything your father envisioned, as well as everything he stands for." She paused to take a deep breath and I was suddenly overcome with feelings of admiration for her. It couldn't have been easy to form The Resistance, and its success spoke of her own personal strength. "It's been a long and difficult five years, Dulcie, but we are stronger than ever before and fully ready to fight."

I gulped, wondering how long it was going to take me to process all of this. "And my father has no idea that you've been involved in The Resistance all along," I continued, amazed that she'd been able to keep her double life from my father, Melchior O'Neil, while working in such close proximity with him. If nothing else, my father was a shrewd businessman and careful, well, as far as I could tell anyway. Apparently he wasn't careful enough.

"I imagine he's got a pretty good idea about where my loyalty lies now," she said and that pretty smile returned to her lips. Yep, right about now Daddy Dearest had to be waking up to the fact that not only did his daughter thwart his nefarious plans to introduce the illegal potion *Draoidheil* onto the streets of Splendor, Moon, Haven, and Estuary, but was helped by his pet, Christina. Right about now my father had to be suffering a very rude awakening.

I heard the sound of someone clearing his throat and remembered that Knight was standing beside (well, more like towering over) Christina, a witness to everything that had just passed between us. Knightley Vander, aka very recently ex-boyfriend, was also part of The Resistance and as far as I could tell, he was now doing a damned good job of resisting the idea that I was anything but guilty of potions smuggling. His eyes were burning with ire, and the normally beautiful blue of his irises was ablaze.

And that was when it hit me that Knight had been aware of who my father was from the moment he'd met me. In fact, Knight assumed I was working for my father all along. His sole purpose in coming to Splendor was to beat my father at his own game, with me as an expendable pawn. Somewhere along the way though, I managed to convince him I wasn't a soulless potions smuggler, (which was the Hades-honest truth!) and he subsequently fell in love with me. Likewise, I fell in love with him.

At this precise moment, however, feelings of love were not first and foremost in my mind. Instead, I was livid over the fact that Knight had always known who my father was and yet he'd kept it from me. Knight had been concealing an agenda from me all along and that was what hurt the most. Well, the fact that he was now accusing me of something of which I was completely innocent smarted almost as bad. But the biggest kicker of this whole screwed-up situation was that I'd basically sold my soul to the proverbial devil in order to keep Knight safe. I'd put myself on the line to protect him ... and for what?

I inhaled deeply, telling myself to ignore my anger, and let it simmer on the back burner because Knight wasn't my biggest concern at the moment. No, I had far bigger fish to fry.

I watched Christina as she faced Knight and shook her head, as if discouraging his foul mood and inability to believe I was anything but guilty.

"We're moving everyone to Compound Three," she said in a matter-of-fact tone. I assumed she meant the other two prisoners Knight had already taken into custody, Horatio and my ex-boss, Quillan. "We're going to move forward with Plan B," she finished, facing Knight squarely before adding: "You can drive her, or I can."

"I'll go with you," I interrupted, glancing at Christina as Knight continued to scrutinize me. Yep, I had way too many conflicting emotions regarding Knight to try to deal with him at the moment.

"Christina," Knight started, his baritone rich and velvety. I felt something catch in my throat, but swallowed it down as I reminded myself now was not the time to bemoan my ruined relationship. No, now I needed to focus on our next steps, on planning a strategy to defeat my father. I needed to learn everything I could about The Resistance.

Christina glanced at him and started for the door. Her lips were tight as she narrowed her eyes. "Call Caressa, and find out for yourself, will you?" Then she turned on her heel, and opening the door, walked into the early morning sunlight.

I'd never heard of Compound Three so wasn't sure where we were headed, but I also couldn't say I cared. Instead, I found my attention riveted outside as we drove down Highway One in a dark grey Chevy Suburban. Ordinarily Christina sported a black Jeep Wrangler, so I guessed this vehicle was courtesy of The Resistance and, as such, probably untraceable. The more I thought about it, the more I had to wonder if The Resistance had lots in common with the CIA.

Knight followed us in a black Yukon Denali, an SUV which had already left a lasting impression on me considering what Knight and I had done in it ... or, rather, on it. But that was another sore subject I wasn't ready to deal with yet.

At any rate, Knight was tasked with transporting Horatio and Quillan. Both would remain in custody due to their associations with my father. I could have given a rat's ass about Horatio but Quillan was another story.

Quillan Beaurigard was originally the Head of the ANC (Association of Netherworld Creatures) Splendor branch, before Knight replaced him. I initially reported to Quill in my position as ANC Regulator (think law enforcement agent), and he and I became pretty tight. Learning that Quill was working for my father during our entire acquaintance was a hard pill to swallow. Almost as hard as me working for my father. But Quill's reasons for serving as my father's right-hand man were very different to mine. While Quill performed his role in quiet desperation, I never did. I never stopped planning my escape and I never, not even for one second, accepted my fate. Truth be told, I didn't do well with ultimatums.

The only reason I ever agreed to obey my father's bidding was because I was forced into it. Yep, I'd been stuck between a rock and a hard place because my father held Knight's life for ransom, promising to kill him if I didn't do as he demanded. Thus, I managed to lead a double life for the last few weeks as both an illegal potions importer, and a Regulator for the ANC.

I felt a sigh escape my lips and focused on the rolling hills outside my window. The splotchy greens of the quilt-like hillsides peppered here and there by sheep or cows were mesmerizing. There was a slight chill in the air, but judging by the lack of clouds in the sky, I figured it would end up another warm California day.

"He'll come around," Christina said softly, offering me an understanding smile. Of course, she was referring to my destroyed relationship, but I remained steadfast in my decision not to think about the infuriatingly stubborn Loki, a creature forged from the fires of the Netherworld god, Hades, and created in Hades's own brawny, large, and stunningly gorgeous image.

"Maybe and maybe not," I responded, taking a deep breath. "But we have lots of way more important stuff to discuss."

"You're right." Christina glanced over at me with a quick nod as we exited Highway One and took a right on Frontier Street, then an immediate left onto an unmarked dirt road. There was a fence and locked gate blocking our path, but Christina didn't seem fazed. Instead, she put the Suburban in park, hopped down and unlocked the padlock, opening the gate wide. She nodded her head at Knight, who pulled up just behind us. Then she jumped back into the driver's seat, put the car in drive and started forward again.

"So all along, you were plotting against my father?" I asked in awe, wanting to understand how The Resistance started. I noticed she hadn't stopped to lock the gate again so I figured Knight must have.

Christina's jaw was tight as her fingers closed around the steering wheel. "Yes. From the moment I was forced into working for him."

"Then that story you told me about him recruiting you as a college student," I started, remembering a conversation we'd had in which Christina said how she met my father in the first place.

"Was all true," she finished. "Well, except for the part about me being okay with it. I was never okay with it."

"So I guess we were both keeping our cards close to our chests," I said, remembering that neither of us trusted the other in the earliest days of our acquaintanceship.

She glanced at me and nodded before returning her attention to the empty road before us. "I wanted to believe you were innocent," she started and then shrugged. "I liked you right off the bat." Before I could respond, she shook her head and laughed as she added, "To this day, I have never met a Jeep owner I didn't like."

I laughed, amused that we really did think alike. But the laugh soon died on my lips as I returned to my line of questioning. "So my father bribed you into working for him and you started thinking of a way out. How did Knight figure into it?"

She was quiet for a few seconds. "I never really knew Knight well. I'd heard of him, of course. I mean, everyone in the ANC knows who Knightley Vander is—his reputation definitely precedes him." She smiled and shook her head, making it pretty clear that she was fond of Knight. I didn't think it was in a romantic sort of way though, more like he was her big brother or something. "When Knight had that altercation with your father and got deported to Splendor, I made it a point to get to know him. Knight was a tough one, though, because he knew who I was and, of course, whom I worked for."

"I'll bet."

"But once I mentioned The Resistance and Caressa vouched for me, he was in. After that, things really started rolling." She smiled at me then. "Knight has single-handedly done more for The Resistance than anyone else."

I nodded, proud of the Loki, while at the same time, still livid with him. "So you and Caressa are tight?"

She didn't pull her eyes from the road. "Very."

"And let me guess, she must have told you I was innocent, which was why you just bailed me out?"

It felt like my teeth were chattering in my head as we drove over a cattle crossing grid. I had no idea where we were; I wasn't familiar with this side of town.

"Yep," Christina replied. "Caressa told me about how you got suckered into working for Melchior and only ever agreed to it in order to protect Knight. And, of course, she also told me about your little flower delivery stunt." Then she glanced over at me and her eyes were wide with mirth. "By the way, she says you look terrible as a brunette."

Christina was referring to the time when I had to change my appearance in order to visit Caressa in the Netherworld, so I posed as a flower delivery person. I secretly told Caressa everything I could about the *Draoidheil* delivery in order to ensure it went off with as many hitches as possible.

I shook my head as I laughed. "Well you can tell her that her left hook needs a little work."

Christina gave me an expression of "what are you talking about?"

"When I was in the Netherworld the first time around, I managed to talk Caressa into releasing me so I could try to free Knight from High Prison. We knew we needed an alibi to get anyone to believe us. So we came up with the story that I'd overpowered her and escaped. Then we figured a few punches should be thrown in for good measure."

"Ah," Christina said, nodding as if she were now on the same page.

"Speaking of Caressa," I continued, "you told Knight to call her earlier. How are you able to keep in touch with her? I'm sure my father has all the phone lines to and from the Netherworld tapped?"

We hit another cattle grid and the entire Suburban vibrated, but Christina didn't seem to notice. "Yep, that he does. He always has—and he's good about monitoring all calls, especially those of his high ranking employees." She raised her eyebrows. "Paranoia anyone?"

I smiled, but my mind was still on my unanswered question. "So?"

"All of us have separate, untraceable phones for Resistance business only. The phones are bewitched and if any of us are on a call, the frequency gets scrambled so no one can pick up on our conversations. The phones continue to change color and shape so they are never identifiable, again through witch magic."

I nodded, impressed. "Seems you've got all your bases covered."

She took a deep breath. "We try."

"So Caressa is in The Resistance, then?" I continued, wondering how many people we could rely on in the Netherworld.

"No, she isn't, but that's merely because it's too dangerous for her to be."

"But you," I started, finding it hard to see how Christina could have been in The Resistance for five years, during which time she also reported to my father, and not consider *that* the very definition of dangerous.

She shook her head with a charming smile. "I'm a daredevil by nature. I not only look for trouble, but welcome it wholeheartedly."

I just laughed, suddenly overcome by the sensation of my strength returning. The void that had been devouring me for the last few weeks was now filling up. It felt as if a huge weight was being lifted from my shoulders, as ridiculous as it sounds. Yes, I absolutely realized what I was now up against, what we were all now up against. But even though our future was far from secure, my improved energy gave me a newly found sense of hope. I had to admit it made me ecstatic to finally be fighting the fight I was destined for. Even though I was now facing a whole new set of obstacles, I was free. I was no longer an indentured servant to the whims of my father. I was now my own person again and it made me want to sing.

'Course, any songs within me were forgotten as soon as I remembered the threat embodied by Melchior O'Neil. My father was a tyrant and delusional, yes; but worse still, he had the entire Netherworld at his disposal. That included ANC officials in the Netherworld, people who were armed and very dangerous. I just had to hope that all Netherworld creatures who lived on Earth were on the side of The Resistance.

"But Caressa is still an ally?" I continued, needing to know exactly how she fit into this picture.

"Very much so. She feeds us information whenever she can, but I'm sure her hands are going to be tied now. We can't rely on Caressa from here on out, Dulcie. She's in the thick of it and it could mean her life."

I nodded, realizing Christina was right. At the same time, I also bemoaned the fact that we'd basically just lost our most powerful ally. "And Gabriel?" I continued, remembering Knight's friend who helped me while I was in the Netherworld.

Christina shook her head. "We're on our own," she said simply as she depressed the accelerator and maneuvered over the rocky terrain, coughing up a billowing cloud of dust behind us and obscuring the Denali.

"How many are in The Resistance?" I asked, my mind racing with myriad questions.

"A few hundred," she responded immediately, braking to ten miles per hour as she took an especially sharp turn.

"And how many support my father in the Netherworld?"

She cocked her head to the side as she thought about it. "We're about neck and neck."

I narrowed my eyes. "I thought the population in the Netherworld was much larger than the population of Netherworld creatures here?"

"It is, but I'm just talking Netherworldians who might be considered a threat. Most of the creatures in the Netherworld don't fight. Most of them are just too scared to resist your father, but that doesn't mean they don't want to see him overthrown." She paused for a second or two before facing me and I didn't miss her description of my father being "overthrown," as if he were a king. For all intents and purposes, he *had* basically appointed himself sovereign. "That's not to say that your father isn't a threat. For as many that don't support him, an equal number do and then some."

"You're preaching to the choir," I said, sighing. "I know exactly how dangerous my father is."

I didn't say anything more, but watched her downshift as we crested the top of an incredibly steep hill. It was so steep, I couldn't even see the road beneath us as we started down the other side. "So what was Plan B?" I asked, remembering Christina telling Knight we were moving forward with our second plan.

She took a deep breath and concentrated on driving, never taking her eyes from the road. "The portals to the Netherworld are all being closed and guards are on duty to prohibit anyone from coming or going."

"And the secret portals?" There were two types of portals that connected the Netherworld to Earth—public portals, which basically acted like airports; and the not so public portals which Melchior used to traffic his illegal potions.

"All portals," she said simply.

"So if there are Melchior supporters here?" I started but she quickly interrupted me.

"They stay here; and likewise, anyone supporting us in the Netherworld stays there."

"So what about spies and moles? I'm sure Melchior has his special touch points?"

"Melchior has plenty of touch points here, as you're well aware. In answer to that, we've had to do a lot of profiling of all Netherworld creatures here on Earth. Those deemed a threat to The Resistance were incarcerated."

"So all the Horatios and Barons of the world?"

"Are either locked up or ... dead," she said with a smile. Baron was the Titan I'd referred to earlier—the one Knight shot through the forehead. "Anyone who isn't loyal to our movement must be taken into custody," she finished.

"If they aren't with you, they're against you?"

"Something like that."

We reached the base of the steep hill and she took a right onto another unmarked road, this one overgrown with weeds. "If I didn't know better, I'd say you were planning on killing me and leaving my body where no one would ever find it," I said with a slight laugh as I glanced outside the window.

Christina cocked a brow in my direction. "Good thing for you that you know better."

I laughed, trying to relax into my chair as I digested all the information I'd just learned. I suddenly felt exhausted down to my core, probably because I hadn't slept well in the last month. I wasn't about to start feeling sorry for myself though. Instead, I focused on how impressed I was—impressed with Christina and The Resistance in general. I'd imagined this Resistance was kind of a grass roots type of organization. But truth be told, they were more advanced and well organized than I'd previously given them credit for. "So what happens next?"

Christina put the car in park and I glanced forward, realizing we were facing the side of a mountain. She smiled, reaching for a garage door opener which was attached to the visor in front of her. She depressed the largest button and the mountain simply opened in half, two doors separating as if it were a garage made to look like a mountainside. When the doors opened, they revealed another dirt road. It led into what appeared to be a compound. The barbed wire fencing and nondescript, white buildings were the first clue.

"What is this?" I asked, looking around myself as I wondered how all of this could have existed, yet I never had any idea about it.

"Welcome to Compound Three," Christina answered with a smile as she moved forward again."It's one of four training bases and prisons." She glanced behind us and saluted to Knight, apparently motioning him forward. Then she faced me again. "Remember how I told you we had lots of people in custody?"

"Here?" I asked, unable to suppress my surprise.

"Yep," she answered, motioning to the Denali behind us with her hand. "This will be Horatio and Quillan's last stop as well."

And on that point, I felt my good humor deflate. Of course, Christina didn't know Quill as anything besides Melchior's right-hand man, but I knew he was so much more than that. I could only wonder if, given the option of joining The Resistance against Melchior, what choice Quill would make. Figuring that was a subject for a later day, I decided to shelve it—right next to the Knight-is-being-an-asshole conversation that was still simmering on the back burner.

I glanced around myself, intent on studying my surroundings in order to distract my thoughts. Razor-sharp wire topped the fences around the compound and I found myself facing three square, asphalt yards. A group of ten or so people jogged by us, led by a werewolf who was yelling orders. Inside the three yards, people were either sparring in hand-to-hand combat, or if they were inclined, magical combat. The second yard revealed people lifting weights; and the last had some sort of obstacle course. Seeing them, I felt like I just enlisted in boot camp.

"You guys sure have been busy," I said in surprised awe, bringing my eyes back to Christina.

She nodded and crossed her arms against her chest, wearing the expression of someone proud. "Yep, you could definitely say that."

TWO

After a tour of Compound Three, I was even more impressed with The Resistance. They were following the lead of the US military and training civilians who, I imagined, could rival any soldiers found in the Netherworld. 'Course, I didn't know much about the military, but I could say The Resistance seemed as though they knew what they were doing, based on their incredible sense of organization, dedication, and perseverance, as well as their infallible sense of discipline. It probably didn't hurt that The Resistance had also recruited a major general from the Air Force (who happened to be a goblin), a lieutenant colonel from the Army (an orc), and a captain from the Marines (an elf) to lead their soldiers. And that was just at this camp.

As far as Compound Three's prisoners were concerned, there were easily fifty or more Melchior O'Neil supporters already in custody, enjoying life behind bars. As I made my way through the prison, Christina heading the tour, I recognized the majority of the prisoners. They were all thugs who were somehow involved in the illegal potions trade. When we finished viewing the relatively small prison (there were only about twenty or so cells), I followed Christina into the front room again. Knight led Horatio and Quill into a nearby cell, which was already occupied by a gnome. He was busily making obscene gestures at Christina and me. I watched Knight's gaze fall on me and he swallowed hard. Since his eyes no longer looked like lethal weapons, I could only imagine he'd lost some of his anger. Maybe he *had* made that phone call to Caressa after all; and now was realizing what a complete and total asshole he'd been to me.

Not dealing with this now! I reminded myself as I immediately glanced away. Instead, I watched Quillan following Horatio into the cell. Quill's shoulders were slumped forward, and as the prison guard released the cuffs from around his wrists, and the manacles at his feet, he massaged his wrists as if the heavy metal had rubbed them raw. He looked up, and upon noticing me, immediately smiled. It was a smile that said he was happy to know I was safe and, better yet, free. It was a smile that said he didn't blame me for blowing the cover of the *Draoidheil* mission and, consequently, landing him behind bars. No, instead, he was proud of me. I could read it clearly in his eyes and the way he nodded at me in silent acknowledgement.

"Christina," I started, turning toward her. If I were going to say something regarding Quill's predicament, I needed to say it now. No time like the present ...

She stopped walking and faced me, curiosity in her eyes. I motioned to Quill and cleared my throat. "I've known Quillan for a very long time," I said as I sidestepped her, aiming for an unoccupied hallway on my right. This conversation required some privacy and I couldn't say I felt comfortable under Knight's scrutiny. Besides, that damned gnome was still making lewd gestures with his fingers while undulating his tiny hips, the little bastard.

"And," Christina prodded as she glanced over at the gnome, lifting an unimpressed eyebrow and shaking her head before following me into the hallway.

I stopped walking, once we were out of eavesdropping range, and took a deep breath as I faced her squarely. "And he was duped into working for my father the same as you and I were."

I couldn't read Christina's response; apparently, she was good at concealing her emotions. Wanting to give her adequate time to process my statement, I glanced over at the handsome elf, who did his best to separate himself from his prison comrades. Now he stood in the corner of the cell with his arms crossed against his chest as he regarded us. And he wasn't the only one who was eyeing our every move. I could feel Knight's eyes on me, but I refused to look his way. Instead, I focused on Quill.

I had always considered Quill a friend. Well, that is, up until I discovered he was working for the bad guys. But life does work in strange ways because once I'd been forced into the same predicament, I found it easier to forgive him and call him my friend again. In actuality, he was the only friend I had while working in my father's employ. And once I was forced into the same situation as Quill, I saw him in a different, and far less damning light. I guess it is true what they say about walking in someone else's shoes ...

"This isn't him. He's a good person," I continued, glancing at Christina again.

Her eyes were hard and unforgiving. "He's been Melchior's yes-man for as long as I've known him, Dulcie."

I nodded and sighed, realizing this was going to be a difficult argument to win. "I know that's how it looks, but I've also worked side-by-side with him for nine years. We were close, Christina. And in nine years, you get to know someone pretty damn well."

"And yet you never knew this side of him existed until recently," she finished, her lips a straight line.

"That's true, but I can also tell you that Quill never would have chosen this path for himself. The only reason he did was because he had no alternative." I swallowed. "Think about it ... if my father was successful in forcing you to work for him, anyone could be forced into it. You know that as well as I do."

She was quiet for a few seconds, but nodded, exhaling deeply. "You missed your calling. You should have been a lawyer." Then she eyed me askance.

I smiled, hoping I was on my way to winning the argument, hoping she'd soon raise her white flag of surrender. "I don't know; I've been told I make one damned good Regulator."

She laughed, but soon the laugh died on her lips and her expression was solemn. "So what do you propose we do?"

I glanced over at Knight who stood a few paces behind us, his large arms folded across his chest and his expression stern. He'd been watching us the entire time and his eyes were still narrowed on me, a void of impenetrable blue. His expression was impossible to read.

I faced Christina again. "I think we need to give Quillan the option of joining our cause."

She laughed lightly as if I'd just made a joke, but then speared me with her eyes, making me feel all of four years old. "Have you joined our cause, then?"

I was surprised and a little taken aback. I already assumed I was now a part of The Resistance. From the moment Christina granted me my freedom, I'd thought I was on board with her cause. "I thought that was understood?"

"You never said yea or nay," she answered, her tone serious. I opened my mouth to say "Yea" wholeheartedly, but she beat me to it. "I hope you realize this is no light matter. If you join us, you will be doing so at risk of your life."

I shook my head as though risking my life weren't a biggie. If the truth be told, I'd been risking my life ever since I first signed up as a Regulator, nine years ago. This was just another walk in a very familiar park. "I'm already living on borrowed time. If I don't join you, I'm a renegade. It's not as though my father would ever take me back and, furthermore, I would never go back." I took a breath. "If I don't join your cause, I'll have to start my own."

She laughed. "Then I guess I should say, welcome aboard." Her laugh died as she turned to consider Quillan, who was leaning against the prison bars, still maintaining his distance from Horatio and the gnome. "As to Quillan, he's still a big risk, as far as I'm concerned."

I nodded, knowing how much of a risk Quill appeared to be. But I trusted him and I would fight for him. Why?

Because at the end of the day, I did consider Quillan my friend and if there was one thing I believed in wholeheartedly, it was protecting those who were close to me. It was only fair and right to give him the option to choose the correct path, to clean his slate, and start over. I would fight to allow Quill the chance he hadn't been offered fifteen years ago when he was first recruited into my father's band of thieves. And I earnestly believed that whatever decision Quill made, he would stick by it. Call me idealistic or just plain stupid, but I believed in Quillan. "All I'm asking is that we give him the option to join us. If he decides to continue to support my father, he stays right where he is—sitting behind bars."

"And if he decides to join us?"

I held my chin high and returned her barbed gaze. "Then we forgive and forget." I didn't hesitate, didn't even blink. "Everyone deserves a second chance, Christina. I know Quill well and I promise you, this isn't the life he envisioned for himself. He's been as much a victim as you and I have."

She was quiet as she faced Quill again, studying him in a detached sort of way. She turned her attention away from him after another few seconds and settled her studious expression on me, the drama of whether or not to trust me playing out on her face.

"He will be your responsibility," she said finally. "If something happens and he maintains his ties to Melchior, it's your head on the chopping block. One mistake, and you both will be taken into Resistance custody."

I nodded, feeling relieved right down to my feet. "I'm willing to take that chance."

"Then go," she said, motioning to the cell holding Quillan. "And while you're at it, tell him what a lucky bastard he is."

"Thank you, Christina," I answered. I turned on the ball of my foot and hurried down the hallway. I could feel Knight's gaze on me as I made my way to Quill's cell. Out of the corner of my eye, I watched Knight immediately ask Christina what was going on, and his face took on a definite reddish hue when he got his answer. He grumbled something about this being "unbelievable," but I couldn't say I cared. Nope, this could just be another instance added to the long list of things Knight had done to seriously piss me off. And the time was fast approaching when I would grant my full attention to that list.

"Dulce?" Quill asked as he neared the prison cells, wrapping his hands around them. "Are you okay? Are you hurt?" He took a breath. "Did they release you?"

"Yes, I'm fine," I replied hurriedly as I summoned the energy to relate my news. "Quill, I was able to talk Christina into giving you a second chance."

His eyebrows knotted as he studied me, his amber eyes beautiful in the low light. And all of a sudden, I remembered how I used to feel about Quillan—how I'd always admired him and, more so, had a strange sort of crush on him. Granted, those feelings were now dead and buried, but the glint in his eyes somehow took me back to another time, when Quill and I were in a very different situation than now, an innocent time that we could never again return to.

"What do you mean?" he asked, his tone soft, exhausted, and, sadly, defeated.

"You have to make a decision, Quill," I responded sternly, hoping in the depths of my soul that he would choose the right path, and take me up on my offer so he could turn his life around. More than anything, I hoped I was right about him—that deep down, he wasn't my father's yes-man. Because the truth of it was: if he did decide to continue to support my father, I could no longer be his friend. Being a victim of circumstances I could understand, but once you were offered salvation and the chance to no longer play the part of the victim, the time for empathy was over.

"What are you talking about, Dulcie?" he asked.

"You have to decide, here and now, whether you want to emancipate yourself from my father and join The

Resistance, or continue serving him, in which case, you'll remain incarcerated." I took a breath. "I am giving you the option to join The Resistance, Quill, and to join me."

He was quiet as he nodded and it felt like years passed as I awaited his response. "Whatever you decide, there is no going back," I continued as I prayed he would make the right decision. "This is your chance to clean your slate," I added. "This is your chance to turn back time and make everything right again." I paused for a few seconds. "My father won't be able to lay claim to you anymore, Quill. You can be free again."

But when his eyes dropped to the floor and he sighed heavily, I felt my heart plummet and the breath catch in my throat. He glanced up at me, his eyes unreadable. "Dulcie, there is no choice to make." He sounded beaten, conquered.

Something within me broke.

How could he still maintain his allegiance to my father? After everything he'd been through, everything we'd been through? How could he make this choice?

"Okay," I started, the timbre in my voice angry. I pushed away from the prison bars and was about to turn around and leave, in favor of some fresh air; but before I could, he stopped me.

"I choose you," he said resolutely, his eyes more serious than I'd ever seen them. "And I will always choose you from here on out."

I swallowed back the anger that moments before had been plaguing me and felt a smile break across my lips. I knew the old Quill was in there somewhere. There was still the flame of a fight left within him, smoldering in the ashes of defeat and subjugation. And that was good enough for me because every conflagration started with the smallest spark. My smile broadened and I felt the fires of my own determination and resistance being stoked within me. "Will you join The Resistance, Quill? Will you stand up with me against my father?" I wrapped my fingers around the prison bars.

His lips were tight as he encircled my fingers with his own. His eyes were piercing, never leaving mine and he suddenly seemed years younger. The downcast strain in his features seemed to melt before me as his strength returned to his gaze and the line of his eyebrows. The Quillan I'd always known was back.

He nodded. "Yes."

I didn't say anything, but held his gaze, and releasing the prison bars, I took both of his hands instead and squeezed them tightly. Moments later, I dropped them and turned toward Christina, eager to tell her of his decision, but his voice grabbed my attention again.

"Dulcie?"

I faced him and felt his eyes boring straight through me.

"Thank you," he said softly.

I didn't respond, but started up the hallway, my gaze resting on Christina. Knight was still standing beside her, his arms still crossed against his chest and his eyes still following my every move. It was more than obvious that he'd watched everything that had just taken place between Quill and me, and he didn't look happy about it. But I didn't care. I forced myself not to care.

"He's in," I said simply. I watched as Christina merely nodded and started toward me, the cell key in her hand. Knight shook his head and clasped his hands behind his head as he cracked his knuckles in the process and sighed deeply. I glared at him before returning my attention to Christina as she passed me and walked to Quill's cell.

"I don't know what you think you're …" Knight started and I turned to find him directly before me.

"I don't see how this is any of your business," I interrupted snidely and propped my hands on my hips, summoning all the willpower I possessed not to deck him right then and there. All it took was for him to open his mouth and I was suddenly infused with anger, raw and irrepressible. It felt as if the blood within me was now

29

burning, bubbling its way through my veins and coloring my vision with red.

"Not my business?" he railed back at me. "I ..."

"Last I checked, Christina was the head of The Resistance," I interrupted him again. "So as far as I'm concerned, I'll take my orders from her, not you." Then before he could so much as utter another word, I turned on my foot, and opening the door, walked outside. I felt as if I'd suffocate if I remained one second more.

The question of whether or not I would be allowed to return to my apartment was a moot one. I'd already figured that I was kissing my old life good-bye. And, of course, Christina furthered that sentiment by informing me it would be entirely too dangerous for me to even set foot into the place. For as careful as The Resistance was in securing the borders between the Netherworld and Earth, as well as ensuring the loyalty of Netherworld creatures on the Earthly plain, there were still unknowns. And it was better to prepare for those unknowns than to be taken by surprise.

As to my dog, Blue, Christina said he'd already been taken into account, and we would be reunited shortly. I didn't have a whole lot in the apartment that mattered a hoot to me, aside from my computer, which held the only copy of my book, *A Vampire and A Gentleman*. It was a book I'd written about my "friend," Bram, and I was in the process of trying to find a publisher for it. I could only hope it would remain safe in my apartment.

But my dog and my apartment weren't my only concerns. I was worried for my friends from the ANC: Sam, Dia, and Trey. According to Christina, they were already relocated to a safer place as well. It seemed that anyone in the ANC was considered a sitting duck and, thus, had been whisked away into hiding. As to the issue of ensuring that the streets of Splendor, Moon, Estuary, and Haven weren't suddenly overrun by mischief-makers, the solution was the soldiers of The Resistance. They had already started patrolling each neighborhood as soon as the *Draoidheil* mission was thwarted. All told, I'd made an understatement when I mentioned earlier that The Resistance was organized. They were *uber* organized.

So now it was a matter of waiting for a ride to some top secret location where I'd be living underneath the radar until things between the Netherworld and Earth settled down. As to what the plan was to ensure that things between the Netherworld and Earth would eventually become less heated, I wasn't in the know. I wanted to approach Christina with more questions on that exact subject, but as I expected, she was more than a little preoccupied. After our little rendezvous through the prison, I didn't see her again.

Instead, she instructed Quill and me to wait in line with five other members of The Resistance for a ride to our new digs. Suddenly realizing I was now high up on the list of most threatened people in the witness relocation program, it was slightly reassuring to know Quill was right alongside me.

"Do you have any idea where they're taking us?" Quill asked as he glanced around, a squadron of ten or so soldiers jogging by us. Quill shook his head in apparent wonder, as if he were impressed. Then his eyes rested on me.

I shook my head. "No, no idea at all."

At the sound of a purring engine, I turned to my left and noticed Knight pulling up in the black Denali. His eyes were narrowed on me and I knew the time for ignoring him was now over.

"Dulcie, we need to talk," he said, rolling the passenger window down. Then he reached over and opened the door, signaling that we were to talk in the SUV while en route to Hades only knew where.

Figuring this conversation needed to be broached at some point, I took a step forward, but was stopped by Quill's hand on my upper arm. Glancing up at him, I noticed his eyes were glued on Knight and his entire body had gone rigid.

"Anywhere she goes, I go," he said simply.

"This doesn't concern you, Quillan," Knight replied dryly, but his eyes warned Quill not to argue with him.

"Apparently, you don't understand English," Quill replied as his eyes blazed in response. "Anywhere she goes, I go."

Before it officially became the war of the elves and Lokis, I pulled my arm away from Quill's grasp and glanced up at him with a warm smile. "It's okay, Quill."

"Dulce," he started, shaking his head, and dropping his tone so only I could hear him. "We are in this together from here on out; and your safety is what matters most to me."

I nodded, but felt something in my stomach instantly sour, not too good with all of this protective stuff. "You know I can take care of myself," I replied sardonically. "I'll see you soon."

I turned around and approached the Denali, climbing into the passenger seat as I eyed Quillan and smiled reassuringly. He just sighed and frowned. I made a mental note to remind him not to suffocate me so much. Once I closed my door, Knight turned the SUV around and started for the entrance of Compound Three.

I'm not sure how long before either of us said anything, but I was already committed to not breaking the silence. This was Knight's conversation to start.

"I fucked up," Knight said finally, his eyes riveted on the road. His voice was deep, and the sound resonated through the SUV.

I said nothing, but nodded, although "fucked up" wasn't even the tip of the iceberg. If he hoped to have a chance in hell at gaining my forgiveness, there was a whole lot more ice to melt.

"All this time, I was convinced you were working for Melchior," he continued. "I guess I was so blinded by it, I couldn't see the truth."

"So, let me guess, you finally decided to talk to Caressa and she told you the truth?" I lashed out, not able to maintain my silence any longer. Fury was simmering inside me, made obvious by the acidity in my tone.

He nodded. "Yes, she told me everything."

"Interesting," I said angrily. "Funny, isn't it? How I first told you to call Caressa before Christina ever did and, yet, did you listen to me? No."

He exhaled deeply. "I couldn't think straight at the time, Dulcie," he said, referring to a conversation we'd had in the Denali, after he took me into custody. "I was convinced you were playing me all along."

"Sucks to be you then, I guess."

He swallowed and then studied me intently. "So this is all falling on deaf ears?" There was an edge to his voice.

I nodded, my anger pouring out of me. "Yeah, you could say that."

"Dulcie, I fucked up," he repeated. "I should never have doubted you." He paused for a few seconds. "I don't know what more I can say except ... I'm sorry."

There were so many thoughts and feelings storming through my head, I felt like my brain was going to implode. My body was rigid and I didn't even realize that I was digging my fingernails into the leather seat until I glanced down and noticed how white my knuckles were.

"Say something," Knight continued.

I glared up at him and swallowed everything that was rampaging through me, trying to find the ability to form words. "Sorry just doesn't cut it," I began, shaking my head in disbelief. "I risked my life for you." I took a deep breath. "Because I was trying to keep you safe, I became something I disdained, something I could never respect."

"Dulcie," he begged, his eyes pools of pain. I held my hand up and shushed him as I faced him angrily.

"Ever since I agreed to work for my father, I've been beaten up and nearly raped more times than I care to say. I can't remember the last time I actually slept more than two hours. I cut myself off from my friends and everyone else I cared about ... but none of that mattered to me. And do you know why? Because what mattered most to me was keeping *you* safe."

He opened his mouth, but quickly shut it again, his eyes downcast.

"And how do you thank me?" I continued as a shallow laugh fell off my lips. "By throwing me behind bars." I felt my heart rate increasing. "And let's not even mention what you did to me while en route to the prison."

He observed me as he shook his head. "I would never have continued, if I didn't think you wanted to."

I couldn't deny that I had wanted Knight when he took me on the side of the road even though there had been nothing but ugliness between us at the time. Even though the moment had been far from ideal, once I felt his touch, not to mention his hands and lips moving all over me, I more than wanted him. That's how it was between Knight and me—our connection was incendiary. Even now, despite my fury, I wanted him. I didn't believe that would ever change.

"Dulcie, if I knew you sold your soul to Melchior because of me, I never would have allowed that to happen. For as much as I fucked up, you fucked up too."

"What?" I repeated, shocked.

"You should never have lied to me. You should have told me what was going on so we could have worked through it together."

I bit my lower lip, enraged that I couldn't argue that issue. Maybe I should have just been honest with him from the get-go. But the time to cry over spilt milk was long gone. "That's beside the point," I said stiffly. "You knew all along who my father was and yet, you kept it from me." I continued to vent, not wanting to think about my contribution to the ugliness between us. "From the moment you first met me, you had a hidden agenda."

"You must understand why I thought what I did?"

34

"Yes," I admitted. "I can absolutely see why you would have thought what you did, but you told me there was a time when you dropped your defenses and believed in me. You realized you were wrong then, and yet, you never told me who my father was."

"Dulcie, I'll be frank with you," he said, eyeing me pointedly. "I never trusted you one hundred percent."

"Despite your body telling you I *was* the one," I snapped, referring to the fact that Knight's body had chosen me as his mate, signified when his eyes glowed.

"It is in my nature not to trust," he responded. "It's what I do day in and day out. I'm a trained soldier, Dulcie. I didn't get as far as I did in the ANC by trusting people. This is who I am." He took a breath. "But do I regret everything that happened between us? Absolutely. Do I wish I could go back and make things right again? Yes, and I mean that wholeheartedly."

I swallowed and stared out my window, trying to avoid the pain in his eyes. I just didn't know how I felt about him now. So much had happened between us, I wasn't sure if the damage was repairable.

THREE

"So where do we go from here?" Knight asked, his expression sullen as he chanced to look my way before returning his eyes on the road. Where we were headed was still unknown to me as I wasn't at all familiar with this area. But wherever we were had to be pretty remote, judging by the weeds popping up through the asphalt and the fact that I hadn't seen another car since leaving Compound Three.

I shook my head and shrugged, answering honestly. "I don't know."

He nodded as if my reply didn't surprise him, then seemed to zone out, staring at the road for a few seconds before returning his attention to me. "My feelings for you haven't changed," he said simply.

"My feelings for you *have* changed," I said just as simply, trying not to notice the chiseled lines of his face, much less how the ends of his thick, black hair curled up over his collar.

My own feelings towards Knight were infuriating, to say the least. I mean, I was more than mad at him—livid, disappointed, and hurt—all rolled into one big grudge that was currently lodged in my stomach. And, yet, for as angry as I felt, I couldn't help seeing Knight's point. I could understand how he hated my father so much that he would want to exact revenge on his daughter. I could also understand how Knight assumed I was in on my father's plan all along. There was a lot of evidence in support of this conclusion (especially everything that happened over the last two weeks). I could also understand Knight's anger since I wasn't exactly truthful about the reasons why I decided to work for my father in the first place. But, given all those exceptions, I also couldn't deny that I was furious that he'd never told me who my father was and, more so, that he wasn't willing to listen to me when I'd told him how and why I was innocent of all his accusations. And those were the sticking points. They were the points that kept jabbing me with their dull blades. Those were the points I couldn't automatically dismiss and which tainted my feelings towards Knight. Basically, his refusal to even listen to me, after I risked my life for him, was the crux of the whole matter.

"So you don't see where I'm coming from at all?" Knight asked, rather astutely.

I nodded quickly, almost wondering if he could somehow read my thoughts as they occurred to me. As a Loki, Knight had numerous abilities and it seemed the longer I got to know him, the more he surprised me with them. "Yes, I do, Knight," I started, exhaling a heavy sigh of despondency. "Of course I see your point of view; but it doesn't change my feeling that the whole course of our ... friendship was all initially based on a complete lie."

"A lie?" he repeated, his voice simmering with anger. He speared me with his beautiful blue eyes before returning his icy glare back to the road.

"If I'd known the true circumstances regarding your reasons for coming to Splendor, I never would have allowed things to progress as far as they did." One of those reasons was him getting kicked out of the Netherworld because he refused to work for my father. In coming to Splendor, he'd intended to track me down and engineer a surprise attack on my father, using me as his vehicle. Yep, Knight had been completely convinced that I was in cahoots with good ol' Dad.

He clenched his jaw and I could see his fingers tightening around the steering wheel. "What do you mean?"

"I mean that had I known all along you were using me as a vehicle in some sort of vendetta against my father, I would never have trusted you. Furthermore, I never would have been your ... friend." I was quiet for a few seconds as I re-contemplated it. "Knight, you were gunning for me from the moment you met me. That's not exactly the ideal foundation for real friendship."

"Stop referring to what we had as a friendship," he ground out, glaring at me. "You are more than aware that we were much more than friends."

At his words, I felt myself flush. Yes, I was more than aware what existed between Knight and me was too hot to touch. That was why I purposely labeled it a "friendship," if only as an attempt to cool my own feelings, which were, even now, heating up. One thing I could say for Knight: the man was sexy with a capital S. Even after everything that happened between us, I couldn't help my irresistible attraction to him. It really stuck in my craw.

"Well, whatever it was, it's done now," I snapped back at him and immediately regretted the words because they sounded so final, so exacting, and they just didn't feel right.

"Well, then, apparently you've just shown all your cards." He shook his head and laughed icily but I could see the pain in his eyes. "But I will have the last word as to your point about me wanting to use you against your father. I already told you that I stopped believing you were involved with your father very quickly after I met you." He returned his attention to the road, his shoulders stiff.

"And yet, you never gave me the benefit of the doubt when it came to my involvement with the *Draoidheil* import," I threw back at him. "When I told you I was innocent, you wouldn't listen to me! For someone who trusted me, you had a really funny way of showing it."

He faced me with raging eyes. "Dulcie, I trusted you up until two weeks ago. Since then, the Dulcie I thought I knew so well was nowhere to be found. I concluded that I must have been duped into believing you were innocent. Obviously, once Christina confirmed your involvement with your father, that was enough for me. "

"But you still could have listened to my side of the story."

He shook his head as if I were dense and couldn't understand what he was saying. Then he faced me again, carefully dividing his attention between the road and me. "What did you expect me to think after Christina confirmed that you were absolutely working for your father? I would've been an idiot if I still believed you were innocent."

I couldn't fault him for that one—especially because Christina hadn't known me from Eve. At the time, she hadn't known the true reasons for my association with my father. As far as she was concerned, I was just one of my father's people. Well, that is, before she talked to Caressa. At any rate, I knew I couldn't win this argument, so instead, I turned to the other issues that still bothered me. "That's all fine and good, but before I ever met my father, when you thought I was innocent of all of this, did you ever tell me who my father was? No. And that was when you quote, unquote, loved me!" I couldn't help the shrill sound of my voice.

"I didn't tell you about Melchior because I didn't want to hurt you," he said earnestly. "I weighed the options and decided it was better for you not to know who and what Melchior was than to know the truth."

"That's a decision you should have left up to me." I shook my head, anger now freely pouring out of me. "Sometimes you have this God complex thing going on and it pisses the shit out of me!"

"Please," he said with a frown. "I'm an alpha male; I have to be in this line of work."

"Alpha male or God complex, they're both just as infuriating," I spat back. "Does it ever occur to you that you don't have the right to make other people's decisions?"

"Dulcie, I didn't tell you about your father because I was protecting you," he said in a hollow voice. "I didn't want to upset you. Think about it—if you had known who and what your father was, how would it have affected your life? You would have wondered why your mother came to Splendor in the first place and if it was to escape your father

39

(which it was). I'm sure you would've always wondered if all of your successes in life had anything to do with you being Melchior's daughter. Not to mention that it would have shattered any idealistic thoughts you might have entertained as to who your father might be. There was no way *I* was going to take responsibility for any of that."

Sometimes Knight was spot on. Sometimes it was difficult to argue with him. "I could have handled it," I grumbled, staring out my window as I frowned. Not wanting to admit defeat, I faced him again. "The point is that it should have been my decision to make, not yours."

"Just like it should have been my decision to make whether or not you ruined your life by teaming up with your father because of me?" he demanded. "How the hell do you think that makes me feel? Knowing that all the shit you ultimately put yourself through was because of me?" He shook his head and sighed. "We could have figured it out together, Dulcie. You never should have taken all of this on by yourself."

I didn't respond, suddenly too tired to think. "What's done is done," I said softly, rubbing my temples as I closed my eyes, fighting the exhaustion that was trying to claim me. I just had too much to think about—The Resistance, what my future held, when I could see my friends again. I really didn't want to add the shriveled remains of my relationship with Knight to the mix. The mix was already dangerously close to precipitating the onset of a complete mental breakdown.

"Yes, what's done is done," Knight continued, his voice much softer now. "But that isn't to say we can't pick up the pieces, Dulcie." He reached over, squeezing my knee reassuringly. "At the end of the day, all we really have is each other, right?"

"I don't know." I glanced down at his large hand that seemed to engulf my knee and felt numb. I lifted his hand and returned it to him, pulling myself closer to the passenger door, suddenly needing more space.

"Dulce," he started.

"You said some really shitty things to me, Knight." Those shitty things included some incredibly rude comments about my friend, Bram. Due to an unfortunate string of events, Knight managed to convince himself that Bram and I were ... intimately involved. And he wasn't discreet about his feelings on the subject. If I remember correctly, he even asked me if I called out *his* name while Bram and I were having sex! That was followed by a few other, just as colorful, statements and/or accusations.

Knight nodded guiltily and sighed again. "I'm sorry. I shouldn't have let my temper get the best of me." Then he stopped himself short as though something suddenly occurred to him. "Then the Rolex wasn't a gift from Bram?"

I shook my head, keeping my lips tightly sealed as I tried to restrain my temper. "It was a portal compass given to me by Melchior."

"Shit," he said. Then, without any warning, he bashed his fist into the steering wheel, which beeped angrily at the assault. "I was jealous, Dulcie," he said once he seemed to calm down. "I was convinced you were playing me before you moved on to Bram. It even crossed my mind that you were with Bram all along." As he said the words, his eyes started to light up with a familiar glow, a glow which said I was his. I felt something inside me blossoming receptively, a yearning deep down in my belly. I swallowed down the sudden desire to feel his lips all over me and felt like slapping myself.

"I was never with Bram," I managed.

Knight nodded, but his expression was unreadable, almost like he hadn't heard me, or like he was reliving his memories. "When I went to No Regrets and saw you leaving his office, he leaned down to kiss you."

"That's just Bram. He always pulls those stunts just to piss me off."

He nodded again, but that same empty expression said the memory still enraged him. "When I watched him kiss

41

you, I just couldn't take it anymore," he said, slowing down. He exited the highway onto "Pineville Street," which appeared to be just as deserted as the highway. With a strange glance at me, he suddenly stopped the SUV in the middle of the road, turning his entire enormous body toward me. "I've regretted all the shitty things I said to you since I said them. I was overcome by jealousy and I couldn't control myself. I wanted to lash out and hurt you because the thought of you and Bram devastated me." He swallowed. "The truth is that thinking about you with any other man makes me sick to my stomach."

And that was when something occurred to me, a thought that left me cold. "Knight, did you ... did you ... do anything with anyone because of what happened between us?" I was thinking in particular of Angela, the bartender at No Regrets, Bram's club. Angela had it pretty bad for Knight; and they'd even dated before things got hot and heavy between Knight and me.

Knight shook his head and laughed, but there wasn't anything happy about the sound. "I thought about it, and to be honest with you, I wanted to. The idea of trying to forget you with another woman definitely appealed to me." Then he shook his head. "But I couldn't do it. At the time, I was in too dark a place to even contemplate being with another woman."

I was relieved, incredibly relieved, but my feelings were just as jumbled as before. Everything in my head was in a tailspin, a whirlwind of thoughts, emotions, and feelings that I couldn't try to begin to figure out. I just needed the proverbial dust to settle so I could sort out exactly how I felt about Knight.

"What are you thinking?" Knight asked.

I shrugged, not quite sure what I was thinking. One moment, I was mad as hell; and the next, I wanted nothing more than to feel his lips on mine. Even worse, I ached to feel him inside me. But then just as quickly, I was livid again. I wasn't sure how to make sense of anything or where

I stood. "Things need to be low key for a while," I said after an uncomfortable silence. "I don't know what to think or how I'm feeling. I've been through a shitload lately."

Knight nodded and stepped on the gas again, driving down Pineville Street, which, true to its name, was canopied by massive Norfolk pine trees.

"Well, I'll be here if you need me," he said quietly. "And no matter what happens between us, I will never doubt you again."

For the next ten minutes, we didn't say another word. The silence was nerve-racking and uncomfortable, but I didn't think there was anything left to be said. Since Knight didn't even say boo, I figured he must have agreed. Left with nothing but the deafening silence, I was forced back onto the battlefield raging in my head, a place resembling a war zone.

Now what would happen between Knight and me? Was this really it? Was it really over between us?

They were questions I couldn't answer although I tried, berating myself for even making the attempt. Why? Because I firmly decided (in the last, oh, five minutes or so) that my relationship or lack thereof with Knight would be relegated, yet again, to the back burner. It was more important for me to focus entirely on The Resistance and creating a plan to defeat my father.

Once I firmly entrenched my feelings for Knight in the quagmire known as "I'll visit this later," relief washed over me. Well, that is, until I realized my future was rocky, if not bleak. Luckily, the drive to Compound One wasn't a long one. I wasn't sure how much of my own pessimism and melancholy I could tolerate at this point. When we reached what I guessed must be Compound One (the heavy gates, topped with barbed wire, and the two guards wielding the latest in automatic weapons were the first clues), I wasted no time abandoning Knight's company, in serious need of my own space.

"Thanks for the ride," I said, jumping down from the Denali with a quick but awkward smile. I just wasn't good at this stuff.

He just nodded, his face still an unreadable mask. I closed the door behind me and stepped back, watching him drive down the road from whence we'd just come. Before reaching the gate guard, however, he took a quick right and disappeared behind the crest of a small hill. I didn't bother wondering where he was going or what he was up to. Now, more than ever before, I needed "me" time, I needed to get back in touch with myself and return to the Dulcie I used to be.

Compound One looked similar to Compound Three with the barbed wire fencing surrounding the place and a nondescript, three-story white building, which loomed before me. As I glanced around, I realized it was the only building in sight. The only difference I could see between the two compounds was that Compound One didn't appear to house a prison, and maybe it wasn't quite as large, well at first glance anyway. I watched as people milled around, dressed in ordinary attire, and appearing, for all intents and purposes, to be ... waiting. No one was especially busy—I watched two weres stroll by, talking about checking around the perimeter. In the distance, six people were playing flag football, while right beside me, three women lazily read beneath a tree. That was when it occurred to me that Compound One was nothing more than a holding facility for anyone who supported The Resistance, and, as such, required protection.

A few minutes after Knight departed, I watched an unmarked, grey bus pull up in front of the building. As the doors opened, I recognized the people who were waiting in line with me before Knight took on the role of chauffer. Quillan was the last to exit the bus. As he emerged, he glanced around himself, a worried expression on his face. As soon as we made eye contact, however, the worry dropped from his eyes, replaced with a wide smile.

"Everything good?" he asked once we were in earshot of each other.

I nodded, although as far as "everything" was concerned, it now lived in a zip code far, far away from "good."

"I guess we register in the front office," someone said from behind us. We both turned to face a squatty elf who had just stepped off the bus. He started walking toward the three-story building, so we followed. I must have taken only three steps before I recognized Sam and Dia walking through the front doors. Trey was just behind them. It felt like centuries passed while I waited for Sam to make eye contact with me. Her eyes rested on Quill first; and with a confused expression, her eyes widened and her attention moved to me. Within a split second, that smile I loved so well lit up her entire face. Dia, who was beside her, was apparently in mid-sentence when she was struck silent as soon as she recognized me. A broad, beaming smile lit up her face as well. Trey was the only one who was still going on about something, focusing his attention on his feet.

Seconds later, I was ambushed.

"Dulcie!" Sam and Dia screamed at the same time as they closed the gap between us. Then I was suffocated by hugs. I pulled myself away from them and took a big breath of air, desperately needing it. Before I could say anything, Sam and Trey took one look at Quill and frowned.

"What?" Sam started as Trey's mouth simply dropped open in astonishment. Or maybe he just couldn't breathe through his nose. Trey was the quintessential mouth-breather.

"It's okay, he's on our side," I said quickly, offering Quill an encouraging smile. "He joined The Resistance."

"Sam and Trey, it's good to see you again," Quill said. He seemed uncomfortable as he cleared his throat. Sam and Trey didn't respond, so Quill turned to face Dia, extending his hand to her. "I haven't had the privilege of making your acquaintance."

Dia took Quill's hand and smiled up at him, her eyes sparkling as she raked him up and down appreciatively. "Honey, I think the privilege is all mine." Then she shook her head in appreciation. "There aren't a whole lotta lookers in this damned place, so you are like a ray of sunshine on a very cloudy day."

I laughed as Quill smiled in response. Dia whistled at him, staring at him wolfishly again before the smile fell right off her face and was replaced with a frown.

"So now that we've gotten past the fact that you missed your callin' as a Chippendale dancer, you better have a damned good reason as to why you're standin' next to my girl, Dulce, and why she's goin' on about you joinin' The Resistance." Then she fastened her hands on her hips and did something with her neck that only Dia could do, something which resembled a snake preparing to strike. Dia did "diva" very well. She was tall and beautiful with chocolate skin and an infectious smile. She was also one of my closest friends.

Quillan laughed, but seeing her expression, the laugh soon died on his lips. For as wonderful a person as Dia was, you never wanted to get on her bad side. Yep, when her temper bubbled to the surface, it could be legendary. Quill cleared his throat and alternated his gaze between Dia, Sam, and Trey as he explained.

"Dulcie thought I deserved a second chance, so she fought for me," he started. "And in true Dulcie O'Neil form, she was able to get what she wanted." Then he offered me a quick wink, to which I just shook my head.

"From here on out, Quill's history is just that," I announced. "He's made the decision to start over and that's good enough for me. I hope it will be good enough for all of you too."

Sam nodded and hesitated only momentarily before reaching out and hugging Quill. "It's good enough for me too, big guy." She pulled away from him, her eyes twinkling.

"It's good to have you back." I was sure Sam was relieved to know Quill was on our side because he was also her boss once upon a time and she used to call him her friend as much as I had.

"It's good to be back," Quill answered before facing Trey and extending his hand.

"What up?" Trey started, jutting out his chin as he tried to act the part of a baddie, but ended up just looking ridiculous. Truth be told, Trey looked like a chubby ten-year-old, grubby and always grimy to the nth degree. Even though there was stubble in various patches around his face (he obviously wasn't adept at shaving), he still managed to maintain an air of Peter Panism, and never quite grew up.

"Good to see you again, Trey," Quill said, a small smile pulling at the ends of his lips.

Trey was quiet for a second or two and I wondered how he'd respond. Then a genuine smile broke across his plump face. "You too, Quill."

Dia took my arm and the five of us started toward the building, ostensibly so Quill and I could check in.

"So, girl, you gotta let me in on somethin'," Dia started as I eyed her, curious to hear her question. "How do you know so many hotties?" I just laughed as she continued. "You an' me need to hang out some more so I can score some of your leftovers."

I faced her and beamed, feeling somehow rejuvenated. I glanced around myself, at my small group of friends and felt so incredibly lucky. They had become my family. My mother died when I was young; and other than my poor excuse for a father, I didn't have any other family. But I had to say that this adopted family was more than enough for me. I felt like I'd just come home again.

FOUR

"I've been taking care of your dog, Dulce," Trey said
as the five of us sat around a table in a coffee house on base.
"Base" was what everyone called this place, and it was
pretty fitting because that's exactly what it looked like.
Complete with soldiers patrolling back and forth, armed
guards at every entrance and barbed wire fences running the
perimeter, it was like a military encampment and then some.
I was wrong about the registration building being the only
building on site—it was merely the biggest. Just beyond the
crest of a small hill, stood a crowded cafeteria, a
Laundromat, and even a bowling alley. There was also a
crudely constructed schoolhouse and an even more primitive
fire station.

"Thanks, Trey," I answered with an appreciative smile.
I tapped my toe to Billie Holiday's "God Bless the Child" as
it poured out of a boom box in the corner. Besides our table,
there were two others in the small room, both crammed with
paper coffee cups and clashing elbows of those busily
chatting.

"It's no prob," Trey said as I thanked Blue's and my
lucky stars that Trey had a soft spot for animals. Otherwise,
Blue could have easily been overlooked in the shuffle of
moving folks from Splendor to this camp.

"How is Blue doing?" I asked Trey, deciding to pay a
visit to my dog as soon as we finished our coffee. I didn't
exactly feel like the ideal dog owner of late. 'Course, none of
that was really my fault, considering recent events and
circumstances; but still, I needed to reconnect with the
yellow lab. The feeling I got from this place was that I'd
have plenty of time for reconnecting. In fact, the idea of just
sitting around here and waiting for further news or

instructions wasn't exactly something I was comfortable with. I wondered how long I'd last before the inactivity caused me to crack. On the flip side, though, a little downtime was probably exactly what the doctor would have ordered where I was concerned.

"He's doin' real good. Right now he's learnin' how to be more sociable," Trey said.

"What?" I asked with a laugh. Sam rolled her eyes and swallowed a sarcastic comment with a mouthful of iced mocha.

Trey offered Sam a discouraging frown before returning his attention to me. "Elsie noticed he wasn't super friendly with strangers, so she got this wild idea to round up everyone's dogs and start a pet sociability class," he finished. Elsie was formerly the receptionist at the ANC in Splendor. Apparently, now she could add "dog whisperer" to her list of credentials.

"Good ol' Blue," Quill said as he shook his head and smiled knowingly at me. "I'd love to see him." Quill had given Blue to me as a pseudo going away gift when I'd first learned that Quill was working for the bad guys. At the time I'd had no clue that the chief bad guy he was working for was my father, but due to that fact, Quill had deserted his post in the ANC and we'd parted ways.

I just nodded, still uncomfortable with the events of the past and, more pointedly, any reminders about my father. Instead, I directed my attention to other topics, such as what the plan was moving forward. It wasn't like I knew much of anything, so I hoped someone could bring me up to speed.

"So, what's the deal?" I started. "Everyone here is just hanging out?"

"Yep, just waiting and then waiting some more, until we're told what to do next," Sam answered with a bored sigh. "We're basically in the same thing as witness protection. Everyone who worked for the ANC is now considered a target, I guess."

"Some of us have already been drafted to fight for The Resistance," Dia added, raising her eyebrow skeptically as she swallowed a mouthful of coffee.

"Drafted?" I repeated, glancing at each of them as I tried to make sense of the word.

Trey nodded. "Yep, I think it's just a matter of time for all of us. Once The Resistance decides it needs us, we get drafted into the cause and have to go through some trainin'. I think it's all leadin' up to the war that's gonna break out with your dad, Dulce."

"War?" Quill asked, sounding surprised. But, my concern was more with the idea that Melchior was my so-called "dad."

"Don't call him my dad," I answered quickly, suddenly irritated that Trey even knew Melchior and I were related. It's not like I ever told him, or anyone else seated at the table either, for that matter. As I glanced around me, and noted everyone's expressions, none of them appeared to be in the least bit surprised. So apparently, Sam, Trey, and Dia were very much aware of my association with my father. I had to wonder what else they knew. "I'm unfortunately related to Melchior O'Neil in name only; but that's it, as far as I'm concerned." Then I speared each of them with my gaze. "And please tell me how and what do all of you know about that anyway?"

Dia laughed, like my question was a dumb one. "Come on, girl, how could we not know?"

"Rumors spread around here fast, Dulce," Sam added. "It's not like we have anything else to talk about all day. Just waiting for word on what's going to happen next."

"When were you all brought here?" Quill interrupted, apparently attempting to steer the conversation into safer waters. It was pretty obvious that if I were anything, it was a private person. I hated having my dirty laundry exposed for everyone to see.

Sam shrugged and glanced at Dia curiously before turning to face us again. "About four days ago maybe."

Hmm, right before the *Draoidheil* import had made its way from the Netherworld to Earth. Christina had had this whole thing finely orchestrated, her timing impeccable.

"And just for the record, Dulce," Sam started, "none of us blames you for the decisions you made."

Trey shook his head. "We all think you were pretty heroic, actually." He took a deep breath. "And Knight will ..."

"I don't want to talk about him," I said firmly, my jaw suddenly tight. "That is one subject that needs to be left alone." Then I glared at everyone in turn, making sure I was absolutely, one hundred percent understood.

They all simply nodded, but I didn't miss Quill's sigh. It told me he was disappointed that I was still upset about the Loki. Well, Quill didn't even begin to know the ins and outs of Knight's and my relationship.

Dulcie, you aren't going there! I reminded myself, choosing to change the subject, and instead, returning to how my life resembled an open book lately. "So all of you know everything about me working for my father?" Then I speared Sam with a glare. "I thought some people were going to keep their mouths shut." Although I had told Sam some of what was going on, I hadn't told her the whole story. I'm not sure how everyone got to know the details, but I figured it was best to start with Sam.

"Hey, don't blame me!" she said, holding up her hands in mock offense.

"I had a vision of most everything that happened," Trey answered sheepishly, glancing up at me through half-lidded eyes, his cheeks flushed.

"Then we just pieced the rest of it together," Dia answered, with no trace of an apology in her tone at all.

"So much for keeping secrets," I grumbled, not at all happy that everyone was in the know where I was concerned. I'd get over it soon enough, but it still didn't make the news any easier to swallow.

"Three can keep a secret if two of them are dead," Dia answered, beaming at me as if she were proud of her witty bon mot.

"Where do you come up with this stuff?" I mumbled, shaking my head as I drowned my irritation with a mouthful of hot coffee.

"Not me, girlfriend," Dia answered. "I got good ol' Benny Franklin to thank for that one." When she grinned broadly, I couldn't help but laugh. Her smile quickly faded into an earnest expression and I knew a "Dia moment of seriousness" was about to unveil itself. She had this uncanny ability to make you drop your defenses with one of her little jokes and then, bam! She'd nail you right over the head with some profound thought."There's nothing for you to be embarrassed about, Dulce," she said quietly. "We all love you and we only want the best for you, so don't you worry that pretty little head of yours."

"None of us judges you, Dulcie," Sam said before turning to face Quill. "And that includes you too, Quill. We're all friends here."

Quill nodded with a broad smile. "I appreciate that, Sam."

"So going back to your comment about a war with my father, Trey," I started, reminding myself I still had lots to learn and time was ticking away. "What were you talking about?"

Trey shrugged and I noticed he had the remnants of his last sip of vanilla shake lining his upper lip. "There's lots of talk about a war with your da ... father," he corrected himself.

"Word is that Christina is going to demand Melchior step down from his office as Head of the Netherworld," Sam started. "She and Knight want to reinstate a democracy in the Netherworld once again."

"But it's not like my father is just going to say 'okay' and lay down his crown," I said, shaking my head at how absurd the idea sounded.

"Well, when he doesn't," Sam continued, "and obviously we're all betting on that fact, then I guess we declare war on the Netherworld."

"You guess?"

Sam shrugged. "It's not like any of this has been ratified. It's all conjecture, but based on the word on the street, that's what's going to happen."

I shook my head, not even imagining how emancipating ourselves from the Netherworld was possible. "We are part of the Netherworld."

Dia glanced at me, cocking a brow. "But do we want to be? That's the question."

Sam shrugged. "The United States *was* once a part of England, right?"

"Thanks for that, Sam," I grumbled, to which she just offered me a cheery smile.

"So The Resistance is going to emancipate itself from The Netherworld?" Quill asked, surprise and worry evident in his tone.

"Apparently that's the plan," Sam said, her eyebrows raised in an expression that didn't say whether she supported the idea or not. "At least, that's what I've heard through the grapevine."

"So we're going to exist as an independent nation then?" I asked, still in doubt. "Because it's pretty obvious Melchior won't step down just because Christina asks him to."

"Well, she'll be askin', but at the same time, she'll have the backing of a few hundred Netherworld creatures in Splendor as well as the surrounding cities," Dia responded.

"And what in the hell does the human government think of this?" I asked, even more shocked than before. Even though we were creatures of the Netherworld, we lived on Earth with humans and they were well aware of just who and what we were. Granted, humans tended to keep to themselves and, likewise, we preferred to keep to ourselves. Splendor, Estuary, Haven, and Moon were all cities with largely Netherworld creature populations—about twenty creatures to every one human.

"The human government doesn't know," Dia answered quickly. "The Resistance decided it was better to buffer the human populations of the affected cities in a magical cloud of ignorance."

"So what does that mean?" I continued.

Dia shrugged. "As far as humans go, life's just the same as it always was. They don't see The Resistance soldiers patrolling the streets, and they don't notice that the Netherworld creature-run stores are closed. They're also unaware if the creatures they considered acquaintances or friends are missing. It's just a regular day as far as humans are concerned."

I nodded, thinking it was a good move on Christina's part because the last thing we needed was for the human government to get involved with our affairs. Sometimes it was good to live in a bubble. I took a sip of my coffee as I tried to digest the information.

"At any rate, it's not for us to worry about," Sam said quietly. "We're given updates every day or so; and once The Resistance is ready for us, we'll be here."

"Ready for you?" I asked.

"To fight," Sam clarified. "That's what it's going to come down to, I'm sure."

"To fight?" I repeated, my jaw dropping as I contemplated it. "Sam, you can't fight." Sam was a witch, someone who had always helped the ANC by casting spells or creating concoctions to help us with our cases. But when it came to hand-to-hand combat, she was clueless. She'd never been trained the way I had been—as a Regulator.

"Well, I guess that's where the training comes in," she said with a frown and fear in her eyes.

I shook my head. "This is ridiculous and what's more, training takes time and it sounds like war might be right around the corner!"

"Well, it's not like I know any of this for sure, anyway," Sam responded, obviously trying to settle me back down again. "It's just what people are saying."

Well, I wasn't okay with relying on gossip and hearsay. I'd already made up my mind to pay a visit to Knight or Christina—whomever I could find first—to demand what *was* going on. Well, that was, after I went to see my dog.

"Hey, don't you think we're kinda like *The Breakfast Club*," Trey piped up. I took a deep breath and shook my head, not even beginning to make the connection. "Come on," he insisted. "Dulce can be that prissy one with the sushi. Quill, you can be that jock dude who dances on the railing; and Sam, you can be that freaky chick who gets the makeover." He glanced over at Dia as if sizing her up to figure out what part she could play.

"Uh uh," she said, shaking her head in a most diva-like way. "Count me out."

Trey shrugged before facing the rest of us again. "An' I'll be that dude who wears the Michael Jackson glove—you know, the rebel."

"Please, Trey," Sam piped up. "You'd be the nerd."

I laughed, the sudden feeling of lightness drifting through me as everyone around me echoed the sentiment, their faces lighting up with broad smiles. In those few, precious seconds, it seemed that none of us carried the weight of the world on our shoulders—that we were boundless and carefree. And as we shared that moment of laughter, a moment free from the angst of worrying about our present, not to mention our future, it was beautiful. I glanced around my circle of friends, suddenly feeling as if everything was right with the world.

"So what the hell is going on?" I demanded as I threw my hands on my hips and glared up at the ridiculously tall

Loki. He was backlit by the bright yellow of the full moon, and his inky black hair almost appeared blue in the light.

Unfortunately, I'd run into Knight before Christina so, true to my word, I blasted him about what we should all be expecting moving forward. After spending the remainder of the day with Blue, who was so happy to see me he wet himself, I stayed busy in my new room. It was a twelve-by-twelve box at the top floor of the registration building. Luckily, my room was next to Sam's and just down the hall from Dia's. Trey's and Quill's rooms were on the next floor down, one of the two floors designated for the men. But going back to my room, it was painted a bland beige, and came complete with a cot in one corner that had a pillow and a brown-and-green-plaid comforter. On the opposite side of the room was a toilet; and just beside that, a sink. Next to the bed, I found a trunk packed full of my clothes—something that surprised me, considering someone must have returned to my apartment in order to get my clothes. And I thought my apartment was a no go …

After taking a quick nap with Blue (who relentlessly refused to sleep on the floor and ended up at the end of my cot, his big head sandwiched between my feet), I tried to amuse myself by playing various board games with Trey, Sam, Dia, and Quill. All the while, I continued to grill them about The Resistance. After obtaining no more information than previously, I decided to give it a rest. Instead, I opted for some fresh air along with some "me" time. Trey asked to take Blue to a party that Elsie was hosting for her new canine students; so I found myself alone, which was just as well. My only other option was to play Bingo with the rest of the base and that thought made me want to go back to bed.

"Nice to see you too," Knight grumbled down at me. There was a small glint in his eye, like he was more than happy to see me. I felt something rising inside me—something that felt happy as well, but I quashed it down. Instead, I kept reminding myself that things between Knight and me weren't resolved yet, and until they were, I wasn't about to sweep the past events under the proverbial rug.

I found him unloading wooden crates of what looked like maple syrup into a makeshift storage facility that was maybe six feet tall and four feet wide. The storage facility was located at the far west of the base, off a one-lane dirt road and under the canopy of an oak tree grove. The only reason I'd actually been able to find him was because I'd decided to take a run around the perimeter of the base and happened to spot the Denali, which wasn't very well hidden on the side of the road. Even so, it wasn't like he was out in the open. Nope, whatever was in the crates had to be something top secret, which was why he was busily unloading it under cover of darkness. Only the moon's light illuminated his way.

I shivered, despite having just run over a mile, but my current getup of sports bra and stretch pants didn't place me on the list of best dressed. "I'm sorry if I seem a little pissy at the moment, but no one knows what the hell is going on around here and it's getting old really fast," I barked back.

Knight took me in from head to toe and smiled warmly as he leaned against the Denali, apparently not averse to taking a break from his unloading. "Everyone is taken care of," he said absentmindedly, devouring my body with his eyes again. "You don't have anything to worry about."

"Yeah, except for the intention of declaring war on the Netherworld in order to excommunicate ourselves."

He raised both brows, obviously surprised. "Where did you hear that?"

I frowned. "That's what everyone seems to think is going on. As I mentioned before, no one really knows just what the hell *is* going on."

He nodded and expelled a pent-up breath of air before hoisting another crate into his arms, and depositing it into the large storage facility at the right of us. "You're welcome for retrieving your clothes, by the way."

I swallowed down an acid reply, but couldn't conceal my surprise. "You went to my apartment and brought my clothes back?"

He placed the crate down and dusted his hands together, offering me a boyish smile. His hair was mussed and a few pitch-black strands obscured his left eye, giving him a rakish, sexy look. "I did."

"I thought there was a reason I wasn't allowed back there, and I assume the same reason applies to you too?"

He leaned against the Denali and wrapped his beefy arms around himself, just studying me for a few seconds. "It does."

"Then it was pure stupidity for you to do that," I said pointedly. I didn't appreciate the wicked gleam in his eye, much less how gorgeous he was. It just wasn't fair.

"You're welcome," he said, his smile still in place as he locked the door to the storage facility and started for the front of the Denali. Opening his door, he turned to face me. "You getting in? Or do you plan to freeze out here all night?"

I frowned, realizing I'd have to take him up on his offer if I wanted to get any of my questions answered. I started forward and watched him seat himself. He closed his door and reached across to open mine. I hefted myself into the passenger seat as he turned the engine on and put the car in drive. The inside of the Denali smelled like him—crisp, clean aftershave combined with spiciness and ... Knight.

"So are you going to answer my questions or what?" I started, folding my arms across my chest and frowning at him. I watched him turn up the heat and silently thanked him as I rubbed away the goose bumps from my arms.

"I'll do you one better," he answered simply.

"What does that mean?"

He shrugged. "I'm about to have a meeting with Christina; and wouldn't you know it? She requested your presence too."

I frowned at him. "Hmm, well then, I guess it's a good thing that I happened to run into you out in the middle of nowhere, isn't it? Who knows what would have happened if I hadn't."

He glanced at me and smiled innocently. "I would have come to get you."

I didn't lose my frown and suddenly felt annoyed that he seemed so comfortable, so nonchalant, especially when things between us weren't exactly kosher. "Why do I find that hard to believe?"

He faced the road as the Denali strained over the crest of the hill, a dust cloud spreading behind us once we were on the dirt path again. "Because you're naturally suspicious."

"At any rate," I grumbled, "what were you up to that required the cloak of darkness? What were you unloading in those crates?" Just call me nosy.

He glanced at me and smiled again, like this was some big game. "Liquid antidote to *Draoidheil*."

"Liquid antidote?" I repeated with surprise. *Draoidheil,* the illegal potion my father had planned on introducing to the streets of Splendor and surrounding areas (the import which I'd flubbed when I'd blown the cover of my father's plan) was the most addicting and potent potion currently available. One whiff caused hopeless addiction, and worse; being airborne, anyone within the immediate vicinity could become instantly addicted. As far as I knew, the only antidote to the miserable stuff was a little white pill. Apparently, however, I was wrong.

"Yep, liquids enter your blood stream faster," Knight responded.

"I'm aware of that," I grumbled as my attention returned to the number of crates Knight had just finished unloading. He'd easily unloaded ten crates that held probably twenty jars of the antidote. Obviously, Christina still considered the *Draoidheil* a big threat. "So you think my father is still going to try and attack us with the *Draoidheil?*"

He nodded. "It's the best threat your father has up his sleeve, which is why we're doing our best to distribute the antidote to everyone on this side." He glanced over at me and smiled. "We figured syrup was the easiest way to disguise it."

"Disguise it?" Then something dawned on me. "You mean you aren't telling people what it is? You're just pretending it's pancake syrup?"

He shrugged as though it was no big deal at all. "Syrup is just one camouflage. It's also in the creamer, and any of the juices you find on all of our bases. It's even in the baked goods you see around. Apparently, it remains as potent baked as it does raw."

"Why aren't you telling anyone what they're consuming?"

"Ask yourself that question, Ms. Regulator," he answered with an expression that said I should already have figured that one out.

I frowned, aggravated that he'd donned his managerial cap. "Because you're afraid of moles."

He nodded and smiled at me handsomely. "Bingo. Trust no one—that's our motto."

"Well, you should be more careful about being inconspicuous when you're unloading the stuff," I replied gruffly.

"Touché," he said with a little laugh, which faded away as he faced me. "Dulce, I really hope you believed me when I told you I regretted everything that happened between us."

I shook my head. "I don't want to talk about it." I had way bigger, more important things on my mind.

"We aren't going to talk about it," he said resolutely. "I just want you to know that I can't get it out of my head; I can't get you out of my head."

I swallowed hard and focused on the bleak darkness outside my window.

FIVE

The "conference room," or so it was termed, wasn't located in Compound One. In fact, just where it was located I had no clue—it was hush-hush, as were the locations of the various other compounds within The Resistance. The fact that I'd even seen another compound (when Christina gave me a tour of the prison on Compound Three) was breaking news, well, according to Knight, anyway. Apparently, Christina took this undercover stuff pretty seriously because she refused to meet Knight and her team of Resistance officials in the same place twice. And, no one knew exactly where she spent her time holed up when she wasn't visiting the various compounds, much less where she slept at night. Knight also inferred that not even he knew where Christina's secret abode lay. According to rumors on base, she never stayed at any one location longer than thirty minutes. But I guess paranoia is survival's best friend, so who was I to judge?

"So you think we actually have a chance in hell of defeating my father?" I asked, growing tired of the uncomfortable silence between us. It was like there were so many proverbial elephants in the room, er the SUV, that I felt claustrophobic, like I was slammed against the window between three trunks and a huge elephant's ass, the air in the confined space evaporating into a vacuum.

"If I didn't think we had a chance in hell, I wouldn't be here," Knight answered rather crassly. I frowned, figuring I deserved that one because my question *was* a stupid one. Well, excuse the hell out of me for trying to break the incredibly awkward silence.

We were driving along a dirt road that led away from Compound One. We'd been driving for maybe twenty minutes before we hit another dirt road that led to the west of Compound One. After being on that seemingly endless stretch of nothing for another ten minutes, we hit a third dirt road, upon which we were now traveling.

"How do you even keep track of where you're going when there aren't any street names and everything looks the same?" I asked. Now, more than ever before, I was hell-bent on starting some sort of conversation that might prevent Knight from bringing up the "us" conversation again. In the last thirty minutes, he'd already attempted it twice.

"I've been doing this a long time," he answered tightly.

I was spared the need to respond when he suddenly stopped in the middle of the road, looking like he forgot something. He backed up maybe five feet and then stopped again, putting the Denali in park as he opened his door. A sudden and persistent beeping blared through the silence, telling us the door was left ajar. He ignored it and walked to the front of the SUV, the headlights bathing him in white light. Turning away from the lights, he held his arms out straight on either side of him, stretching them wide. Then he dropped his head back and closed his eyes. A split second later, he let his arms fall and turned around to face me, beckoning me forward with a wave of his hand. Although I found his display strange, I possessed neither the curiosity nor the energy required to investigate it. I just shrugged and unbuckled myself, jumping down from the Denali and walking toward him.

"Was that your best impression of *Close Encounters of the Third Kind*?" I asked with an irreverent laugh once I caught up to him.

He offered me an unimpressed raised eyebrow.

"Scanner just below that tree," he replied while jerking his head to the right. I followed his gaze and noticed a pine tree in close proximity to us, along with about twenty others. Given his less than precise directions, it wasn't a big wonder that I couldn't locate the so-called scanner.

"Well, if Rand McNally needs new recruits, I'd advise you not to apply," I said in an irritated tone.

I got the same unimpressed expression, this time with the opposite eyebrow raised. I just smiled pleasantly and waited for him to explain exactly what in the hell he was talking about. But instead of an explanation, he grabbed my hand and pulled me forward, until I was standing beside him, in the middle of the headlights.

"Stand here and stretch out your arms like I just did," he said hurriedly.

"Why?"

Knight rolled his eyes and shook his head as he exhaled a breath of visible exasperation. "Damn, Dulcie, just do it, will you? Do you always have to question everything?"

But I made no move to do anything. It wasn't in my nature to blindly do as I was told. Instead, I glanced up at him and slowly crossed my arms against my chest, giving him a mirror image of the raised eyebrow expression he'd just so graciously shown me.

Knight shook his head again. "To get access to the Conference Room, everyone has to be scanned. It's protocol to make sure you don't have weapons on you."

"Was that so hard?" I demanded and stepped wide while I hoisted my arms in a perpendicular angle from my body, dropping my head back. I noticed a small lens that was hanging just below the immensely tall pine tree closest to us. It's not as though the scanner was attached to the tree, though. Nope, instead it was just hanging in the middle of thin air, obviously by some magical incantation. The point of using the tree was just to disguise the scanner and it worked incredibly well. The pine needles and branches managed to obscure the thing so perfectly, I had a hard time finding it, even after I knew what to look for.

Apparently recognizing me, the lens started shifting in an up and down motion, while emitting no sound at all. A red light at the very top of the scanner began to flash.

"Hold still," Knight said, evidently cognizant of the meaning of the red light.

Before I could say "boo," the red light beamed against my forehead, suddenly spreading wide as if encompassing my whole body. Then it began running the length of my body, bathing me in a wide red laser light, from my eyes to my feet, and then back up again. Once it finished scanning me, it flashed green, which, I supposed, meant I was good to go. I dropped my arms and started forward, but Knight shook his head, holding me at bay.

"Gotta pat you down," he said in explanation.

"What?" I asked, pissed off that I was about to be subjected to more of this treatment. It just seemed like overkill and then some. I threw my hands on my hips. "Didn't that little scanner just prove I'm not packing anything?"

"Protocol," Knight answered evasively.

"This whole thing is ridiculous anyway, considering I'm on your side and have no interest in hurting anyone."

He shook his head. "Procedure is procedure." Realizing I wasn't buying his explanation, he continued. "I'm the number two guy in The Resistance and you just saw me get scanned, so what does that tell you?" He paused when I didn't respond. "It tells you that we take all this stuff very seriously; and besides, we won't be granted entrance unless we both subject ourselves to these security measures."

I glared at him, but said nothing. Instead, I just took a wide stance again and held my hands out straight on either side of my body, allowing him to frisk me. I wasn't sure if it was really protocol, or if he just wanted to touch me. As soon as the thought arose though, I realized how silly it was. Knight wasn't the kind of guy to go for cheap thrills. On the flipside, however, I was no dummy, and yes, this might be the usual protocol, but I also wasn't convinced that he wouldn't enjoy it. I just hoped I wouldn't.

He stood in front of me with his eyes trained squarely on mine, and started running his hands down the tops of my arms very slowly.

"Um, I don't have sleeves, in case you didn't notice," I said snidely. I was referring to the fact that as I was still clad in my sports bra; it wasn't like I could conceal anything on my upper body.

But Knight didn't falter. He continued running his hands along the skin of my upper arms. "Magic has a funny way of tricking the eye," he said simply. He had a point—I mean, I could have a grenade strapped to my arm; but in using fairy magic, I'd be able to disguise it as nothing more than skin, silky smooth and uninterrupted—sort of like trick photography. 'Course, the question remained as to why I would even want to do something like that in the first place; not to mention what the point of this whole thing was. But I figured the answer would still remain the same: "protocol."

Upon reaching my shoulders, Knight rotated my arms around and started patting them, going north into my armpits. Once there, he held my arms up, beside my head, as he cupped each one. I assumed it was because they offered a handy little place to hide something (magically speaking, of course), if I were so inclined. After he seemed convinced I wasn't packing anything, he brought my arms back to my sides and ran the palms of his hands down the sides of my upper torso, to my waist before patting me around the middle of my upper stomach. Then he gripped my hips and gently turned me around until my butt was facing him. I wasn't sure why, but it made me nervous. I felt like a racehorse being sized up before a derby. It was probably just a matter of time before he inspected my teeth. He ran his hands up my legs after carefully patting down my shoes and fishing inside my sneakers as well as my socks with his index fingers. When he reached my thighs, I felt myself shudder and the goose bumps that suddenly arose on my naked skin had nothing to do with the chill in the air.

"I have to pat down your, uh, your butt," he said apologetically, as if preparing me for it. Or maybe he was preparing himself for it. As uncomfortable as I felt, he didn't look much better.

"I understand," I replied gruffly, my voice sounding somehow deeper than normal. It seemed like an eternity before he touched my butt. His touch was soft as he ran his hands across my backside, although what erupted inside of me was anything but soft. It felt like a volcano suddenly blowing its top while fiery lava pumped through me. Just at the touch of his hands along my backside, my whole body tensed, letting me know just how much I wanted him, no, yearned for him. I shut my eyes and tried to replace the intense feelings of lust with feelings of anger—trying to subdue my sexual needs with guilt over feeling them in the first place.

It didn't work.

Knight turned me around again. Sitting back on his haunches, he glanced up at me apologetically. "I have to do the same on this side."

I just nodded while hoping he couldn't read my eyes, which were shouting that I was melting under his touch. He started at the base of my stretch pants, where they met my socks and frisked me quickly, his hands moving upward, to my thighs and then my hipbones. When he reached my middle, he gripped each side of my waist, wrapping his large hands around me until I seemed to vanish underneath them. He didn't move his hands, but tightened his grip around my waist. About that time, I realized this had nothing to do with a weapons pat-down. His touch became heavier, almost as if he knew he shouldn't be doing it, but was unable to resist. The naked skin of my upper stomach, just above my stretch pants, suddenly felt as if it were on fire. It was a reaction to the sensation of his fingers as they brushed against me. The breath caught in my throat and I could already tell my eyes were wide.

Dulcie, wake up! I chided myself. *What is wrong with you? Now is not the time for this!*

But I couldn't honestly say I was paying any attention. Losing myself, I found Knight's eyes utterly intoxicating as he stared down at me. His hands were still wrapped around my waist and neither of us said anything, not one little, insignificant word. Apparently, neither of us could find our tongues. With our eyes still locked on each other and neither one emitting so much as a breath, I felt Knight's hands releasing my waist. His fingers skimmed my upper waist, to the junction of my arms, where they met my chest. He traced the line of my collarbone and paused just above my breasts. I nearly closed my eyes with the thought that I wanted nothing more than to feel his warm hands on my naked breasts, his fingers pinching my nipples. Thankfully, I managed to keep my eyes open. Somewhere in my overwhelmed mind, a little voice still urged me to keep my cool. But that isn't to say that I could open my mouth and demand Knight stop. For as much as that little, nagging Puritan inside me was still carrying on her one-person mission by decrying everything that was happening, a choir of voices rose up in unison, drowning out her voice by singing in glorious harmony how good this felt and how … right.

Once I felt Knight's palms moving below my collarbone and resting against my breasts, I had a feeling that the time for stopping was dripping through my fingers. He rested the flat of his hands above each of my breasts and stared down at me, his eyes glowing with a whiteness that told me just how excited he was. The glow in Knight's eyes was primitive—an instinctual, animal-like reflex responsive only to me, and to my body. It was his way of broadcasting to the world that I belonged to him—a warning to other men to stay away from me or suffer the Loki consequences.

He pushed against my breasts, cupping his palms around them. I opened my mouth, trying to regain my wits enough to tell him to beat it; but that's not exactly what I said. Well, in all honesty, I didn't say anything at all. Nope, instead I ... moaned.

Even though it was only the very beginning of a moan, and more like a split second of a whimper, or a tiny mouse's squeak, that was all it took. Instantly, Knight thrust me toward him and kissed me. The touch of his lips on mine was like kerosene to fire. Whatever was building inside me broke through the weak dam that was restraining it and now took full dominion over my entire body. Without any hesitation whatsoever, I opened my mouth, allowing his tongue full access. But he didn't need any invitation. His tongue met mine violently and we lapped at each other with an incendiary urgency. He looped his hands around my shoulders and pulled me into him, into his hardened shaft. He was most definitely stirring beneath his pants, pressing against my navel. I met the thrusting of his tongue and we kissed one another with so much fervor, I wasn't sure where my mouth began and his ended.

He lifted me and carried me the few feet that separated us from the Denali and I was suddenly aware of the cold steel of the door against my back. The feel of the Denali beneath me was all it took for me to come to my senses, to come back to reality. It was as if the sharp coldness of the steel completely obviated the sexual waves of bliss that were previously consuming me. Instead, a montage of memories from the last time I got up close and personal with the Denali overtook me. However, those weren't memories that I cherished, by any stretch of the imagination. No, they left me feeling angry and depressed. Although the sex that night was one of the most passionate we'd ever had, it went well beyond angry and turned out to be one of the chief reasons I didn't know how to feel towards Knight.

I brought my hands up to his chest and pushed him away, breaking the seal of our lips as he stared down at me in surprise. "Stop," I said weakly. "We can't do this."

"Dulcie, if it feels right," he started.

I shook my head. "It doesn't feel right." As I met his eyes, I could see the hurt in their depths as he seemed to realize things hadn't changed between us, that our kiss didn't mean I forgave him for everything that happened before. "There's too much baggage between us."

I was beginning to wonder if this was going to be a repeat of the last time we found ourselves alone on an empty stretch of road with only the Denali for company. Would Knight be able to restrain himself? What was more, would I be able to restrain myself? As it was, my self-control was hanging by a thin thread. But one thing I knew for sure was that I would never allow myself to have angry sex with Knight again. The pain and guilt afterwards were just too much.

"I don't want what happened last time," I started but he interrupted me.

"That will never happen again," he said sharply and I could see the self-loathing in his eyes at the mere memory of it. It was clearly evident that Knight hated himself for what happened. I could see as much in his eyes; he couldn't accept knowing that he lost control of himself and took advantage not only of the situation, but also of me.

Without another word, he pulled away from me, even taking two steps back, as if to assure me that nothing more would happen. His eyes were still glowing, and clouded over with naked desire. It was taking all of my self-control not to surrender to him, and allow him to claim me. Even now my body was begging for it. The yearning deep within me had grown into an endless stinging—something that was becoming painful. Basically, my brain was in an all-out war with my body.

Knight shut his eyes tightly and took another few steps from me.

"Get in the car," he said gruffly, sparing me the need to question him as he quickly continued. "I can sense you, Dulcie, everything you're ... you're feeling and ... you're not making things easy on me."

No more explanation was necessary. I completely got his gist. Apparently, this was yet another of his Loki abilities: sensing my desire for him. Maybe he could somehow smell my pheromones or something similar. I could see that whatever it was that he was picking up on, was taking every ounce of his fortitude to resist. As much as I'd been wrestling with my own needs, Knight was doing the same. Judging by his pinched lip expression, his battle was much more difficult than mine was.

He glanced up at me and as his eyes met mine, they glowed fiercely white. He immediately dropped his head and rubbed his eyes. It was as if he was trying to rub the glow right out of them. When he looked over at me again, his eyes were back to their brilliant blue, with only a few specks of white. He took a few deep breaths, his already broad chest inflating until he looked unbelievably large. After exhaling, and apparently regaining control of himself, he faced me again.

"I'm sorry," he started. Then he seemed to be at a loss, making no motion to do anything.

I nodded my acceptance to his apology, and suddenly felt the urge to sit down. I hurried to the passenger side of the Denali, throwing myself into my seat as I wrapped my arms around my chest and berated myself for losing control. I couldn't look at Knight. Instead, I focused on my knees as they nervously bounced. From the periphery of my vision, I watched Knight settling himself into his seat. He closed his door and turned the heat up as high as it would go. My guilt, confusion, and anger with myself all made me forget that I was freezing cold until the heat enveloped me.

"Dulce," he started.

"No," I interrupted. "Let's just pretend that never happened."

He cleared his throat and sighed, putting the SUV in drive and starting forward. Evidently, the scanner had opened some sort of portal or passageway because as soon as we drove past the pine tree, which housed the scanner, there was a popping sound and the terrain completely changed. Instead of miles and miles of flat, open land, we were suddenly in the center of a city.

"We're going to have to talk about things, Dulcie," Knight said. "If we're going to continue working together ..."

"As far as I'm concerned, nothing happened," I answered with steel resolve. "There are way bigger things on the horizon for us to worry about. Whatever is going on between you and me isn't important right now, Knight," I finished, suddenly realizing how icy my words sounded.

His lips were tight, but his eyes burned. "Understood."

Although I wanted to tell him that I didn't really mean that our situation was unimportant, I couldn't bring myself to utter the words. I just didn't possess the wherewithal, or the energy, or whatever the hell it was to allow me to open up. Instead I gazed outside my window, losing myself in the cityscape, the blaring of loud horns, and the flickering of skyscraper lights. The gentle hum in my ears told me there was a freeway somewhere close by.

SIX

"Shit, we're late," Knight said as he led me down a long hallway with white linoleum floors that terminated in two steel doors. The building was in the center of the city, but just what city I didn't have a clue. And, apparently, Knight wasn't about to tell me anytime soon since keeping it secret was "protocol." Judging by the intense traffic and the number of people scurrying to and fro in the city streets, I had to imagine we weren't anywhere near Splendor or the vicinity.

But back to this building, there were twenty-two floors and we took the elevator to floor fourteen. What I found interesting was that although there were twenty-two floors, it didn't seem as if the building was occupied. There were no lights on in any of the windows and the whole thing had an unkempt feeling of neglect to it, with cobwebs in the windows, peeling paint and dust covering everything. Once we reached the fourteenth floor, the elevator spat us out into the dank hallway, which smelled like mildew. I immediately noticed two guards, standing in front of each door. They were tall, almost as tall as Knight and nearly as broad. Both were armed with *Zoobs*, something akin to a machine gun, only these were packed full of dragon blood bullets: instant death to any Netherworlders.

At our approach, each of the guards saluted Knight and started to step aside, ostensibly to grant him entrance through the double steel doors. Once their eyes landed on me, however, they hesitated.

"She's with me," Knight grumbled as he reached behind, grabbing my upper arm, and yanking me forward as if to prove it. "She's already passed security."

The guards just nodded as one of them reached over and opened the door nearest him. The other did the same, but added a licentious smile right after he checked me out from bust to butt and back up again.

"Thanks," I said acidly as I walked through the doors, now faced with an incredibly large and mostly vacant room. The ceilings had to be twenty feet high; and the stained glass windows emitted fragments of light from the skyscrapers across the way, giving it a churchy sort of feel. Knight started forward, his heavy footsteps sounding like thunder against the ancient, dusty hardwood floors. I brought my gaze down from the ceiling and focused on the conference table in the center of the room. Six people sat around the table, and at our entrance, all of them glanced over at us. I immediately recognized Christina at the head of the table and … Dia sitting just beside her?

"Dia?" I asked out loud as I approached the table, my surprise obvious by my tone.

"Hi, girl," she responded with a little laugh, pulling out the chair next to her, and patting it encouragingly. "Funny meeting you here."

I immediately took the proffered seat, not waiting for Knight to offer me one. "What are you doing here?" I whispered. "Did you just get recruited or something?"

Dia laughed as she shook her head. "No, no. I've been a council member of The Resistance for a few months. I just couldn't tell you, especially in front of everyone else. We're top secret, you know?"

"Yeah, I know," I muttered, frowning as I attempted to piece together the latest revelation that Dia was part of this team. "I thought you lived on Compound One? Your room is right down the hall from mine?"

She nodded. "Yep, I live on base. I stay in the mix for intel and security reasons."

I took a deep breath as the surprise inside of me started to fade away and curiosity over what was soon to unfold took over. I glanced around the table, wondering if there might be any other surprises awaiting me. But I didn't recognize anyone else. Sitting at the opposite head of the table, and beside me, was a man. He was older, maybe in his early fifties, and based on my itchy palms, I could detect that he was a Drow.

Drows were in the same family as elves, but where most elves were known for doing good, Drows were known for just the opposite. They were generally regarded to be nefarious in all their dealings so I was pretty surprised to see one sitting here. Similar to their elf cousins, Drows were generally tall and slender and dignified looking with pale skin. This one was dressed in black slacks and a deep purple sweater, which complemented the lavender hue of the dark circles beneath his navy blue eyes.

Knight took the seat on the Drow's other side as he offered Christina an apologetic smile. "Sorry we're late," he said.

Sitting next to Knight was a woman I also didn't recognize. It took me a second or two to place her heritage, but then it hit me over the head like an anvil. She was a nymph. Nymphs shared the same lineage as fairies—they even had the same pointy ears. And just like my own kind, nymphs were also associated with nature, mainly streams and rivers. But there were also land nymphs and this woman was of the land variety—I could tell by the brown roots of her hair (the rest of her hair was aqua blue). Water nymphs were either blond or redheads. Nymphs were definitely magically inclined but usually only when they were in the natural environment because they had to draw their power from natural resources. Nymphs and fairies alike were always famed for our youth, vitality and good looks, and this woman didn't contradict that reputation. She was young--in her mid to late twenties, if I had to guess--and very pretty with her mahogany brown eyes and short, bobbed hair. The only thing that distracted from her nymph mold was her striking aqua hair. Interesting.

74

"No problem. We waited for you both," Christina answered, seemingly not in the least fazed. She cleared her throat and smiled at everyone around the table.

"Who's the new addition?" the Drow asked while glaring at me as if I were rude and should have already introduced myself. I returned his glare, finding him less than endearing.

"Dulcie, why don't you do your own honors?" Christina said with her eyebrows raised in a rendition of "good luck."

I nodded, getting her gist, and took a deep breath as I glanced around the table. All eyes were on me and the only friendly ones belonged to Dia, Knight, and Christina. "I'm Dulcie ... O'Neil."

The nymph sucked in the air so loudly, she sounded like she was choking, while the Drow said nothing. But his silence definitely wasn't an indication of his disinterest. Instead, his cheeks were well on their way to turning a deep shade of crimson and the tips of his ears already resembled a third degree burn. No one said a word, though, so I just leaned back into my seat and waited for someone to speak, presumably after they made the connection between Melchior and me.

"Seriously?" the nymph started, dragging her angry eyes from Christina to me. "Christina, you didn't tell us about this." Once her gaze settled on me, she appeared to get even angrier and maybe I was just imagining it but it seemed her hair turned a darker shade of teal.

"This is an abomination!" the Drow yelled out at last. He slammed his bony fist into the top of the table for emphasis, his skeletal fingers so rickety, I half wondered if they might shatter. "She is our enemy!"

"Hey, don't soil your panties," I started, holding my hands up in mock surrender. "I'm not working for my father."

"What the hell? I thought we agreed to discuss this, Christina?" the nymph barked out, clearly uninterested in whatever I had to say. She refused to remove her furious and condemning gaze, just continued glaring at me as if she thought I might melt into my seat, and drip through the floorboards toward certain escape.

"Y'all are overreacting," Dia started, shaking her head as she held out her manicured hands in a mock display of surrender. I glanced at Knight and found him leaning back into his seat with a smile on his sumptuous lips as if he were enjoying himself ... the bastard.

"She's ... she's *his* daughter!" the Drow shrieked in response to Dia's comment, his mouth hanging open and his lips shivering with outrage.

"First of all," I started, standing up when I decided I'd had enough. I smacked both my palms onto the table and leaned over, alternately staring at the Drow and the nymph. "I'm sitting right here so I'd appreciate it if you called me by my name. And, speaking of my name, which seems to offend you so much, I'm related to my father in name only."

"You worked for your father," the nymph piped up accusatorily.

"Caressa confirmed Dulcie's innocence," Christina said in a tone that brooked no arguments. Her lips were pressed in a straight line, which matched the line of her eyebrows. "Caressa's word is good enough for me."

"It's good enough for me, too," Dia said in a steely voice. "I can vouch for Dulcie's credibility."

"It should be good enough for all of you," Knight said, finally coming to my defense. And it was about damn time. He leaned forward and eyed the two naysayers coldly. His eyes were narrowed and his jaw was tight, giving him a daunting appearance by anyone's count. "I've worked with Dulcie and I know her well. She's an absolute asset to our mission."

"The Loki's got that right," Dia said in a stern voice, nodding her head in a most diva-like manner. "Anyone who's gotta problem with my girl's gotta problem with me." Then she held her chin up and crossed her arms against her ample chest. "And trust me when I say that you don't wanta have a problem with me."

"Amen to that," Knight said with a flirty smile in Dia's direction.

"Thanks, D," I whispered and glanced at her with a grin. Yep, it was definitely a good thing to have Dia Diva Robinson in my corner. I relaxed and sat back in my seat.

"I got your back," Dia whispered in response as she winked, offering the same wink to Knight only this time there was something sexy about it. Sigh.

"Anything else you want to say?" Knight asked, spearing the Drow and the nymph with his ferocious stare.

"We should have been consulted," the Drow grumbled, but dropped his eyes once Knight's gaze landed on him. It was pretty obvious that Knight intimidated everyone.

"Sometimes, I don't have time to consult all of you. Sometimes, decisions have to be made," Christina responded defensively after pausing for a few seconds. "Anyway, we're moving on from this now," she finished with a glance at the Drow. "Dulcie, this is Fagan. He's in charge of The Resistance soldiers."

"Pleased to meet you," I said with a wide and artificial smile. He grumbled something unintelligible, refusing to so much as look at me. I glanced up at Christina and shrugged but she seemed uninterested. Instead, she faced the nymph who was sitting beside her.

"And this is Erica Comacho. She's in charge of the relocation efforts and the safety of all our people."

I smiled at Erica and was surprised when she nodded in response and offered me a succinct smile, mumbling: "C'est la vie."

Christina glanced down at Dia. "And you are well acquainted with our diva, I see?"

I laughed, amused that Dia's diva-bility seemed to follow her wherever she went, like a shadow, only way cooler. "I am."

"Dia is in charge of recruiting any magically sentient creatures to our cause so we can utilize their abilities," Christina continued. It was a good role for Dia to play because as a Somnogobelinus, or sleep goblin, she was magically sentient herself, being able to invade people's dreams.

"And what are you in charge of?" I reluctantly asked Knight with a frown. We'd made the rounds and he was the only one left and it was glaringly evident that he was waiting for me to ask him that exact question.

"Knight is second in command," Christina responded, granting him a proud smile. "I don't know what I would do without him."

I couldn't say I enjoyed knowing Knight was teacher's pet—mainly because it just gave him another reason to be so damned smug all the time. "Looks like a good team you've got assembled here," I said, returning my attention to Christina.

"It's better now," she responded with another broad smile. "We're happy to have you on board."

Well that seemed to be debatable, but I wasn't in the mood to argue. "Thanks," I managed.

"Now that introductions are done, we've got lots to discuss," Christina continued, referring to a notebook sitting on the table in front of her. It was covered in scribble. She faced the nymph. "Erica, any word on the portals?"

Erica nodded. "Yeah, everything is still secure. There haven't been any breaches."

Christina nodded and seemed pleased with the information. "Have there been any recent attempts?"

"At Miller's Crossing there was a small uprising by a group of O'Neil supporters who somehow managed to slip under our radar." Erica dropped her eyes to her fidgeting hands and didn't seem especially happy to be the bearer of this news.

"What were they attempting?" Knight asked, spearing her with his disappointed expression.

"They were trying to break through our portal so they could return to the Netherworld," Erica answered. Seeing the raised eyebrows and frowns around the table, she quickly added, "Anyway, the uprising was stopped almost immediately."

"Was anyone killed or injured?" Christina persisted, the look of someone concerned.

Erica shook her head. "No one was killed. The worst injury was a broken arm. Other than that, we took the bad dudes into custody and they're now in prison at Compound Five." She cleared her throat and added. "That was the only incident where any portals were threatened; and our response was swift and successful and...basically awesome." She definitely had some sort of So Cal girl flair about her.

"Good job. Please extend my kudos to those involved," Christina said with a nod, apparently pleased with the information. "Any reports on attempts to break through the portals from the Netherworld side?"

Erica shook her head. "None. The Netherworld seems to have gone quiet, like worryingly so. In the first day of the portal closures, there were attempts to break through constantly, but in the last day or so, everything has been pretty silent." She paused and glanced down at her fingernails, sighing. "I'm pretty sure it's something to worry about."

Christina nodded and picking up her pencil, bobbed it against her lips as she apparently contemplated it. "We need to make our demands soon," she said after a protracted silence. "Melchior's up to something."

"What does that mean?" I demanded at last, finally feeling like I was caught up sufficiently to where I should involve myself in the conversation.

"We're in the process of deciding how to move forward with the Netherworld, in terms of how we want to divorce ourselves from it," Knight answered. "We need to formally declare war on the Netherworld, but in order to do that, we have to demand Melchior step down as Head of the Netherworld."

"We don't want to invade without due reason," Christina added. "We want it to be known that we were forced into this position, rather than go on the offensive."

"And it's not something as simple as a phone call to Melchior," Dia continued, as if reading my expression.

"It must be a formal request that every Netherworlder can see, so they know what's coming their way," Christina finished before facing the others again. "And I've decided the best way to move forward with it is with *The Netherworlder Today*."

"The what?" I asked.

"It's the chief newspaper of the Netherworld," Knight responded. "Think *New York Times*."

"So, what, they'll run an article or something?" I asked, still not completely understanding the point.

Christina nodded. "This is something that the entire Netherworld needs to know about. If we just go to Melchior, he'll never alert the public, because he doesn't want them to know what's going on. He'd be too afraid that they might demand that he step down rather than wage war against us."

"People are too afraid of him; they would never demand that," Dia said in argument with Christina.

Christina nodded. "I know that, Dia, but Melchior is the type who won't take any risks where his supremacy is concerned. If the *Netherworlder Today* runs the column, it's our safest bet to ensure that word gets out about who we are and what our demands are."

"If my father is some supreme dictator in the Netherworld, wouldn't he be able to censor the newspaper?" I asked, frowning because it seemed so obvious.

"Yes, ultimately, he's able to censor anything, but if the article runs without him seeing it first ..." Christina started.

"And how do you propose to do that?" I interrupted, my voice sounding dubious. It just seemed like a long shot, especially when their whole plan depended on this newspaper to be the sole herald of the event.

"Sometimes it's good to have friends in high places," Christina answered loftily. I just smiled and shook my head, figuring my doubts were probably irrelevant. I mean, they knew what was going on way better than I did. And, yes, usually it *was* good to have friends in high places.

"Your friend's life won't be on the line?" I asked.

Christina shook her head and laughed. "If anyone gets away with anything in the Netherworld, it's the newspapers. Besides, if your father tried to go after them for running the piece, it would only better illustrate his despotism; and that's the last thing your father wants."

"He's going to be working overtime to convince the Netherworld population that his rule is ultimately better for them," Knight added and nodded in agreement.

"So let's say I can make sure our article runs in *The Netherworlder Today*," Christina continued, still tapping the end of her pencil against her lips. "The question is: how soon do we run it?"

"Now," Knight answered as he leaned forward, his elbows on his thighs. "What else are we waiting for?"

"We could wait for Melchior to make his first move; that way, we're justified in our retaliations," Fagan piped up, alternating his gaze between Christina and Knight. "That way it would look like he's attacking us, rather than vice versa."

"Oh, geez...What does it matter anyway?" Erica asked. "It's not like anyone in the Netherworld will stand up to Melchior regardless of whether he attacks us first."

"She has a point," Dia said with a frown. "When Melchior goes silent, it's not a good thing."

"I think we run the article ASAP, as in yesterday," Knight announced before leaning back into his chair, and crossing his large arms beneath his head. Then he glanced at me and smiled. I felt my cheeks flush and immediately glanced at Christina, trying to quell the rising tide of heat within me.

Dia glanced over at me after ogling him and fanning herself. "Good Lord, Hades did us all a big favor with that one," she whispered.

"I'm not sure I'd call it a favor," I whispered back. Knight glanced at me and raised one eyebrow. It was pretty evident he'd either overheard our conversation or was adept at reading lips. Either way, he was annoying.

"Okay, done," Christina said, slapping her hands together. "The article runs tomorrow. I'll take care of the preparations today." Then she eyed her notebook, which I assumed was a list of agenda items, and crossed off the top two. "Okay, the other issue I wanted to talk about is spies. It's becoming more and more evident that we haven't done a good enough job at sniffing out the loyalists." She took a breath. "The incident at Miller's Crossing is just another example that we should be doing our job better. Loyalists are an absolute threat to our cause. They need to be identified and dealt with."

"Loyalists are the folks who support your father," Dia whispered to me. "We call ourselves the rebels."

"That's an understatement," Erica pointed out. "Loyalists have been the biggest threat any of us have come across so far. Probably next to Melchior, himself. I've been telling people lies just so I can see if the lies get out, and then I track them back to the source. I've already caught a crapload of moles that way." Then she glanced over at me and smiled. "Good times."

Christina nodded. "Just be very careful. Don't give out any information to anyone who isn't sitting around this table. Got it?"

Everyone nodded as Knight rubbed his chin and leaned forward. "Speaking of moles," he started, settling his gaze on me as his jaw tightened. "I think we need to keep a strict eye on Quillan."

82

I felt my heart stop as I glared at him. "Quillan gave me his word, Knight."

"This isn't about pinky promising," he spat back at me, narrowing his eyes. "Quillan was Melchior's right-hand man for how many years?"

"That's beside the point," I threw back.

"Wait, Quillan Beaurigard joined The Resistance?" Fagan asked in a tone that belied his incredulity. "Are we no longer consulted on anything anymore?" he demanded of Christina.

She just shrugged. "It made sense to grant him absolution."

"Um, how did it make sense?" Erica asked in a loud tone, seemingly irritated again. One thing for Nymphs--most of them were bipolar.

"He was the closest person to Melchior; and, yes, he did work with Melchior during the entire time I did," Christina started. "So he knows how Melchior thinks."

"But don't you think Melchior is aware that Quillan is one of us?" Erica asked with a frown as she shook her head, clearly uncomfortable with the revelation. "I mean, hello McFly!"

"No," Christina answered. "As far as he's aware, Quillan could be rotting in one of our prisons."

"Which is where he should be," Knight added, and I made the decision to ignore him.

"Until word gets out," Dia said and shook her head. "It's just a matter of time before Melchior is made aware that Quill has joined us. And then he'll have to change his tactics 'cause he'll be more than aware that Quillan knows everything about him." She paused for a second and sighed, glancing down at her fingernails as she buffed them against her bright red blouse. "This could come back to bite us, y'all."

"It's all the more reason for us to act now rather than later," I said sternly. "We have to beat my father at his own game and the only way we're going to do that is with timeliness. We have to take him by surprise."

Christina nodded. "Dulcie's right."

"This is the most ridiculous thing I've ever heard!" Fagan yelled, slamming his fists against the table again. "You talk as though the elf has actually joined us! When he could be the biggest mole among us!"

"So lemme get this right," Erica started, a frown marring her pretty face. "We've been working our asses off trying to separate the loyalists from the rebels and you just decide to bring Quillan on?" She continued, glaring at Christina and then me.

Christina glared right back at both of them. "I've informed Dulcie that Quillan is her responsibility. And if she feels he's worthy of our trust, then I'm going to give him the benefit of the doubt. And I refuse to hear another word on the subject."

"He must be kept under strict surveillance," Knight said, leaning back against his chair as his attention rested on me again. I refused to look at him. Anger freely flowed through me, but I tempered it. There was no point in reacting because it wasn't like I could ever change Knight's mind where Quillan was concerned. The others, however, I was less sure about.

Christina faced him. "I'll leave that subject for you and Dulcie to figure out." Then she turned to the team assembled around the table again. "On that note, you're all dismissed. We'll meet again tomorrow after the article runs, in which case, we need to prepare for Plan A immediately. You'll receive notice of where we'll be meeting an hour before we meet. Until then, please be very careful."

SEVEN

I was so angry, I couldn't even force myself to look at Knight as we drove in the darkness. It wasn't like I was surprised though—I should've guessed he'd never give Quillan the benefit of the doubt. So, really, I wasn't even sure why I was so mad to begin with. This was just another one of Knight's shortcomings—that he couldn't find it within himself to forgive and forget. Yeah, yeah, I know—that's the pot calling the kettle black, but so what? In this instance, I would play the role of the pot all day long since I still wasn't prepared to forgive Knight for everything that had happened between us.

We'd already driven out of the portal from the city where we'd had our meeting with Christina and team, and were now on our way back to where we'd first come from, complete with a barren landscape against the velvet background of dark blue sky and yellow stars. I'd hoped Dia would have accompanied us, but unfortunately, we weren't going in her direction; so now it was just Knight and me.

As I glanced out my window, I caught a shooting star sailing across the sky. The beauty of the night, however, was lost on me. I was still utterly consumed with how pissed off Knight and the whole Quillan debacle made me; or maybe, it was just leftover resentment about what nearly happened between us in the Denali. The more I thought about it, the more I realized the Denali episode was the primary culprit. I just couldn't swallow my anger at myself. It was overflowing now, gagging me with a cornucopia of guilt and disappointment.

Why do I always lose control of myself where Knight is concerned? How is it possible that I still find him so attractive while being so pissed off with him at the same time?

It was like both sides of me were in constant conflict. One half kept reminding me that this was what happened in relationships—you'd get screwed over, turned inside out, and left a mere shell of your former self. But the other half of me couldn't stop picturing Knight's brooding gorgeousness, his smoldering eyes, and how they seemed to consume me with just a glance. And my first half wanted to murder my second half. But both halves couldn't deny how I longed for the feel of Knight's hands on my body and the taste of his lips. Not to mention how his spicy and clean scent drove me absolutely insane.

"So are you just going to ignore me for the rest of the drive back or what?" the asshole in question asked. He glanced over at me with his eyebrows raised. I had to wonder if during his creation as a soldier of the Netherworld, his incredible good looks were just part of the package. Seduce your enemy with your handsome charm and then … whack! Finish them.

I folded my arms across my chest with a frown. "Ignoring you is less harmful to your health than the other things going through my head."

"Is that so?" he asked with a hearty chuckle. His eyebrows lifted in what appeared to be genuine amusement. "Well, I'm game, hit me with your best shot, sexy."

"Okay, Pat Benatar," I snapped, refusing to look at him because his smile managed to aggravate me to no end. "And don't call me sexy."

He shook his head. "Ah, Dulcie, you are sexy, so why fight it?" Then he narrowed his eyes as if studying me. "In fact, to this day, I have yet to see another woman who can rival you in the sexiness department." He allowed his eyes to follow the lines of my body while I slowly simmered with anger. "All that fairy beauty rolled up into one delectable, little package. Sexy, sexy, sexy and then some."

"Enough," I said, glaring daggers.

"Hmmm, and you're even sexier when you're angry."

"If you're trying to piss me off, you're succeeding," I responded, unable to deal with his impish grin any longer. Instead, I tried to divert my eyes to the view outside my window. It didn't amount to much more than pitch darkness, occasionally punctuated by the halo of the headlights against a tumbleweed or lonely tree.

"Okay, okay," he said. "You win. No more sexy talk."

I didn't say anything, but tightened my arms around myself as I continued staring outside, wondering how much longer it would take to get wherever we were going.

"Come on then, out with it. What's got you so pissed off?" Knight pressed.

I glanced over at him and felt my jaw clench. "Do you really need to ask?"

"Are you mad about the Quillan thing?" Without waiting for me to respond, he continued. "Because if you are, you can stay pissed about it. I'm never going to change my mind about him no matter what you or anyone else says. I think he's a rat and wouldn't trust him as far as I could throw him."

"Because you're jealous as hell of him," I spat back before even thinking about it. And, after I did think about it, I regretted it. Why? Because I didn't have the patience or the interest, really, in getting into some long-winded argument about whether or not Knight was jealous of Quillan.

Knight remained quiet for a second as he cocked his head to the side and appeared to ponder the thought. Then he frowned. "Maybe I am."

I was so surprised, I didn't even respond; although Knight also didn't allow me the chance.

"I'm not so sure I'd call it jealousy though. I think it's more because I don't believe he deserves your forgiveness, or your kindness." He glanced over at me then. "He's like something that just crawled out of the slime compared to you."

"Getting a little dramatic there, don't you think?" I muttered, not appreciating hearing him talk that way about someone whom I considered my friend.

He shrugged. "Call it whatever you will, but I'm not going to change my mind." He took a deep breath and faced me again, apparently not concerned with safe driving. "Dulcie, I know you think he's your friend and you're all about protecting those you're close to, but I think you're wearing blinders in this case."

"Well, lucky for you, we all have a right to our own opinion," I answered snidely.

He didn't seem fazed by my comment, though. "That's the beauty about you, Dulce—you want to give everyone the benefit of the doubt and you believe in second chances." Then he paused. "I, however, do not."

I looked at him, my eyes blazing. "You don't believe in second chances?" I repeated. He nodded, but before he could respond, I added, "Funny, but that's exactly what you're asking me to give you—a second chance."

He shrugged, then nodded again. "Yes, I guess you could say I am. But, giving me a second chance and giving Quillan a second chance are two totally different subjects."

"How are they any different? A second chance is a second chance regardless of whom it's for. And, let me remind you that according to you, you don't believe in second chances."

"Where Quillan is concerned, I don't," Knight said emphatically. "I don't trust him and I don't like him. I don't like knowing he could rat us out at any second; or that he knows exactly where you are, should your father ever decide to come after you. There are too many unknowns with Quillan and you mean too much to me to ever gamble on Quillan being a decent person. That is a bet I would never take. So go ahead and be pissed off with me all you want, but at the end of the day, your safety means more to me than some insignificant ... elf."

"Then I guess we can agree to disagree," I said, falling silent. Neither of us said anything for a few seconds, until the quiet began to make me uncomfortable. I reached over to turn the radio on, but Knight grabbed my hand, apparently not in the mood for music. I pulled my hand away.

"So is that why you're pissed off with me? Because of him?" he persisted, eyeing me with those undeniably beautiful baby-blues.

"Yes," I grumbled. "I guess so."

"I'm not convinced."

"Ugh," I ground out, irritated that he could read me so well. I mean, yes, the whole Quillan thing still bothered me; but really, there was so much more. "There are so many things you do that piss me off, I'd have to start a list!"

He looked at me again with a strange expression, one that didn't appear in the least bit offended or upset. In truth, he looked amused—like he enjoyed ruffling my feathers. "How do I hate thee? Let me count the ways?" he asked with a boyish grin.

I took a deep breath, suddenly losing the wherewithal to respond. Instead, I focused on my fingers, mindlessly tapping them against my knees. If a genie in a lamp could have granted me one wish, I would have wished that we'd already arrived wherever it was that we were going, just so I could take my leave of the infuriating Loki.

Luckily, I was spared the need to respond when the lights on the dash suddenly started spazzing out, glowing incredibly bright and then dimming away to nothing. They flashed five or six times intermittently before dying altogether.

"What the hell?" I started, alternately looking from the dashboard to Knight's surprised expression.

"Weird," Knight responded as the humming from the engine suddenly stopped. I half wondered if the car was even still running.

"Did it stall?"

"Shhh," he answered, holding out his hand just in case I didn't understand English. Before I could tell him where to stick it, the Denali slowed to coasting, losing all of its momentum as the seconds ticked by. Knight turned the key in the ignition, which resulted in only a clicking sound. Apparently, the thing was dead. He pumped the brakes a few times until we came to a stop, then put the car in park and tried to start it up again. But, as with his former attempts, it clicked a few times and … nothing.

"You're kidding," I started as Knight pulled the keys out of the ignition and sighed. Then he relaxed back into his seat. I could read the question of *what do we do next?* playing over his face. "Did we run out of gas?"

He frowned at me. "Do you really think I'm such an idiot that I'd run out of gas in BFE?"

"I won't answer that question," I answered as my mind raced with what course of action should be taken next. "Where's your cell phone?" I asked, realizing mine was still in my room on base. Since our business was labeled "top secret," all cell phones that weren't Resistance-issued were banned.

Knight fished inside his pocket and produced his cell phone (which was Resistance-issued), but after he tapped it and held it up to the windshield, I realized he didn't have any cell service.

"No bars," he said grumpily.

"Jumper cables?"

He shook his head. "It's not the battery. I think it's the starter."

"Great, this is just freaking great."

Hopefully, no one was planning on traveling this road because it wasn't like we could pull to the side of it. There was no side. Instead, we were stopped dead in the middle of the road. On either side of us lay the uneven terrain of large rocks and dirt. The moon and stars twinkled down at us through the sunroof, almost as if to say, "Hey, at least it's a nice night."

"Unbelievable," I muttered while unbuckling my seatbelt, suddenly feeling the need for some fresh air. Who knew how long we'd be stuck out here? Probably all night, if I had to guess. It wasn't like we were on a well-traveled road and neither of us had any way to call AAA for a jump-start, or failing that, a tow. Nope, we were shit outta luck and then some.

"You're magical; you can fix it," Knight said, glancing over at me with a hopeful smile.

I frowned, feeling more irritated because there was no way I could fix it. "In order to fix it, I need to know what the problem is, and I know zip about cars."

That was one of the limitations of fairy magic— although I could heal myself, defend myself, and sometimes even make things out of thin air, if the task involved required background knowledge of the subject, it made things tougher. And to say I knew nothing about engines was an understatement.

"All you can do is try, right?" Knight asked, raising his brows in question. "Besides, I can guide you. Together, we should be able to fix it."

"What a shame that you aren't magical," I said, frowning. In this instance, it was a real shame for both of us.

"I seem to have other tricks up my sleeves," he said, but there was no humor or playfulness in his tone. No, he seemed worried—I could see it in his eyes. And wondering why he was worried started to worry me. Why? Because there were only a handful of times that I'd witnessed anxiety in the Loki and it wasn't something that filled me with confidence.

I didn't say anything more but took a deep breath, guessing he was right. Maybe together, we could figure out how to start the engine again. I leaned over to open my door, assuming we should look under the hood to better understand what the problem might be. When I tried to open my door, it was locked. "Um, in order for me to fix the problem, you need to let me out," I said, tugging on the door handle, as proof it was locked.

Knight wore a puzzled look on his face and seemed to move in slow motion as he hit the unlock button. When I retried the handle, it still wouldn't open. His frown deepening, he tried his door, but it, too, was locked.

"What the hell is going on?" I started. Watching Knight shake his head, I got a sinking feeling deep inside my gut.

"Use your magic to break the glass," he said in a serious tone. "Now."

I didn't wait for him to explain why. The look on his face told me something wasn't right, but just what the "something" was was the scariest part. Instead, I shook my hand until I felt a mound of fairy dust slipping through my fingers. Facing the window, I threw the dust at it, and watched the moonlight glint off the shimmering particles as they bounced against the glass. I closed my eyes tightly and imagined the glass busting out, with all the pieces dropping on the ground outside. I was also careful to imagine all the broken shards disappearing, leaving nothing but a safe, clean sill. Opening my eyes, I knew what was coming next, and covered my face with my hands as I heard the sound of glass shattering.

"Go," Knight said. I glanced over to find him right beside me, clearly ready to climb through the window behind me. I started to push myself through the large opening, but being faced with a big ass potential fall once I got to the other side, I paused. At that same moment, I heard what sounded like the monotonous ticking of a clock. Confused, I suddenly felt Knight's hands on my back, thrusting me through the window. I blinked, and in that brief millisecond, felt the cold night air against my face. That feeling was soon replaced with the rocky terrain of the road. Hitting the ground knocked the wind out of me. When I felt Knight's body on top of mine, I forced myself up, completely at a loss as to what was happening. When I tried to sit up though, Knight held me down, covering my body with his.

"It's going to blow!" he yelled into my ear.

Before I could ask him what the hell was going on, I heard the explosion. It was so loud, I felt my brain rattling between my ears. For a moment, I half wondered if my eardrums had just been blown clean out of my head. I squeezed my eyes shut tightly in an automatic reaction and felt Knight tightening his arms around me. He pushed my face into the ground as he shielded me with his body. The sounds of flying shrapnel were thick in my ears. Knight jerked against me and I could hear the thrumming of his heart.

"Have you been hit?" I screamed out against the blaring din.

"Don't move!"

I'm not sure how long we stayed like that, probably mere seconds, although it felt like hours. The ringing still blared, deafening me. Finally, Knight rolled off me and got onto his hands and knees. I sat up, shaking my head against the dull pounding in my ears that made me think the explosion must have injured my eardrums. It sounded like I was underwater, like there was a dribbling brook nearby. I shook my head again, then brought my hands to my ears, cupping them to see if the sound lessened. It didn't.

Knight grabbed my hand, bringing my attention to his face. "Heal yourself," he yelled. I didn't really hear him, but I could read what he was saying.

I nodded, shaking my hand until my fairy dust appeared. I threw the dust over my head, closing my eyes and imagining my ears healing themselves. When I opened my eyes again, the ringing had dissipated and I felt as good as I could hope for, given the circumstances. I glanced at Knight and noticed he hadn't changed positions.

"Are you hurt?" I asked in a tremulous voice.

"My back," he said. I stood up and walked around him, stopping in shock when I noticed the long and angry gash across his upper back. It spanned the top of his neck all the way to his middle spine. It was so deep, I could see the white bone beneath it; well, that is, through all the blood. The wound must have resulted from the shrapnel—it looked like a piece of something had split his back in a long, clean stroke. I shook my fist until I felt it fill with dust and sprinkled the glittery particles on top of him, like drops of rain. At the same time, I closed my eyes and pictured his wounds healing, weaving themselves closed as if with an invisible thread. But when I opened my eyes, his wound was just as raw as before.

"What?" I started.

He sat back on his haunches and seemed to bend forward a bit, panting as he did so. I walked around to face him, noticing how he winced with pain. He closed his eyes and appeared to be concentrating, his lips tight and his eyes clenched. I peered over his shoulder and watched the angry, red swelling of the cut slowly give way to his tan skin. The skin then seemed to stitch itself together, the seam of the gash slowly giving way to nothing but an uninterrupted canvas of perfect skin. That was when I remembered that he *could* heal himself, something he'd artfully demonstrated for me when I first met him.

"That'll have to do," he said, straining to get to his feet. I immediately took his arm and braced myself to support his weight as he used me for his crutch.

"You aren't all the way healed?"

He nodded. "I am, but I lost a lot of blood," he answered in a shallow voice. When I glanced up at him, I could see the truth of his words. Blood soaked the remnants of his shirt back and his face was paler than usual, beads of perspiration dotting his hairline. His hands were clammy against my body. Only pockets of tan skin peeped through his tattered clothing, which was utterly drenched in blood. Even the backs of his pants were also stained red.

"Will you be okay?" I asked, my voice belying my worry.

He simply chuckled deeply, rubbing my head with his knuckles, like I was a little kid. "Should I take that to mean you're actually worried about me?"

"Just answer the damn question," I muttered.

He eyed himself, as if assessing the damage, then looked at me, smiling. "Never better."

I shook my head and sighed. "I should have remembered that you can heal yourself and survive fire."

He beamed widely but he still looked exhausted. "Forged by the fire of Hades, Dulce. Keyword: fire."

"Yeah, yeah," I said, sighing as we both turned toward the direction of the Denali, or what was left of it. Now it looked like the burnt-out remains of some kind of enormous beast. The steel was so blackened and bent, it no longer resembled a car. "So what the hell just happened?" I asked, looking up at him.

Shaking his head, he attempted to stand up straight, as if summoning all his power. He separated himself from me and then took a few steps forward, stretching his arms above his head as if to check his handiwork on his back. "It was a botched assassination attempt."

"Botched ... *assassination* attempt?"

He shrugged and bent forward, stretching his arms out in front of him. I couldn't help noticing how his muscles bulged despite the bloody remains of his clothes.

"Botched. The thing should have blown from the moment we stepped into the car. Somewhere, someone's magic went wrong." Then he glanced up and smiled at me. "Luckily, for you and me."

"How would anyone know where to find us?" I asked and watched him pick up a piece of debris that looked like it was once a part of the door. He clutched it in his hand and motioned for me to approach him. When I did, he draped his arm around me again and we continued forward, albeit slowly.

"Loyalists. They make it their business to know." He kicked a piece of metal beside his foot and the metal clanked as it came into contact with another piece of the Denali. "There are spies all over the place. This is just their calling card. The hard part is going to be tracing it back, and finding out who is responsible."

"Were they targeting you or me?"

He sighed and shook his head. "No way of knowing. Maybe both of us."

I nodded, realizing there was no point in asking him questions because all we could do was speculate. "So what now?"

He shrugged and smiled down at me. "You up for a little stroll?"

EIGHT

The so-called "stroll" became a four-hour hike with nothing but the moon and a blanket of stars to light our way. The dirt road seemed never ending, comprising miles of flat land on either side with only the outlines of spotty pine trees to break the monotony. It seemed the longer we walked, the colder the air became; and eventually, I could see my breath. Knight helped to keep me warm though, owing to the fact that he was using me as his crutch and consequently, enveloping half of me in his body heat. After we managed to cross all of BFE (or so it felt), we reached an equally desolate highway. While the highway didn't look as though it promised more civilization than the dirt road from which we'd just emerged, at least Knight now had cell phone service. And that was a godsend, as far as I was concerned.

After rejoicing over the single bar of connectivity, Knight managed to reach Christina and explain what had happened over the last several hours. I could hear her shocked exclamations, and from what I could make out, she was in the process of assembling her team for an emergency meeting. Thirty minutes after Knight hung up, a black Lincoln Town Car appeared. I didn't recognize the driver, but Knight did, so I figured we were in safe company. And it was about damn time! My left shoulder felt like it was crushed, after having supported Knight's massive weight for the last few hours.

Once we were seated in the cushy Town Car, Knight didn't say anything to the driver, or to me, for that matter. I wasn't sure if it was due to his exhaustion and pain or maybe he was just in an introspective mood. Not that his silence bothered me particularly. I cherished any quiet time where I could retire into the privacy of my head and get lost in my own thoughts. During the last few days, I couldn't say that I'd had any "me" time at all, so this was just what the doctor ordered.

I relaxed into the plush leather seat and closed my eyes, suddenly feeling fatigue's claim on me. It threw me temporarily, when I thought how my adrenalin was on overdrive a mere few hours before; but now I wanted nothing more than the solace of sleep. Sleep, however, continued to elude me because there was way too much going on in my mind. My thoughts were a jumbled mix of fear, anger, and concern over what had just happened, and what sort of threat these so-called Loyalists now posed.

Why were Knight and I nearly been blown to smithereens? How could someone have known where we were? And, furthermore, who was that "someone"? If Knight and I were such easy targets, what did that mean for the rest of Christina's "A" Team? Were we just sitting ducks? Each one of us doomed to extermination in only a matter of time? Just how pervasive was my father's authority?

Being so consumed by my thoughts, it took me by surprise when the Town Car suddenly stopped. I opened my eyes and glanced beyond Knight to observe what looked like another military base. The eerie glow of the overhead floodlights illuminated a narrow guard station where several immense, concrete pylons outlined the entry through a pair of huge, wrought-iron gates. I pulled my attention away from the pylons and focused on a man in a dark grey uniform as he approached our vehicle. He was clutching a *Quig 300*—a weapon most similar to a semi-automatic machine gun.

"Where are we?" I asked.

"Compound Two," Knight answered in a worn-out tone. I didn't say anything, but watched the driver roll down his window as the guard leaned over and stuck his head into the Town Car. First, he studied the driver, then Knight, and then me. Based on the whiff of dog that suddenly rose up into my nostrils, I figured the guard must have been a were.

98

"Louie," he said, addressing the driver. Then with a glance back at Knight again, he said, "Vander."

"Greetings," Knight replied drolly. "We're in something of a rush, so let's get on with it."

The guard said nothing as he reached into his pocket, withdrawing something that looked like a cigarette lighter. Knight simply nodded and rolled his window down as the guard approached. The man leaned in and held the lighter directly in front of Knight's eyes. A red, laser-like light suddenly emitted from the front of the object and the guard moved his hand very slowly from left to right, allowing the red of the light to scan both of Knight's irises. The whole thing took maybe two seconds; then the guard gave a nod of approval before returning the laser pen to his pocket. He then faced me.

Who's she?" he asked.

"She's with me," Knight answered evasively. The guard eyed me once again with a frown.

"She'll have to be checked just like everyone else, Vander."

Knight sighed like he didn't have the time, much less the interest, in getting me "checked." "Make it quick—we're on borrowed time."

"What's he talking about?" I asked in a concerned tone, wondering if I was to be victim number two of the cigarette laser scanner. Not that it looked painful in the least, but anyhoo ...

"Don't work yourself up," Knight answered as he further reclined into his seat. He smirked at me as if he were extending an invitation to climb onto his lap. "It's best to remain calm. Breathe in slowly and breathe out slowly. The more your heart rate increases, the harder it is for the *Magreew* to confirm your innocence."

"The what?" I repeated, frowning as I narrowed my eyes at him. Before I could demand an explanation, I heard the sound of my door opening. I immediately turned to find the guard standing in front of me. There was a black box in

99

his hands. It appeared to be about two feet long by a foot wide.

"Please stand up," he said in a monotone.

"What is that?" I asked, making no motion to stand as I folded my arms against my chest and did my best to appear nonplussed.

"Dulcie, it's policy," Knight said as I glanced over at him. "Just trust me, okay?" He smiled that charming boyish smile of his, which I supposed he thought would put me at ease. It didn't work.

I didn't respond, but after considering how limited my options were, I stood up and took a step toward the guard and the black box. Apparently accepting my silence as acquiescence, the guard opened the box and reached into it, producing what looked like an enormous slug. The thing was puke-green and the length of my forearm. It glistened in the moonlight, slime covering every inch of it. It looked like Slimer's smaller cousin.

"What. Is. That?" I asked with undisguised revulsion.

"That's a *Magreew*," Knight responded from behind me, making no attempt to conceal the chuckle in his tone.

The bastard.

"This will only take two minutes," the guard said, clearly observing my disquietude. Two minutes never sounded so long.

"What will only take two minutes?" I asked. My attention was riveted on the nasty thing as it rolled its head from side to side, its banana-shaped body slithering across the guard's hand and leaving a trail of bubbly green goo that looked like baby snot.

"Extend your hand," the guard demanded. I wasn't sure if I imagined it or if he actually avoided looking at the creature. I mean, he had to be just as grossed out by it as I was. The abomination was the unabridged definition of disgusting.

"There is no way in hell I'm letting that thing anywhere near me," I said, eyeing it suspiciously. "It's repulsive."

The thing cocked its head (I think it was a head, but since both ends looked exactly the same, it was hard to tell). I had to wonder if it somehow understood me.

"You can wash your hands afterwards, Dulcie," Knight said, still sounding amused. "It's just a little ectoplasm, so grow some balls and let's get this show on the road."

"Yeah, says the guy who only had to deal with the laser pen," I barked back. He chuckled in response as I took a deep breath in preparation for the slug's application. "If this thing has teeth, I'm out," I said, glaring at the guard.

"No teeth," he answered evasively.

Figuring I wasn't going to advance beyond this point if I didn't submit myself to the ministrations of the slug, I said nothing more. Courageously, I thrust my hand out, palm open and facing upward. The guard brought his palm onto mine and the *Magreew* slid one of its ends (I still had no idea which end was head or tail) onto my hand. It seemed to sniff my palm—one end moving up and down as it inspected me. Then, it simply slid off the guard's hand and into mine. It was incredibly warm and strangely heavy, feeling incredibly dense in its wet heat. In fact, its weight surprised me so much that I nearly dropped it. Gripping my wrist, I held my hand up straight again as I eyed the abhorrent creature curiously. It began to roll its body slowly from side to side, which reminded me of one of those paper-thin, plastic fortune-telling fish. It stopped rolling and seemed to flatten itself against my palm, while bubbles of hot goo fizzled up from underneath it.

"Um, what's it doing?" I asked in tremulous wonder.

"It's reading you," Knight answered. "It's figuring out what your intentions are and whether you're any threat to The Resistance. It's a sympath."

So the odd creature did possess a high level of intelligence. Sympathetic creatures were very rare, and in the wrong hands, could become dangerous. They could read a person's character just by touching the person in question. This one must have been imported from the Netherworld as I'd never seen one before.

It continued to gyrate against my hand, becoming warmer and warmer until it actually became pretty hot. "Um, this thing is getting really warm," I said in a concerned tone.

"It's okay," the guard answered. "It's almost finished."

I glanced down at it again right before it suddenly went cold and stopped fidgeting. It simply lay still in my palm. "Yeah ... I think it just ... died?"

The guard didn't say anything as he nodded and reached for the vile thing. He rolled it back into his palm before opening the black box and depositing it inside.

"It's not dead," he answered at last. He closed the box and reached inside his pocket, wiping his hands on what looked like a hankie before offering the same one to me. I accepted it, figuring it was better than wiping the gooey remnants on my clothes. 'Course, right about now, I also considered wiping my hand right across Knight's smug face, but figured that probably wouldn't go over too well. "Thanks," I grumbled.

The guard opened my door wider for me, tacitly urging me to return to my seat. I did so and glanced over at Knight glumly. He was beaming from ear to ear.

"Now was that so bad?"

I cocked a brow and regarded him coolly. "I'd say it ranked right up there next to the botched assassination attempt."

"Dulcie, Dulcie, Dulcie," Knight chided as he shook his head, adding. "Oh, I'd advise you to wash your hands once we get inside the compound. Those things don't ... smell very good."

I didn't even have the wherewithal to respond.

###

An hour later, we (as in Christina's Team) were all assembled in what I assumed was a library. Upon further inspection, though, the books were all fake—mere facades to make it appear that the owner of the library was well read. Whoever owned it and where we were remained mysteries to me. I knew we'd arrived in Compound Two, but upon entering the only building in sight, I guessed we must have traveled through a portal because we were now in a house, or so it appeared.

"We" was comprised of Knight, Christina, Dia, Erica, the still foul-mooded Drow, and me. The Drow sat next to Erica while Dia sat on the opposite side of the room. She kept herself busy by inspecting one of her many fabulous earrings she was renowned for making. These were huge, colorful circles with feathers attached at the bottoms. Christina stood right beside her, pacing back and forth as if in obvious distress.

"So sounds like you guys nearly met your maker?" Erica piped up from across the room. Her hair was now canary yellow, but still short and bobbed, and still super cute. She had one of those faces and skin tones that could get away with just about any hair color.

"Hi to you too," Knight said, frowning at her in a playful sort of way.

"No need to get your feathers ruffled, handsome," she threw back with a knowing grin. "You know, I think you're the sexiest creature south of the Netherworld."

"Oh, here we go," Dia muttered, but seconds later erupted into a giggle as she faced me. "That nymph's got it somethin' bad for your Loki, Dulce."

The Loki glanced over at me with the expression of "Yeah? So what are you planning on doing about it?" pasted on his face. I just frowned, facing Erica. "He's not my Loki, so have at it."

I didn't miss Knight's frown or the way his eyes narrowed in obvious offense. But there was something in his eyes that gave me cause for pause, something that hinted to the fact that my comment really bothered him—a lot. I felt a moment's twinge of guilt before I shook the feeling loose, irritated with myself. I mean, I never said I'd forgiven Knight for everything that transpired between us, and as far as I was concerned, I still hadn't forgiven him. Besides, it wasn't like I'd actually even had the time to think through my confusing thoughts to arrive at a decision regarding Knight anyway. Nope, it just became one of those subjects relegated to the back burner, where it could boil and bubble, just like every other subject that had the misfortune of being back-burnered in my overwhelmed mind.

"Loyalists were responsible for the near deaths of Dulcie and Knight," Christina started. She faced everyone in the room as she propped her hands on her hips, only to bring them to her head and clasp them behind her hair as she started pacing again. "I've called Henrietta to join us so she can tell us more."

"Who's Henrietta?" I whispered to Dia, getting dizzy from watching Christina making the rounds of the room again.

"She's a witch," Dia responded out of the corner of her mouth.

"No," I piped up, facing Christina as I felt myself standing. "The only witch I trust is Sam."

"Henrietta is one of the best," Christina started as she stopped walking and turned to face me.

I adamantly shook my head. "If a witch is going to be involved in something that happened to me, I want that witch to be Sam. And while you're at it, Trey should be brought in as well, because he can be just as useful as Sam is."

Christina was quiet for a second or two before she nodded and picked up her cell phone, speed dialing someone. "I need Sam and Trey from Compound One." She was silent for a few seconds before she nodded. "Yes, they are to be brought through the portal to the library." She paused again. "Yes, standard security protocol." Then she hung up and faced us again. "They'll be here shortly."

I nodded and smiled as I imagined Sam's expression upon arriving at the security gates to this compound. I could just picture her repugnance when she found herself up close and personal with the *Magreew*.

I didn't know if portal travel merely occurred from Point A to Point B, or if it also meant manipulating time; but within ten minutes, Sam and Trey walked through the double doors of the library. They were now facing all of us curiously and both of them seemed not only surprised, but concerned.

"Dulce?" Sam asked as soon as she recognized me. "What's going on?"

I stood up and approached them both, putting my hands on each of their shoulders as soon as I reached them. "Everything is okay," I started, but frowned as I thought about the comment. "Well, as okay as can be expected, given the circumstances."

"What do you mean?" Sam asked, eyeing me askance. Trey didn't mutter a word, and instead just focused on the people assembled in the room, as if memorizing their faces.

"Welcome to The Resistance," Christina said with a warm smile as she approached us.

"The Resistance," Trey echoed as he eyed everyone again and looked, for all intents and purposes, star struck.

"Then this is The Team?" Sam asked, glancing first at Christina and then at me before her eyes searched the room and landed on Dia. "Dia?"

"Hi, girl," Dia called back with a little wave.

"I requested that you both come," I started as I led them to the center of the library where Knight stood up. He offered his chair to Sam, doing his best impersonation of a gentleman. Sam took the proffered seat and I took the empty one next to her. She glanced around, as if taking stock of the room, the fake books, the furniture, and everyone in it, before facing me again.

"Why do you need Trey and me?" she asked as she chewed on her lower lip. "And are you part of The Resistance too?"

"Yes, I am," I started, taking a deep breath as I tried to figure out where to begin. "Knight and I were nearly killed yesterday."

"Nearly killed?!" Sam exclaimed, her eyes wide.

"There was an explosion in the Denali that was meant to kill us, but failed to detonate in time," I said quickly, not wanting her to worry unnecessarily. I mean, Knight and I *were* still alive...

"Oh my God," Sam cried, her mouth dropping open.

"We need for you to determine whether there were any potions involved in the explosion," Knight added, alternating his gaze between the two of us. It seemed his strength had finally returned as he was able to walk around unsupported. Good thing for me because my shoulder was still aching like a son of a bitch.

"Of course," Sam started, looking at me with her doe-eyes. Then she threw her arms around me and buried her face in my neck. I could feel the heat of her tears against my skin.

"I'm okay, Sam," I whispered as I patted her on the back, uncomfortable with being the center of everyone's attention. Some situations call for a little privacy and this was certainly one of them.

She looked up at me with watery eyes. "You were nearly killed, Dulce, that's far from being okay."

I didn't say anything because I didn't know what to say. Why? Because Sam was right. Things were far from okay. Things were more in the realm of super fucked up and probably quickly on their way to getting worse.

"Sam, can you detect any residual signature or anything else on this?" Knight asked as he held out a piece of debris from the Denali. Sam nodded and dragged her shirtsleeve across her nose as she tried to get herself in order. "Take as much time as you need," Knight added in a soft voice with an encouraging smile.

"The library has everything you might need," Christina said. "This is an alchemist's library," she finished.

Sam nodded and gave Christina a smile of thanks before reaching for the piece of metal in Knight's hand. She glanced down at it and sighed before taking her seat again and running her finger down the length of the cold metal. Searching the room, I noticed everyone had broken up into smaller groups and were making idle conversation, probably to allow Sam and me some privacy.

"I need a white out," Sam said, addressing me. I looked up at Knight in question, obviously not knowing enough of our location to even begin to try and find the tincture, which would announce whether or not a potion had been involved in the detonation of the Denali.

"White out, white out," Christina repeated as she scanned the myriad of bookless spines along the wall. "Aha," she called out as she pushed the spine of one very beaten-up book that was written in what appeared to be Latin. The book facade popped forward, revealing a shelf behind it. On the shelf were several vials of white powder. Christina reached for one of the vials and handed it to Knight, who then gave it to Sam.

Accepting it with a nod, she opened the vial, depositing a small mound directly onto the metal. Then she recapped the vial and spread the white powder across the surface of the metal as we all looked on in silent anticipation. The white powder began to bubble within seconds.

"Yep, it's charmed," Sam said with a sigh. She glanced up at Christina. "I need some *Renneen One,* if you have it."

Christina nodded and started scanning the book spines again as Erica stood up and approached her, offering to help.

Smiling in response, she and Erica started searching the bookcase on the opposite side of the room.

"Looks like we've got *Renneen Two*," Erica called out. "But I don't see *Renneen One*."

"Two will do," Sam answered.

Erica nodded and pushed against the book spine, which then plopped open, displaying a large chunk of what looked like butter. There was a small knife next to it and about four baggies beside the knife. Erica picked up the knife and cut a small slice of the stuff off, bagging it immediately. As soon as she dug the blade into the mound of buttery stuff, it began to ooze out a green liquid, almost as though it were bleeding.

Erica handed the bag to Sam and Sam opened it, smearing some of the buttery-like stuff against the piece of the Denali. The butter melted into the metal, which began to glow with a pinkish hue in the areas where the butter stuff dissolved into it.

"Looks like it could have been a *Maegon* bomb or possibly a *Jaffroodi*," Sam said. "It's definitely an illegal concoction, but I'm just not sure which one."

Knight nodded and approached her, his eyes on the metal. "*Maegon* or *Jaffroodi* could mean the difference between an East Coast Loyalist or a West Coast one. Can you be a little more specific?"

Sam paused for a second or two and eyed the piece of metal as she thought about Knight's question. Not finding an immediate answer, she turned to face Trey. "Trey, can I borrow you for a sec?"

"Sure thing," Trey answered, peeling himself off the wall where he'd been watching Erica. He smiled at her apologetically before trotting over to us. Glancing over at Erica, I just shook my head as I realized she was probably Trey's newest crush.

Once Trey reached Sam's side, she turned to face him. "Can you see if you get any feelings about this?" she asked, handing the piece of the Denali to Trey. "See if you can get any sort of hint as to where the potion might have come from."

He nodded and opened his palm as Sam dropped the twisted hunk of metal into his hand. Closing his fingers over it, he shut his eyes. His pupils began to race side to side behind his eyelids, like someone experiencing REM sleep.

"The potion definitely didn't originate on the East Coast," he said softly. "I'm not getting much from it, but I can tell you it's a *Maegon*."

"Then it's West Coast," Knight said, never pulling his eyes from Trey.

"Wait," Trey said as he held up his hand. "I'm sensing that it wasn't a potion on the black market, but a home concoction."

No one said anything; we all just waited to see if Trey was going to receive anything else about the strange potion. The fact that it was a home concoction was definitely an interesting point. It wasn't common to come across homemade potions. Why? Because illegal potions were relatively cheap and plentiful on the black market and what was more, they were highly dangerous to create. But going back to this particular potion, I chewed on the fact that it was apparently created in someone's backroom. The question was why?

After another few minutes, Trey shook his head and opened his eyes. "I got nothin' else," he said simply.

I faced Knight, only to find him already staring at me. "So?" I asked.

He cocked a brow and continued to study me before his sumptuous lips broke into a solid line, a sure indication that he was frustrated. "I'd bet my ass that someone we know is behind this; not some random Loyalist."

Christina stepped forward, as her eyes narrowed and her jaw grew tight. "Why?"

Knight pulled his gaze from me and faced her. "Someone had to know what car I was driving and more importantly, where the car was located. A *Maegon* potion won't keep long, which means that once he'd created the potion, the perp had maybe two hours to dust the Denali with it."

"How do you know the perp is a 'he'?" I asked.

Knight faced me and swallowed hard. "I don't." He took a deep breath. "But what I would bet my ass on is that it's ANC."

"Let me guess ... the ingredients for *Maegon* are sitting in the vault of the ANC?" I asked as I tried to make sense of his comment.

Knight nodded.

"And *Maegon* ingredients are near impossible to find on the streets," I continued, shaking my head against the fact that someone in the ANC could have done this.

"Yes and no. You can find the ingredients, but it's incredibly difficult to do so; and, yes, there was a shipment sitting in the ANC vault which was never destroyed, owing to everything that happened within the last twenty-four hours," Knight finished.

"Not only that, but *Maegon* is very difficult to make; and as part of our potion training, only highly ranking ANC Regulators and officials have the knowledge," Christina added. "So it *would* seem someone in the ANC was involved for sure."

"Doesn't this seem way too convenient though?" I asked as I shook my head again, eyeing everyone in the room. "Whoever did this would be more than aware that we would be able to figure out it was a *Maegon* and then trace it back to the ANC. I really have a hard time believing that someone could be so stupid."

Knight raised his brows and shook his head. "Criminals don't necessarily have to be smart, Dulce."

I rolled my eyes and grumbled something under my breath because I was convinced there was more to this situation than what was so readily apparent on the surface.

NINE

After our impromptu meeting ended, Christina informed me that it wasn't safe for me to continue living on base. She was convinced that whoever tried to kill Knight and me was one of her people and also an ANC employee. Apparently, the idea that the perp was a Loyalist had been quickly abandoned because there was just too much evidence pointing to the fact that this must have been an inside job. As an inside job, it meant the would-be killer could be living in any of The Resistance compounds or, worse yet, he or she could even be part of Christina's Resistance Team. Either way, Christina considered me a walking target if I continued to proceed as if nothing happened. This was quite artfully demonstrated by Knight's and my near fatalities in the Denali. So I had to be relocated, but as to where I would soon be spending the majority of my time, I didn't have a clue but figured I'd find out shortly.

Christina ordered Knight to re-test the loyalty of all residents of the compounds, as well as her own team members. If paranoia were Christina's second cousin, it now became her sister and for good reason. All those loyal to The Resistance movement had to be subjected to rigorous lie-detectors, which involved incantations and spells from our resident witches. Once that task was completed, everyone would next be subjected to the application of the *Magreew*. The final gauntlet was a human polygraph. In so doing, Christina figured she had all her bases covered—magic by way of witchcraft, sympath, and no magic at all.

As expected, Christina insisted her team of officials undergo the tests first. It took two hours to assemble our team, the witches, the *Magreew,* and the polygraph. We also had to determine a proper location to perform the tests. After

111

a couple of hours, during which time we sat in the library in complete silence, I felt like I was playing the real-life version of Clue. Our wait in the library felt like an eternity, especially since no one said much to each other. We just eyed one another as if sizing each other up as we wondered if someone present in the room was responsible for the murder attempt on Knight and me. While my natural instinct was to point my finger at the Drow, given his obvious aversion to me from the start, I didn't imagine he was guilty. Why? Because the reason for his distrust was solely due to my being Melchior O'Neil's daughter. 'Course, he also could have been a good actor ...

Moving my eyes from the Drow to Dia, I shook my head as I even considered her involvement. There was no way Dia could have plotted Knight's and my assassinations. Of that, I was more than sure. Excluding Knight, since I didn't imagine he wanted anything to do with a suicide bombing, that just left Christina and Erica. As the leader of The Resistance, I had to imagine Christina's loyalty was obvious. So that left Erica.

What did I know about her? Nothing really. She seemed to emphasize the Drow's anger when she first found out I was my father's daughter ... Yeah, but what could that mean? Maybe she was just playing the part of concerned Resistance team member to throw us off the fact that she was really working for my father?

I sighed at the realization of how completely useless this task was, not to mention how wrong it was. Rule number one in the ANC: Do not point accusatory fingers at people before knowing all of the facts. And furthermore, I couldn't imagine the verdict being as simple as a big, red flashing sign above someone's head announcing his or her guilt. No. Whoever this person was, he or she had to be good. I mean, none of the sympaths (Trey included) picked up anything out of the ordinary. That was a sure sign that the perp had somehow manipulated the magical force field that allowed sympaths to pick up on feelings and visions of situations and events.

After another hour, each of us was shown into separate rooms where we underwent the prescribed tests of our loyalty. Even though it certainly occurred to me, I didn't point out the non sequitur of testing Knight and me for our loyalty—I mean, it wasn't like either of us planned to blow ourselves up. But, as Erica would say, *C'est la vie*.

The room was small—maybe ten feet wide by twelve feet long and incredibly dark, owing to the fact that there weren't any windows. The only light was afforded by a yellowed, old light bulb, suspended from the ceiling by a wire. It looked like the setting for some hideous torture scene, or maybe, an interrogation, guerilla-style. Swallowing my own sense of foreboding, I forced myself to take a deep breath and banish my morose thoughts. Instead, I glanced around the room and noticed that there were two plastic chairs with a small school-style table between them. I took the chair closest to me and started to fidget, my knees bouncing with nervous anticipation of what was to come.

I was alone for probably another five minutes before a witch I didn't recognize entered the room. She looked like a Soccer Mom. Her hair was very short—that asexual, boyish haircut women often relegate themselves to once they hit forty. Apparently the big four-oh made women feel like they had to eviscerate all signs of being women. But back to the witch, she was tallish—five foot six or so, and maybe thirty pounds overweight. She wore dark jeans and a pink, amorphous T-shirt that made her look even boxier. She carried what looked like a bowling ball bag, but when she plopped it on the table and zipped it open, it was not a bowling ball, but rather an enormous hunk of crystal. It was close to the size of my thigh. The bottom was milky white, which slowly yielded to long and lustrous clear crystals.

She didn't so much as offer me any form of greeting, not even a smile. She simply dropped the bag on the floor and, lifting the crystal, took a seat, while placing it on her

113

lap. Then she closed her eyes and held her palms up towards the crystal as her lips moved. She was chanting something, but given her Soccer Mom appearance, to me it looked more like she was singing the lyrics to some Justin Bieber song. She opened her eyes and focused on me, but remained silent. Reaching for my hand, she folded it beneath her fleshy fingers, and resumed her incantation, which now sounded foreign—something like what I imagined Latin might sound like. Well, for all I knew it could have been pig Latin.

After finishing incantation number one, she opened one eye briefly, glanced at me and then immediately shut it again. She started chanting something else, her grip on my hand tightening. As she finished her Bieberesque humming, she opened one eye again, almost as if she were checking to make sure I was still there. Apparently pleased that I hadn't made like a bird and flown away, she performed a third charm on me, which was in English. It described a whole lot of mumbo-jumbo about nature and the goddess and the seasons. Before I could say "hocus pocus," she grabbed the index finger of my right hand and speared it with the tallest point on the crystal.

"Shit!" I yelled out in shock and pain as I withdrew my injured digit into the haven of my chest and glanced down to appraise the damage. My finger looked like the victim of a hole punch. "You could have at least warned me!" I lashed out with a frown. It still hurt like a son of a bitch and blood coursed down my finger, pooling into the palm of my hand. She handed me a tissue from her pocket and I quickly staunched the blood flow, but I didn't say thank you.

She sneered at me like I was overreacting (which I probably was), but said nothing. Instead, she returned her attention to the crystal on her lap. I watched the gold drops of my blood run down the rough edges of the crystal, where they dissolved into the base entirely, as if they'd never been.

"You passed," the Soccer Mom witch said simply.

"Great," I grumbled with a fleeting glance at my still bleeding finger. I shook my palm until a mound of fairy dust

114

emerged. Then I sprinkled the dust over my wound and watched as the blood dried up and my skin began to sew itself back together. Eventually, the wound vanished into my skin.

The witch stood up and collected the gargantuan crystal into her bowling bag, saying, "Wait here for the *Magreew*."

With that, she simply waddled to the door and closed it behind her. I sighed as I thought about reuniting with the *Magreew*. While I couldn't say I was looking forward to it, at least it wouldn't make me bleed.

Forty minutes later, I'd successfully completed all three trials to test my loyalty to The Resistance. I'd braved the spells of the witch, suffered the slime of the *Magreew*, and tolerated the unsophisticated polygraph machine, and I'd passed. To my surprise, at the conclusion of my polygraph test, I was told to remain in the dismal little room. Why? I didn't have a clue, but I didn't argue. Instead, I just stayed put. Yep, I was doing a damn good job of being a team player.

The next time the door opened, which was maybe ten minutes after the conclusion of my polygraph test, I was relieved to see Knight.

"Congratulations, it appears you weren't behind the plot to assassinate yourself," he said with a cocky smile.

"Ha ha, Mr. Comedian," I replied grumpily. "Thanks for making me wait ten minutes just to deliver that surprising news." I stood up and started for the door, having already decided I'd had enough.

"Not so fast, Speedy Gonzalez," he said, adding a chuckle. "Unless you plan to walk yourself to your new hideaway."

I turned around slowly, shaking my head as I cocked a brow and let him know how unamused I was. "Let me guess, you're my chauffeur?"

With a nod, he smiled that devil's smile. Even in the relative darkness of the room, he was exquisite to behold. The shadows played with his features, darkening his already tan skin, the whites of his eyes in stark contrast. His handsome, albeit rakish, smile gave him the look of an absolute rogue. As much as I dared not admit it, in the entire course of my history with Knightley Vander, there was never a moment when I felt the longing to kiss him more. Somehow, though, I managed to subdue my more carnal, primitive urges in favor of appearing more civilized.

"We've got a smart one," the Loki said in a suggestive sort of way.

"Okay, so what now? Where are we going and how long will it take? Do I have time to get my things?" I asked, throwing my hands on my hips. I had to discourage myself from noticing how broad his shoulders were, and how his hair was the exact same shade as his black T-shirt. I definitely didn't want to draw my attention to the swells of his biceps, which his T-shirt did a terrible job of covering. Never mind his long legs and incredibly tight ass …

"To answer your montage of questions—yes, I'm your chauffeur. I can't tell you where we're going, but it will take about an hour or so to get there. Your things have already been packed for you."

"You can't tell me where we're going?"

He cocked his head to the side and studied me for a few seconds. "I could."

I sighed, long and deep. "So?"

"But then I'd have to kill you," he finished, smiling even more broadly.

"I keep wondering if one of these days you might actually grow up."

"Nah, growing up is for adults."

"Exactly." I took a deep breath, wondering if I'd be able to get anything out of him. "So what *can* you tell me about where we're going?"

He shrugged. "I can only tell you I'm taking you somewhere Christina believes you'll be safe. I couldn't tell you where exactly because I actually don't even know, myself. But once we get to wherever it is we're going, you'll need to get some shut-eye."

I hadn't even thought about sleeping, but as soon as the thought crossed my mind, I realized I hadn't slept in ... a while. My body suddenly appeared to deflate with just the mention of sleep. It became clear that I was beyond exhausted. "Okay, then what?"

"Then you wait for further notice," he answered simply with another shrug. His rebellious smile was still fully manifested. It was a smile that characterized Knight all too well; and the perfect example of how cocky he was. He seemed incapable of taking no for an answer, and could undress you with a simple glance.

"And what about you?" I insisted.

"What about me?"

I shrugged, thinking the question was obvious and he was just delaying answering. He was just playing with me. "If I'm being relocated to a safer place, I hope you're also considering your own safety? It's not like you can go back to any of the compounds. I mean, I wasn't the only target when the Denali blew."

He smiled even more broadly, his eyes twinkling with undisguised mirth. "Wait a second, did I hear you correctly?" He pretended to clean out his ears. "So, does this mean you really do care about me?"

I shook my head and sighed, glancing down at the floor as I rubbed the back of my neck and felt sorry for myself. Why were things always a pain in the butt where Knight was concerned? Why couldn't things be easy?

When I looked up at him again, I wore the expression of someone far from amused. "Why do you always have to make everything so difficult?"

His smile faltered, instantly replaced by a frown as he folded his large arms against his chest. "Well, remembering how you told Erica to 'have at me,' I'm confused about where you and I stand ... and understandably, I might add."

I was in no mood to argue, nor to discuss the hot mess otherwise known as *what in the hell is going on between Knight and me.* "We're not getting into this right now," I answered, showing my intent to prove it by walking past him.

I didn't get far. He grabbed my upper arm and stopped me, his eyes imploring. He didn't say anything for a few seconds, but stood there with his fingers wrapped around my arm. I didn't say anything either. It was as if his touch had completely stolen my ability to form words. There *was* something between us. It was as obvious as the nervous energy working its way up my stomach.

He relaxed his fingers from around my arm and dropped his gaze from my eyes to the skin of my upper arm, gently stroking it as goose bumps erupted. When he glanced up at me, his eyes were dark pools, bottomless in their depths.

"I know I made a huge mistake and I know I hurt you," he said in a soft voice. I shook my head. I could hear a loud voice shouting that I didn't have the time or the stamina to get into this right now. But he interrupted me. "I know that whatever happened between us can't be wiped away, Dulcie; and believe me when I tell you that I regret it more than I've ever regretted anything in my life." He dropped his eyes to the floor and shook his head, sighing as he thought about it.

"Good, I'm glad," I said and pulled my arm from his grasp, trying to convince myself that this air of detached indifference was really and truly how I felt. But I was smart enough to realize I wasn't detached or indifferent where Knight was concerned. Instead, there was something inside me that kept screaming at me to never trust Knight again, to never ever find myself in this position again. There was something inside me that insisted the only person I could truly rely on was myself.

"Something has to give, though, Dulce," he said, bringing his face up close to mine, so close that I could feel his breath fanning against my cheek.

"Nothing has to give."

"I know you don't hate me," he started.

"No, I don't hate you."

"And there are moments when I can tell you aren't thinking about the past—moments when you and I are just ... us."

I couldn't deny the truth in his statement. I mean, it wasn't like I was constantly rehashing the past, and reliving everything that ever transpired between us. I didn't even think that was possible. "There's a lot that's going on right now, Knight. I've got lots more on my mind than nostalgia from the past."

He nodded as he closed his eyes, inhaling deeply. I felt something within me thawing, and I had to keep myself from touching him. I had to tamp down the thoughts that raged inside my addled head, thoughts that urged me to reach out and feel how hot and smooth his skin was ... thoughts that told me to touch his lips, feel the hot wetness of his tongue ...

"God, just being around you does something to me," he whispered. His eyes started to glow a fiercely possessive white. "I hope you know that this ... this silence between us is killing me."

I gulped, propping my hands on my hips. I was suddenly overcome with anger because I didn't like awakening old urges and needs. Just as something primal and passionate was emerging from him, it was also emerging within me. Even now, it seemed as if I were drowning in my own sea of need.

"I don't know what to tell you, Knight." My voice was harsh and cold.

"Tell me we can move on," he said quickly as he reached out to touch me again. Knowing what that meant, I took a step back. His hands dropped to his sides. "Tell me things between us can be the way they were before." He paused for three seconds and just stared at me. "I will never doubt you again, Dulcie, and I swear to you that I will never hurt you again." He swallowed. "Tell me you forgive me."

I hesitated, but then shook my head, knowing I wasn't ready for this; I still hadn't fully examined my own thoughts on this subject. "I can't."

He started to say something, but thought better of it and cleared his throat instead. Suddenly, panicking and nauseous, I couldn't fight the urge to flee, to get as far away from this room and Knight as I could. With my heart in my throat, I lurched forward again. I felt the cold of the doorknob on my palm, feeling like I was in slow motion as I turned it. I could think about nothing but escaping.

Knight's voice stopped me.

"I will make this up to you, Dulcie. I will prove to you that you can trust me again."

"Knight," I started, but he shook his head, his eyes hard.

"I love you."

It felt like my feet were suddenly mired in heavy tar. My breathing had been escalating so quickly that I started to hyperventilate and now I couldn't catch my breath. I felt suddenly light-headed, my chest constricted and tight. I closed my eyes and released the doorknob, suddenly feeling a sharp pain in my palms as I dug my fingernails into them. Without another word, I extricated my feet from their invisible binds and forced myself through the door.

TEN

Not surprisingly, the drive to my new digs was quiet and completely uncomfortable. I mean, I'd just attempted that whole escape act after hearing Knight tell me he loved me, so things weren't exactly cheery in the Dulcie-Knight camp. To defend my actions, though, I never wanted to get into the conversation in the first place. There was still just too much up in the air regarding The Resistance and my father. And let us also not forget that in the course of the last six hours or so, I'd been the unfortunate victim of the Denali detonation in which I came way too close to turning into a fairy shish-kebab, only to learn that the killer was one of our own. So as far as my guilt was concerned, if the truth be told, I wasn't really feeling any mainly because there wasn't any more space in my already overwhelmed head.

Luckily for me though, Knight didn't say another word. He just sat behind the steering wheel and looked ... glum. Yes, something within me told me I should have said something, or at least made small talk. But at this point, I figured small talk would be more of a slap in the face than silence, so I chose silence. Besides, I had a splitting headache and wasn't in a talking mood anyway.

Instead, we both quietly listened to the navigation in the Suburban as it barked out, "take a right turn here" and "take a left just ahead." How it even knew where we were was a shocker in and of itself, considering we were still in the middle of BFE. Furthermore, the locations of these Resistance compounds were on a need-to-know basis only and I couldn't imagine Garmin or Tom Tom needed to know. As soon as the thought crossed my mind, though, I realized that the navigation unit was no doubt "charmed" as were most things supplied by The Resistance.

We'd left the library about an hour earlier and were now driving down an unmarked highway that seemed to stretch into oblivion. As we crested the only hill yet, I noticed the highway T-boned into a dead end. We had to go right or left. The nav unit ordered us to make a left turn, so we did. Once we took the left, the entire car wobbled like a tightrope walker in a high wind on a faulty wire. Seconds later, we were no longer on the lone highway that stretched for miles with nothing but the early morning sun to greet us. Instead, we were suddenly plunged into the midst of a dark forest, complete with traces of moonlight that lit up the interior of the car through the heavy branches. It took me a second or two to realize what just happened, but before I could speak, Knight did.

"That must have been a portal," he said simply, as if it were no surprise at all and the news was so humdrum that it didn't even require commenting.

"So what do we do now?" I asked as I glanced around myself and realized I couldn't see anything beyond the trunks of the seemingly never ending trees. The moonlight cast eerie shadows that soon became great, hulking trolls and monsters.

"Looks like driving is out of the question."

I agreed, considering there was now a huge pine tree directly in front of us that even a forty-point turn couldn't allow us to weave our way around.

"So?"

He didn't respond, but faced the navigation with concern all over his face.

"You will finish the remainder of your journey on foot," the thing said in that same highfalutin', accent-free sort of way. "Step out of the vehicle. Walk forward three paces; make a ninety-degree turn to your right, and walk forward six paces."

Knight reached forward to remove the navigation device from its holder, which was suction-cupped to the windshield. Turning toward me with a sigh, he raised his eyebrows in a rendition of "What other choice do we have?" I nodded as I undid my seatbelt. I tried to open the door, but found it butted up against another tree, leaving me maybe two feet of clearance to wiggle out. Luckily, I was small enough to squeeze my way through.

"You could have crawled out on my side," Knight offered as soon as I worked my way free of the door and jumped to the ground in front of him.

"And miss that daring adventure?" I asked, forcing a smile even as I wondered if things between us would ever again feel comfortable. I wasn't at all okay with how things now were, but I also couldn't imagine things improving—not anytime soon anyway.

Knight didn't say anything, but glanced down at the nav again. The moist smell of the forest infiltrated my nostrils as I leaned up on my tiptoes and eyed the device in his hands. It revealed a road map view of a forest, which I figured was the forest we were now in, and the X in the center must have marked our current position. There was a red arrow pointing straight ahead, which then veered to the right.

The sounds of crickets and frogs were thick in the air as I took a step forward, my shoes squeaking against the mossy undergrowth. "Three paces, huh?" I asked with a slightly hesitant smile.

"Guess so," Knight answered, and together, we took three steps forward, just like the nav instructed.

"Prepare to make a ninety-degree right," the voice called out, apparently satisfied with our obedience.

Neither of us said anything as we turned to our right and took six steps forward. Knight's gait was obviously much longer than mine, so I did my best to keep up with him before the thought occurred to me that maybe the six strides specified were referencing a normal-sized person, not a shrimp like me, or a giant like Knight. But, I guess I'd just have to find out the hard way if and when the portal didn't open.

123

"You will now have exactly three seconds each to cross over," the navigation said with detached authority.

Knight glanced at me and nodded, a dark smile on his lips that seemed to match the muddied expression in his now navy blue eyes. "Ladies first."

"Thanks," I grumbled, thinking in this case, I'd prefer ladies second. But I didn't argue and, instead, thrust myself forward, just like I'd done every other time I had to travel via portals. I felt the difference in the air almost immediately. The now familiar feel of balmy air that was both thick and heavy, hugged me like an old friend. Before I could take another breath or blink, I felt myself slipping through the air. A second or so later, I unceremoniously landed on my ass, shrouded in cold. I caught a glimpse of my surroundings—a smallish room, painted black with thick, black carpeting to match. A yellowish glow emitted from a floor lamp in the corner—the only furniture in the room. The scent of something foreign, but clean and crisp, stung my nose, but before I could take stock of anything else, I remembered Knight. I managed to roll out of the way just as he came through the portal, landing in exactly the same spot I'd previously occupied. Talk about a close call!

"Well, well, well," came the aristocratic voice from behind me. "Look what the portal dragged in."

I turned to see him, although I recognized his voice before he came into view.

"You've gotta be fucking kidding me," Knight said as he lurched to his feet and he settled his eyes on Bram.

"I am quite overjoyed to see you as well, Vander," Bram said with a polished smile as he slapped his hands together artfully, and approached us from the far side of the room. Glancing around, I realized my first hunch was correct—there wasn't any furniture in the room aside from the floor lamp. I figured the room must have been dedicated to portal travel, given how landings could sometimes be ... unpredictable, and furniture might prove to be dangerous.

124

Knight ran his hands through his hair as he cracked his knuckles and scowled at our vampire host. I managed to stand up, my heartbeat in my throat. It took maybe another few seconds for the shock to wear off and as soon as it did so, the reason for why we were here dawned on me.

"What the hell was Christina thinking?" Knight continued, still glaring at Bram, even though the question was directed at me ... I think.

"It makes total sense," I said simply, although I was awed and amazed by how smart this move actually was. I turned to face Knight and noticed him studying me quizzically. "If the offender is one of our own, Christina figured that I'd be safer somewhere they would never expect to find me."

"Yes, quite so," Bram said, nodding vehemently as he eyed Knight, as if he presumed the Loki were slow. "As I am neither a member of The Resistance nor a foe," (he said as his eyes rested on me), "you would do well to find yourself under my roof, Dulcie, sweet." Then, narrowing his eyes at Knight, he added, "And please note, my dear Loki, that my invitation of hospitality only extends to the fairer of our sex."

Knight frowned. "Of course it does, Bram." He gritted his teeth. "But as to whether or not I'll accept your invitation on behalf of our fairer sex—it remains to be seen."

Bram held his long fingers in front of him as he appeared to inspect them, something he always did for added drama, and something which absolutely drove me nuts. He didn't say anything, though, so I took the opportunity from him.

"Knight, I can take care of myself," I spat out, suddenly angry. I wasn't sure whether I was more irritated by Knight's display of machismo or Bram's obsession with his damned nails. Men could be so frustratingly exhausting.

"Well said, my dear, well said," the vampire finally spoke before turning his stringent gaze on Knight and addressing him pointedly. "You would not want to contradict any command from your superior, would you?"

"Enough, Bram," I snapped before turning to face Knight. "I'll be fine here. It's short term, anyway."

"I'm not convinced you're going to be fine," Knight answered. "We could be making a big mistake. You have no protection here—no soldiers patrolling, no barbed wire fencing, no guards, nothing."

"None of those things mattered a damn anyway," I argued. "I had all of those things on base and look what good it did! Someone still managed to sabotage the Denali."

"And as to Sweet's protection, I am most certainly considered a formidable ally, but an even more formidable enemy," Bram piped up, apparently insulted by the idea that Knight had little faith in his skills.

"Against an army of Melchior's men, you are nothing," Knight spat back at him, his eyes raging.

"It might please you to know," Bram continued, in a level tone as he faced me and turned his back on Knight, "your leader has graced my quarters as an estimable guest, more than once." Then he turned to face Knight again. "And I do believe if the leader of The Resistance finds sanctuary beneath my roof, it should be deemed safe by anyone else's accounts!"

I couldn't say my mind was focused on Bram's question, though. Instead, I was still stuck on the point he made about Christina staying with him. I had to wonder which quarters he was referring to—a random room in his house or his own private bedroom quarters? Somehow, I didn't want to know the answer.

"That doesn't change the fact that I don't trust you, Bram," Knight spat back.

"And yet you trusted me enough with our Dulcie sweet while we were in the Netherworld on your business?"

"It was hardly Knight's business," I grumbled but Knight interrupted me, his eyes narrowed and his jaw tight.

"I had no choice in the matter. I was in prison, if you recall."

Bram made a big show of exhaling a pent-up breath, as if he were too busy to bother himself with the mundane, trivial details of Knight's whereabouts in the Netherworld. "At any rate, I was given express instructions to ensure that Sweet receive a comfortable shelter and bed on which to lay her pretty head in preparation for tomorrow's activities," Bram finished.

"What does that mean?" Knight demanded, his tone becoming increasingly agitated.

Bram simply shook his head and dropped his eyes onto his fingernails again. "It is not for me to repeat, Loki," he said simply. "That information must come from your leader, herself." Then he turned to face me with a polished smile. "Now, if you will excuse us, I must insist on showing Sweet to her bedchamber; and rest assured, I will protect Sweet and guarantee her safety in whatever way becomes necessary."

Knight stepped toward the tall, gallant vampire until the two were maybe three inches apart. Apparently sensing Knight behind him, Bram turned around slowly. Knight was fuming and Bram seemed slightly ill at ease, which was no surprise, given that he had an incensed Loki staring him down.

"If you so much as lay one finger on her, you'll have me to answer to," Knight sneered. "No, scratch that, if you so much as look at her with anything other than respect, I'll make sure you regret it. Got it?"

"Affirmative," Bram answered acidly.

"I don't trust you and I don't like this arrangement one bit. I'm counting on you to keep Dulcie safe and I don't want her to have to worry about trying to fend off your advances on top of everything else we have going on."

"Knight, it's fine. I can take care of myself," I started, although neither one seemed to hear me.

"As I understand, you no longer have any claim on our Sweet?" Bram teased, egging Knight on.

Knight was about to say something, but his words seemed to dissolve on his tongue. As for me, I was shocked because I didn't know how Bram could have found out about Knight's and my falling out. I guess it came down to bad news traveling fast. One thing I could say about Bram was that he was a nosy bastard. He made it his business to know everyone else's.

"Dulcie's and my relationship isn't any of your concern," Knight said at last, taking the final step separating them until they were nose to nose. "Touch her and you won't be happy with the consequences."

Bram stepped away from Knight and narrowed his eyes at the larger man before turning to face me, a false smile of bravado pasted across his handsome face. "My goodness, it seems your caveman has snapped his tether."

"Take that as a warning, Bram," Knight continued before turning to face me again. "If you need anything, call me, Dulcie." Then, addressing Bram again, he added, "I want her room in the most remote section of this house. There should be more than one exit point; and I want a guard posted outside her door, day and night." He took a big breath. "Her door should not only lock from the inside, but also have a deadbolt. I'll send Sam over to charm the place and make sure it's as safe as it can be."

"No need, my good sir," Bram answered. "My entire home and estate have already received the benefit of multiple witches' charms."

"I don't care. I'm only interested in Dulcie's safety."

Bram frowned. "Sweet's bedchamber has been charmed three times by three different witches to ensure its safety." It was Bram's turn to narrow his eyes and assume the role of someone ticked off. "I believe the sky is the limit when Dulcie's safety is concerned."

"Okay, I've had enough of this now," I barked out, holding my head because it was beginning to throb. I'd have to magic the pain away as soon as Knight left. But at the thought of him leaving, I felt my stomach drop. "Where are you going to go?" I asked in a shaky voice as I again realized he was as much of a walking target as I.

"I don't know," he answered simply. "But I do know that you need to save your strength for whatever Christina has planned. I have a feeling it's going to be something big that will have to come together quickly."

I simply nodded before I approached him. "Be careful, Knight."

He seemed surprised by the worry in my voice, but simply smiled down at me. "I will." Then he started for the portal again, turning with one final boyish grin. "I'll see you soon, Dulce." I watched him study Bram purposefully, his eyes issuing a silent warning before he turned toward the portal and vanished.

With a new sense of niggling worry in my gut, I faced Bram, intent on making him understand that Knight's warnings were legitimate. "Don't think I'm going to grant you any sexual favors just because I'm staying under your roof. My coming here is only as a last resort and I don't want you to turn it into an opportunity to benefit yourself."

"Sweet, you cut me to the core," he said in mock offense, dramatically bringing his hand up to his heart. "Although I might remind you that you still have yet to deliver on your end of our agreement."

I rolled my eyes just as I realized the truth in his statement. Our "agreement" was comprised of Bram's list of demands which he'd created in exchange for serving as my guide to the Netherworld. My part of the agreement, which I still hadn't upheld, amounted to five dinner dates. Hades be damned.

"Perhaps you do not recall the stipulations regarding our agreement?"

"No, Bram, I haven't forgotten," I started, still shaking my head at the injustice of it all. I mean, I was just so exhausted and the thought that I could relax, at least for one evening, had been music to my ears. Music that had now soured.

"I shall enlighten you regardless," he said, holding his chin up high as if he were an orator about to captivate his audience. "You consented to dine with me five separate times upon our return from the Netherworld. If you also recall, I stipulated that each of those occasions would require that you dress in something no longer than three inches above your knees. Furthermore, the upper garment, blouse or the northern end of your gown must plunge into a very low "V", thereby fully displaying your breasts, thereby permitting me to appreciate your ... assets."

"Obviously you aren't taking Knight's warning seriously," I muttered, irritated because I knew he had me. We *did* have an agreement and I still hadn't held up my end of it.

"I care not for the Loki, much less his silly warning." He paused for a few seconds before a villainous smile took hold of his entire face. "All I do care about, Dulcie sweet, is our dinner this evening. I will escort you to your accommodations, where you will find a suitable gown hanging in the closet." He sighed deeply as he studied me, clicking his tongue against his teeth in apparent appreciation. "Until then, I must leave you as I have some personal business to attend to." Without pulling his gaze away from me, he added, "I will send for you in three hours."

"Didn't Christina tell you I needed my rest also?" I muttered, even though I started following him out of the room.

"Yes, of course, my dear; and you would do well to enjoy your brief respite now as you and I have an evening engagement awaiting us."

"You're impossible to argue with," I grumbled.

"Yes, I am quite aware, sweet, so why even start?"

And that was the twenty million dollar question.

ELEVEN

Just as I'd expected, the "gown" Bram had so generously donated wasn't exactly to my taste. As I stood in front of the full-length mirror in my makeshift accommodations, heat was already warming my cheeks. And it wasn't the type of heat that comes with gratitude or excitement. Nope, this heat was completely dedicated to the fact that I was mortified over being seen in the horrid thing but, more so, that I was pissed off Bram had the gall to expect me to wear it in the first place!

I gritted my teeth as I faced myself, almost not believing my own eyes. For one thing, the dress was cut in a low "V" just as Bram had promised, although he hadn't been very forthcoming with just how low "low" was. This thing plunged clear down to my navel and the "straps" coming back up barely covered either of my nipples, let alone my breasts. Unfortunately, I could clearly see the swell of both sides of my breasts beneath the narrow strips of gold fabric. The way the material shimmied against my skin, I had a feeling it wouldn't be very good at staying put over both of my nipples, which was probably exactly as Bram intended. I tied the two straps behind my neck as tightly as I could, hoping and praying I could somehow secure the fabric tightly enough to where there was very little, if any, wiggle room.

As to the rest of the catastrophe known as Bram's taste in women's clothing—the "gown" was short, just as Bram had instructed in his original list of demands. The fabric dusted the tops of my thighs and bending over was completely out of the question. The gold of the dress matched the honey gold of my hair as well as the room perfectly. Yes, the entirety of my room was "gilt" with dark gold chenille wallpaper meeting hardwood floors that were almost a yellow gold. The floral pattern of the drapes was in hues of yellow and orange curlicues while the molding along the ceiling looked as if it were actually made from gold— especially how it reflected in the low light of the burnished bronze candelabras on either side of my massive Louis XIV bed which was, yes, also sculpted out of gold. And knowing Bram's expensive tastes, I wouldn't have been surprised to learn the bed was constructed of solid gold. 'Course gold was known for being less than strong so maybe it wasn't solid. At any rate, it was expensive and it was ... gaudy.

With a defeated sigh, I heaved my mass of hair over one shoulder, so I could better see the shoes Bram had intended for me to wear, which he'd left just beside my bed. I stepped into the ridiculous heels, which were a coppery color, and had to be over six inches high. The laces crisscrossed clear up to my knees and gave me a sort of Roman look. Yep, the shoes accompanied with the dress that was so small it looked like it was intended for a Barbie Doll, made me look like a Roman whore. Once I'd fastened the shoes to either of my feet, it took me a second to find my balance, and once I did, I attempted to walk, all the while afraid that I might trip and break an ankle. Fashion and crime fighting weren't exactly bedfellows.

"Are your accommodations to your liking?" came Bram's voice from behind me.

I twirled around so fast, I lost control and had to stabilize myself against the handrail of my poster bed. "My accommodations aren't occupying my mind at the moment," I grumbled in response.

Bram smiled handsomely and showed himself into my room, eyeing me from head to toe as he did so. Then he shook his head and his eyes narrowed, filled with something that resembled passion. "I have never wanted to undress a woman as fiercely as I do now."

I raised my eyebrows at the same time that I made a show of fending him off with my palm, making sure to keep

132

my other hand firmly locked around the bedpost because I didn't trust myself on my stilts. "Save it, Romeo. This is not my idea of a good time," I mumbled, taking a few unsteady steps in his direction. "And nice work with this hankie," I finished, glancing down at myself in obvious distaste.

I expected him to at least laugh but he didn't—instead, he continued staring at me as if he were a deer caught in the death grip of a car's headlights. "I hand selected that gown and had it flown in from Florence, Italy," he said at last, his tone affronted. "Not to mention that I returned the dress five times until I deemed it adequate to grace your lovely skin."

"Tell your tailor he forgot the rest of it!" I snapped, in no mood to seem in the least bit gracious ... because I wasn't ... not in the least bit.

Bram just continued to stare at me, his gaze roving over my breasts as his fangs visibly lengthened until they were indenting his lower lip. He held his hand out and with his index finger, appeared to outline the swell of my breasts in the air, looking like a conductor who'd lost his baton.

"The lines are exquisite," he said breathlessly. "Rossi managed to capture your body flawlessly." He continued tracing the dress or my body, I wasn't sure which, in the air. He looked ridiculous. "It is a work of art. The way the gown reveals the swell of your lovely breasts and hints at your stomach just beneath, only to obscure the admirer's view with the skirt which then hints at your muscular thighs, leaving your stunning legs as a cornucopia of sexuality on which I can feast my eyes."

"I just threw up a little." I frowned as I tried to hobble forward again, feeling like I was on ice skates.

Bram arched an unimpressed eyebrow and scowled at me. "Sometimes I do wish you would refrain from speaking, Sweet."

"Ditto," I replied grumpily before throwing my hands on my hips at the reality of how much time and thought went into creating this "dress" in the first place. "So how did you figure out what my size is, anyway?" I eyed him narrowly as I further considered it. "Did you steal something of mine?"

Bram chuckled and shook his head, looking at me as if I were dumb. "It is not so simple as your size, my dear sweet. And, no, I have never stolen anything in my life and do not plan to start. The simple answer is that I have memorized your body—the flow of your neck to your shoulders." Then he drew a line in the air which I supposed represented the line of my neck to my shoulders. "The flow of your breasts to your stomach, your stomach to your hips ..."

"Yeah, yeah, I got it, Dr. Grey. I don't need an anatomy lesson."

He dropped his fingers from their escapade into air-writing and faced me squarely. "You do realize you are the only woman who refuses to adhere to my ... sensuality."

I laughed. I couldn't help it. "Adhere to your sensuality? What, like a piece of tape or maybe some glue?" I laughed even more loudly, finding his comment and this whole situation increasingly funny. Maybe I was just at the point of losing my mind because it did feel as if my grip on sanity was slowly fading.

Bram frowned, crossing his arms against his chest. "I fail to see the humor in my pointing out how delectable you are and how I desire you, though it pains me to admit it."

"Come on, Bram, this whole thing is ridiculously funny if you think about it." Then I started for the door again, feeling like I was going to face plant at any second. "I'm dressed like a bimbo on stilts, which somehow, and I still don't understand how, seems to sexually frustrate the hell out of you. And the cherry on this completely screwed up cake is that we're probably about to go into war with the Netherworld." I started to laugh even harder. "Now that is the best damn punch line I've heard in a while."

Bram regarded me coolly, one of his brows drawn in admonition. "Dulcie Sweet, sometimes you are quite bizarre."

134

I shook my head and sighed, thinking the only people who seemed to really get me were Sam, Dia, Trey and, okay, Knight.

Bram held out his arm and I took it, figuring my balance needed all the help it could get. He led me from my bedroom, down the stairs, and into his dining room, although it took us probably twice as long to make the trip because I had to cling to the banister with one hand and his arm with the other. When we reached his dining room, a goblin dressed in black and white was waiting for us and hurriedly opened the double doors, revealing the most enormous table I'd ever seen, sitting atop an enormous black rug that matched the black of the walls perfectly. The only lights in the room were offered by a chandelier made of elk or deer horns which looked as if it were fifteen feet wide and nine feet tall. The table was easily the size of my apartment, a place setting at each of the chairs.

"Um, are you having a party tonight?" I asked as Bram motioned for his butler (I supposed the hairy goblin was, anyway) and the man shut the double doors behind us, leaving us to our privacy, much to my chagrin.

"Yes, Sweet," Bram said simply and eyed the room as if he were bored.

"How many people are you expecting?" I asked, glancing down at the table as I tried to get a place setting count. It was futile because my brain didn't work that fast. Especially now when I'd had such little sleep.

"One," Bram said simply and turned his broad grin in my direction. "You, Sweet, you are the extent of the diners to fill my evening."

"Then why all the place settings?" I asked, facing the enormous table again.

Bram shrugged as if the answer were obvious. "I was not certain as to where you'd prefer to sit." Then he started around the table, glancing forward and side to side as if to judge which position offered the best view.

"Um, overkill anyone?" I asked, shaking my head. "You didn't have to go to so much trouble, Bram, I'm fine sitting anywhere."

He nodded and pulled out a chair in the dead center of the table. "This seat offers the best view of the room, I do believe."

I said nothing but took the proffered chair and felt Bram push it up to the table as my eyes fell to the wall directly across from me. Staring back at me was Bram, only this Bram was memorialized in oil. The painting had to be ten feet high and when I took the whole thing in, I had to keep myself from laughing. It was Bram dressed in what appeared to be armor although it wasn't the type of armor commemorated in cartoons and the like. Instead, it looked like something ancient—something real for lack of a better word. Next to the knightly Bram, who wore a steel expression in his eyes and an almost obscene smirk (like he was going for the Mona Lisa but never quite made it), was a black horse. But what really tickled my funny bone wasn't the morose expression of a Bram whose shoulders were actually much broader than they were in real life or whose jaw was a bit more square and whose nose was a bit more Roman. No, what was even now making me clear my throat so I wouldn't erupt into a fit of giggles was the fact that the oil painting depicted Bram with one foot on the decapitated body of a dragon, the beast's head hanging from Bram's hands.

"So this is the best view in the room, is it?" I asked, turning to face him with unconcealed humor.

But his attention wasn't on me. It was on the painting. "Astonishing, is it not?" he asked in a faraway voice. "An absolute masterpiece."

"Um, Bram, you're dressed like a knight and you're holding a dragon's head."

My statement seemed to pull him from his reverie and he shook his head, as if just waking from a deep sleep. "Yes, I was known as the dragon slayer."

I suddenly felt exhausted—so exhausted that I didn't even want to get into the whys and hows of Bram's days as a dragon slayer. Sometimes there was just a point where life became too much to deal with and I was now at that point.

"Would you prefer I sit beside you, Sweet, or across from you?"

"Across from me," I answered automatically.

"Very good, as I prefer to view all of your lovely face as opposed to just your profile." Then he started the long walk around the table, taking even longer to work his way up the other side, pausing just before the painting so he could admire it ... again. Everything Bram did was for show—it didn't matter who he was with or who he wasn't with. I was almost convinced that he thought he was constantly being videotaped or something—like he thought he was on his own show with a myriad of viewers just dying to find out what Bram was about to do next. He never seemed as if he wasn't "on."

Once he reached the seat opposite mine, he pulled the chair out slowly and made a show out of seating himself and pulling his chair back up to the table again. Then he eyed me purposefully, saying nothing for at least three seconds.

"You surprise me, Sweet," he said at last.

"Why is that?" I answered with a yawn, double checking my breasts to make sure the straps, which amounted to Band-Aids, basically, were still in place. They were. Phew.

"This is the first you've seen my house and yet you have not commented?"

I cocked my head to the side as I digested his comment. Yes, this was the first I'd seen of his home. I'd always understood that he'd lived in the building that housed No Regrets, but learning he'd bought a house wasn't exactly thrilling news. "It's a moot point anyway," I started, shrugging.

"And why is that?"

"Because whether or not you have a house doesn't concern or interest me. It's where this house is located that I might find even mildly interesting. The moot point is that I doubt you'll tell me our whereabouts?"

Bram laughed. "You do know me well and, no, I will not divulge such information."

"Then I'll save my comments for another day."

He eyed me as he tapped his manicured fingernails against the mahogany table. "It is for your own good, Sweet. Your leader chose to station you here for a reason, privacy and safety being her foremost concern."

"I understand," I said simply.

Bram eyed me for a few more seconds before he stopped drumming his fingernails against the table top. "In other news, I am working on a painting of you as we speak."

"What?" I barked. "What the hell are you talking about? *You* are painting a picture of me?!"

"No, I am not the artist," he said and shrugged. "Although I am commissioning the painting so I choose to refer to it as my own."

"Okay, all of that is beside the point. The better question is why you're commissioning a painting of me?"

"I choose to surround myself with objects of beauty, hence that incredible painting." Then he glanced up at the Bram-Dragon canvas again, as if worried it had melted into the wall. He turned to face me again and smiled widely. "You, my dear Sweet, are the most beautiful woman I have the fortune of knowing, so naturally I should want to memorize your understated loveliness by way of oil."

"Did it ever occur to you to ask my permission first?" I asked, somewhat put out as I tried to imagine a portrait of me hanging in Bram's home. It definitely wasn't an idea that thrilled me by any stretch of the imagination.

"I do not care for permissions, Sweet," Bram said and then raised his eyebrows loftily. "I have hired the best oil artists from France to do your honors, my sweet, and I am told the masterpiece known as the 'Fairy Law' will be finished shortly. We shall have an unveiling party, if you would oblige me."

As long as it would take care of another of the outstanding dates I still owed him, sure, I was game for anything. And as to insisting Bram divorce himself from the undertaking of the "Fairy Law," that was another moot point because as far as I knew, there weren't any laws disabling people from painting other people. Damn it to Hades.

"So moving onto more important subjects," I started, but Bram interrupted me by shaking his head and ... pouting.

"Sweet, you wound me."

"Here we go again," I grumbled, mostly to myself. "What did I do now?"

Bram glanced behind his shoulder at the atrocity known as the dragon slayer. "Are you not even in the least bit curious as to the story behind the painting, my dear?"

I took a deep breath, feeling exhausted all the way down to my toes, but by the same token, I had to admit that somewhere inside me I was interested in the story that had born the hideous painting—at least a little bit. "Okay, shoot."

He shook his head. "No, if you are uninterested in the particulars, I do not care to brow beat you into listening."

I shook my head, tired of playing Bram's idiotic games. "Stop acting like a five-year-old taking your ball from the sandbox and tell me the story ... please," I added. "I would love to know, really, I would."

Then he beamed like a child on Christmas morning and turned his chair to the side so he could take turns gazing at me and then at the painting. "It was the latter part of the eighteenth century in England. And plaguing the countryside of the village in which I lived, was a band of murderers, thieves, and rapists," he started.

"This was in London?" I asked, trying to seem actively involved even as I doubted London could be referred to as a "village" even in the eighteenth century.

"Just outside of London, Sweet. At any rate, I disposed of this band of troublemakers and I am quite certain you can imagine how," then he winked at me like it was a big secret, but his fangs were fully lengthened as if to offer a very obvious hint. "Needless to say, I was considered to be quite the hero among my kinsfolk and to show their gratitude, the townspeople hired the most famed portraitist of the time to paint the masterpiece you see before you."

I didn't say anything for a few seconds because I wasn't sure if that was the end of Bram's story or not. Once the discovery that it was the end of the story dawned on me, I couldn't help frowning. "That's it?" I blurted out. "That is the worst story ever! You completely forgot the part about why you're wearing armor and, hello, what about the dragon?"

Bram shook his head and sighed as if he were agitated. "The dragon and the armor were merely symbolism, my sweet. Both were symbolic of the fact that I possessed the fierce determination and courage of a dragon slayer, that I rid my village of a threat no less than a dragon, himself."

I didn't say anything else because I really didn't know what to say. I mean, not only was the painting ridiculous in every aspect of the word but, more so, it was a complete sham. I'd thought I'd at least get a hilarious dragon story out of it, but nope. "That's great," I said simply.

Bram didn't say anything else but clapped his hands together and the goblin reappeared within seconds. I figured he'd been waiting just behind the double doors. The man was short—maybe five foot six and solidly built. He wasn't handsome but nor was he unattractive—just had a bland sort of nothingness about his face. He was someone you wouldn't remember.

"What do you care to dine on this evening, my sweet?" Bram asked and offered me a sugar-coated grin that revealed the very tips of his fangs.

"What's on the menu?"

Bram shook his head. "There is no menu. Whatever you desire is at your disposal."

Talk about being put on the spot. I wracked my overwhelmed brain but nothing seemed to come forward. Finally I just settled for a filet of salmon and a Caesar salad. Not exactly a culinary delight, but I was too tired to come up with anything fancier.

"Very well," Bram said and then eyed the goblin who very quickly retired through the double doors again. "So you find yourself under my roof, my sweet," Bram said and eyed me speculatively.

"Don't get any ideas," I reminded him again to which he just laughed heartily.

"I have been getting ideas, as you call them, about you from the moment I first laid eyes on you in your tight, little ANC uniform." He grew quiet then as if he were stuck in his memories. "How long ago was that, my sweet?"

"Too long," I answered and took a big gulp of water once the goblin returned with a large jug of ice water with lemons and poured me a glass.

"At any rate, you and I have been friends many years, my dear."

"Are we friends, Bram?" I asked, suddenly wondering where this conversation was headed. And, really, that was the ultimate question. *Were we friends?* I'd always considered Bram an acquaintance, definitely, but our relationship had never firmly traveled to the land of friendship mainly because Bram also maintained ties with the less savory members of Splendor society.

"I have always given you the unpleasant details of those who live and work in the Underground, have I not?"

I nodded. "Yes, you have, but sometimes I wonder if it's because you prescribe to the idea of keeping your enemies closer than your friends."

Bram eyed me suspiciously almost. "Very advantageous words to live by."

I smiled, suddenly feeling fuel behind my fire. One thing I could say for Bram was that I could always speak my mind with him. "Why do you insist on playing the middle ground, Bram?"

"Middle ground?" he repeated, feigning ignorance, but I was more than aware that he was simply buying time. Bram didn't care for conversations such as these because he didn't like demonstrations of the errors of his ways, as most narcissists don't.

"Yes, you walk a tight line between doing good and doing not so good." I took a breath. "I always find myself wondering if and when you will ever cross over and if you do, which way you'll cross."

Bram laughed and started drumming his fingers against the table again as I wondered if maybe he was nervous. "I am a businessman, first and foremost, Sweet. And as all good businessmen do, I hold my cards very close to my chest."

I nodded but I wasn't placated. "There will come a day, Bram, and that day is coming closer and closer, where you'll have to take a side."

"Against your father?"

I nodded. "The margins are slimming. You're either with us or against us."

Bram smiled more widely. "Is not your sitting at my table an example of where my sympathies lie?"

I smiled just as broadly. "It wouldn't surprise me to know you harbored Loyalists in the very next room. That's the thing about you, Bram, you're unpredictable."

"That I am, my dear," he said, eyeing me pointedly. "But is unpredictability not the very measure of mystery and is mystery not the very measure of intrigue?"

I leaned forward. "I don't want to mince words here, Bram, but your tightrope walking days are going to come to an end ... very soon."

He just watched me, appearing amused. "Then I daresay it will be an interesting moment when you learn which side I shall choose, will it not?"

I leaned back into my chair and nodded. "As long as you choose correctly, Bram."

TWELVE

After my dinner with Bram, which was beyond exhausting, I was more than pleased to retire into the "comfort" of my temporary room. Bram accompanied me up the stairs and down the hallway. I noticed a guard stationed outside my door and greeted him with a quick nod. Apparently, Bram *was* taking this safety and security stuff pretty seriously, which was reassuring. After saying good night, Bram loitered in front of my door for a few minutes, obviously waiting for an invitation to enter. When he didn't receive one, he bid me a quick and unenthusiastic "Good evening," before retiring to wherever he kept himself occupied. I didn't waste any time in closing the door behind him and dead bolting it as I eyed my bed with sincere appreciation, even though it was way too ostentatious for my taste.

Because my clothing hadn't yet arrived from the compound, I was left with no other option but to search through the only chest of drawers in the room. It matched the Louis XIV bed with its intricate detailing and brash gold color. Not surprisingly, I found an assortment of women's clothing, which, upon further inspection, were of various sizes and diverse tastes—a rainbow of choices as I'm sure Bram maintained a rainbow of variety when it came to his dalliances with the opposite sex. Some men kept track of their "scores" by way of "notches" on their bedposts; Bram appeared to "notch" by keeping random articles of women's clothing. Yep, of one thing I was certain regarding the handsome vampire, was that he was a total and absolute man slut.

I searched drawer after drawer, looking for something that resembled pajamas or even a loose T-shirt, but after finding only a slinky, red negligee and an even slinkier black-lace teddy, I opted to sleep in nothing but my panties.

Trying to beat down my second wind, which was just now making itself known, I approached the enormous windows on the opposite side of the room, curious to see what lay beyond them. The curtains were thick, heavy, and difficult to open, but once I managed, I was rewarded by a beautiful view of a wrought-iron balcony just above Bram's enormous pool. The moonlight reflected against the dark water in ripples. I thought about standing on the balcony for a while, just to feel the touch of the breeze against my skin, but in this instance, I ignored the urge, figuring it would be too cold anyway.

Instead, I gazed out at the moon, which was full, round, and shining like a son of a bitch. Thoughts began circling my mind regarding Bram. Our conversation tonight had really sparked questions and the more I considered just how Bram fit into the larger context of Loyalist vs. Rebel, the more I had to wonder about Bram's allegiance in all of this. I mean, at what point was it no longer okay to remain uninvolved and detached? At what point would Bram realize he needed to make a decision as to what side he favored? Furthermore, what did it mean when he said he was a "businessman, first and foremost"?

Everything was coming down to the wire and the time for choosing sides was long past. Thinking more about it, I had to wonder whether Bram could really be considered a friend to The Resistance, especially if he was, to use his own words, primarily a businessman? Was he referring to the business of running the biggest nightclub in Splendor? Or was there more to this picture?

Ultimately, when it came down to it, what did I really know about Bram?

I mean, I knew he owned and operated No Regrets, and that he definitely held hands with the criminals of Splendor as often as he held hands with the ANC. Yep, I'd always been able to rely on Bram for juicy tidbits regarding

145

the less than law-abiding citizens of Splendor. But I could only imagine that while he fed me information about the goings on in the streets of Splendor, he also fed criminals information about the ANC. Otherwise, he could never have been able to remain in the middle, regarded as neither a model citizen nor a criminal by the ANC and the law breakers alike.

I also couldn't ignore the fact that Bram had been in business with my father once upon a time. Of course he'd also said that he'd come to Splendor to escape my father's tyranny, but who knew if that story was entirely accurate? And furthermore, Bram *did* have his own portal to the Netherworld ... Granted, Bram's portal looked as if it hadn't been used in over one hundred years (which was also the story Bram gave me), but just having a private portal to the Netherworld that was still operable had to mean something. Right?

Now I wondered if maybe Bram wasn't as innocent as he professed to be. But what exactly did that mean? Did I think Bram was responsible for the Denali explosion? No, I couldn't wrap my mind around that one. As much as I couldn't imagine Bram shedding a single tear over Knight's demise, I also didn't think he would voluntarily plot my assassination. Besides, Bram was no insider of The Resistance so he wouldn't have had any way of knowing the whereabouts of the Denali, or Knight and me ... unless, of course, he had an informant.

But regardless of whether he had an informant or not didn't change my belief that Bram didn't want to see me dead—not after the way he went on and on about his interests in me. As much as I never wanted to admit it, Bram was obsessed with me. But didn't obsession lead to crimes of passion and violence? Wasn't everything fair in love and war?

I shook my head, because it just didn't ring true. If Bram wanted me dead, he'd already had many opportunities to see his goal to fruition, especially after taking it upon himself to become my guardian in the Netherworld. No, if Bram was guilty of anything, it sure wasn't planning my end.

My brain continued to find reasons for Bram's innocence or lack thereof, and I was suddenly reminded about Bram's statement that Christina had stayed with him on more than one occasion. What did that mean? With all certainty, I believed in Christina's innocence, since she was the leader of The Resistance. But maybe the answer wasn't so complicated. Maybe the answer was as simple as Christina falling in love with Bram? And if she were in love with him, maybe she was feeding him information without even realizing what she was doing. How many times did I hear that love was blind? Well, maybe love *was* blind! Maybe in this case, Christina's blind love for Bram was responsible for her blabbing information she otherwise would not have. Maybe she trusted Bram because she loved him and failed to see the danger involved by trusting him?

Thinking more about it though, I didn't buy it. Why? Because one thing I'd learned about Christina during the course of our association, was that she was one bad ass chick. And last I checked, bad ass chicks didn't fall head over heels in love with candy ass vampires. Not only that, but I couldn't imagine there was a chance in hell that Christina, even playing the devil's advocate and accepting that she was in love with Bram, would ever give up any information about The Resistance, since she held it so close to her heart.

Hmm, so if a love tryst between Bram and Christina didn't seem likely ...

What if Christina, knowing that Bram walked the fine line between good and bad, didn't trust him and as part of her distrust, stationed me here, under his roof on purpose? What if this move on her part wasn't so much to secure my own safety as it was for me to keep an eye on Bram? Maybe it was an attempt to get up close and personal with the goings on behind Bram's closed doors? And, finally, to get to the bottom of whether or not Bram was somehow involved in the assassination plot, and more pointedly, somehow involved with my father?

That made sense. Christina, being my father's pet before all of this Resistance stuff hit the fan, would have known those who were closest to him. Moreover, Christina would have all the background history between Bram and my father. And, knowing that history, she'd want to make sure Bram didn't pose a threat. Or maybe it was even simpler than that—maybe Bram was involved with my father all along, and Christina was also aware of it?

'Course, if Bram had been in cahoots with my father recently, then he would know about Christina's fall from my father's grace. Moreover, she'd also be fully aware that Bram knew. And if they were both aware of what happened, there wouldn't be a need for the two of them to play games. Instead, Christina could have simply taken Bram into Resistance custody, or Bram could have fled Splendor for the Netherworld a long time ago.

As far as I could tell, Christina and Bram seemed to be dancing around one another. Bram wasn't a member of The Resistance, but seemed to be considered a friend. Toward that end, Christina paid her own visits to Bram, just as Bram admitted. But the more I thought about it, the more I was convinced that those visits weren't social calls. No, Christina was trying to decipher whether or not Bram could be considered friend or foe. After all, Bram was a wild card and Christina couldn't count on a wild card in her deck. It was just too dangerous. So, rather than come right out and let Bram know she was sizing him up, she'd orchestrated the genius excuse of my needing protection. In doing so, she was putting me directly in his lair where I could watch his comings and goings, and keep track of him in order to decipher if he really was a threat.

Aside from not appreciating being left to my own defenses in the enemy's lair (if that was, in fact, what Christina considered Bram to be), I didn't fail to see the beauty of the arrangement. The only risky part for Christina was betting that I would experience this epiphany in the first place. But then again, it must have been a bet that Christina was willing to take. And, not to toot my own horn, but given my ANC record for weeding out the facts, I was the perfect candidate for this job. Not only that, but I believed Bram trusted me. I'd never given him any reason not to.

Hmm, so Christina might be suspicious of Bram continuing some level of involvement with my father. While I couldn't say I wholeheartedly wrapped my brain around the idea, I also couldn't deny it. Thinking about it, though, upset me. Granted, although I never considered myself to be close to Bram, at the same time, I always enjoyed our awkward relationship. When it came down to it, I didn't want to believe Bram was guilty of associating with my father and supporting his cause. I wanted to believe Bram was innocent, but I'd also been trained well enough to leave my personal feelings out of it. As an ANC Regulator, I had to focus on the facts, to focus on the cold, hard truth, the black and white ... just as I'd always done.

One thing I did know, though, was that if Bram was a Loyalist, in cahoots with my father, and (for the sake of argument) partially responsible for the detonation of the Denali, there had to be someone else involved. Why? Because Bram was too separated from The Resistance itself in order for him to even get an inkling of information about the internal goings on. That could only mean one thing—someone was feeding him information.

My mind was swimming with "what ifs" as well as feelings of anger, betrayal, and sorrow if the "what ifs" were actually valid. Deciding to sleep on everything, I closed the curtains and started for the bed. Yes, it did occur to me that if Bram was behind the Denali detonation, I was now basically as good as dead. But I abandoned the thought because I imagined Bram wouldn't show his hand quite so quickly. Besides, Christina and Knight knew the location of my whereabouts, which meant there would be too many witnesses. Nope, Bram would opt for stealth if he were behind the attacks. Killing me now would be too convenient and way too obvious.

Besides, I wasn't wholly convinced of Bram's involvement in any of this anyway ...

I removed most of the pillows from the headboard, noticing how much bigger the bed appeared when it wasn't overflowing with fluff. Then I crawled under the covers, while a yawn seized my entire body. I closed my eyes and felt the luxury of sleep invading me.

It was one of those dreams where you realize you're dreaming, but you can't wake up so you end up just going with the flow. In it, I saw myself lying in an enormous and god-awful golden bed. It took me a second or two to realize it was the same bed I'd gone to sleep in and my room was also the same: an ornately overdone gold bedroom.

I felt as if I were floating at the top of the room, glancing down at the enormous bed where I could just make out the top of someone's head. Her hair was a wavy, honey-gold and when she turned to her other side, I immediately recognized her profile. She was I and I was she. As soon as the thought occurred to me, I felt a great swoosh of air against my face, as if I were in a wind tunnel. When I opened my eyes, I noticed my vantage point had changed and I was now no longer floating along the ceiling, but firmly planted on a bed, with my cheek against a satiny pillow.

I've been sucked back into my body.

At the revelation, a sudden wind gusted from an open window at the far side of the room. It was a window that hadn't been open when I went to bed. The gust of wind blew out the candle beside the bed which was concerning since I didn't recall going to bed with the candle lit, or, for that matter, a candle even being on the bedside table. The drapes rustled in the cold breeze and I felt myself sitting up, my eyes swollen with sleep. I watched the curtains dance suggestively with the breeze and didn't feel threatened in the least, even though I imagined I should have, considering windows couldn't open themselves. Instead, I enjoyed the feel of the cold night air against my cheek. I yawned and urged myself to stand up in order to close the window and the drapes, but somehow couldn't quite motivate myself to do it. Instead, the breeze against my cheek felt icily delicious and I pulled my knees into my chest, loving the fact that I felt so warm beneath my covers.

Forgetting the window and the drapes, I closed my eyes again and willed myself to go back to sleep. Almost immediately, the temperature in the room dropped until it became painfully cold, like an ice locker. I rolled onto my back, trying to convince myself to get up and shut the window, but my body was still completely in Morpheus' grip and I couldn't wake myself up.

Dulcie, close the window! I yelled at myself.

I opened my eyes, feeling irritated that I'd have to leave the haven of my warm covers in order to brave the freezing room on an errand that I still hadn't convinced myself was even worth it. I noticed the moonlight streaming in through the window, where it highlighted the gold of my coverlet until it appeared to glow. Following the rays of the milky moon, I watched the curtains while they danced this way and that, as if in the throes of a passionate affair with the wind.

I felt my eyes growing heavy as I watched the heady dance of the curtains. I thought it must have been an optical illusion, but as I watched, the air just at the end of my bed began to grow opaque, almost as if mist were rising up from the floor. As I watched, the mist grew slowly denser and thicker. What was more interesting, it now embodied the shape of a man. I could clearly see shoulders, a head, arms, and legs.

I wasn't sure why, but the manifestation of the mist didn't frighten me. Instead, I just stared at the outline of the man in awe. And somehow, I felt it staring back at me—as if we were both in the throes of a dream-like stupor, where warning and worry don't enter into the equation. The mist seemed to grow even more opaque. What were once mere wisps of smoke, now became a thick fog.

I watched the fog man moving toward me, his legs losing their outline as if someone turned a fan on them. I could see him resting his fog hands on either end of my bed, and even though he didn't have eyes, I could clearly feel us staring at one another. The fog man seemed to reach forward and as I glanced down, I noticed my coverlet hovering over me, as if being picked up by invisible fingers. When I glanced back up at the apparition, it was gone.

My gaze dropped to the end of the bed and I watched the covers continue to ripple, growing taller as if covering a large rock. I watched as the last wisp of mist dissipated outside the covers, and I was suddenly aware that the mist now lay beneath the bed sheets. Somehow, I still wasn't frightened, though. Instead, I felt myself giggle as the fog moved past my feet, tickling me with its airiness.

The cold mist traveled up my legs, encircling them playfully. The covers continued to move this way and that, looking like a giant snake was beneath them, coiling and uncoiling its massive body. The fog reached my knees and encircled them as goose bumps invaded every inch of my being. Before I could wonder what the fog was going to do next, I felt my legs being pushed apart, as if hands were on the insides of my thighs, pushing outward at the same time that hands on the outsides of my thighs pulled.

With the realization that the fog was now intent on knowing me intimately, I felt nothing but a sense of aching excitement in the pit of my stomach. As soon as the feeling struck me, I felt the fog release its hold around my knees as it began to fill the space between my thighs. The air between my legs grew even colder until it felt as if I were sitting on a block of ice. Somehow, though, it wasn't painful.

When I felt a weight on top of my panties, I arched my back and felt a sigh forming on my lips. I could feel the fingers of air, only somehow tangible, somehow heavier, as they massaged me. Next the fingers of mist gently peeled away the fabric of my panties until I was bare. In response, something exploded deep down from inside me, something repressed and carnal, something that caused a moan to escape my lips.

The fingers of fog paused a moment, as if studying me, or staring at me in all my nudity. Then before I could so much as breathe, I felt the mist rubbing me with its coldness. I moaned in response and felt the fingers traveling down toward my entrance. They skimmed my opening and then died away, as if teasing me. In response, I arched my back again, moaning. I clenched my eyes shut tightly as soon as I felt the fog lapping at me with what I could only characterize as its tongue. I could feel fingers touching me, delving inside me and out again. First one, then two.

My nipples suddenly perked almost painfully when I felt the mouth of the mist instantly on them, caressing and stroking with a tongue made of air. At the moment that I reached orgasm, I screamed out, waking myself up.

Realizing what just happened, I sat bolt upright, surprised to find I was completely alone in the dark room. I glanced down at the bedclothes and didn't notice them moving with a faceless fog.

I had dreamt the entire thing.

I shook my head against the very idea that I'd imagined everything. It had just seemed so real! I glanced up and noticed the curtains fluttering in the breeze of the open window.

"That was quite delightful, my sweet," came the English accent. I turned to glance at Bram, who smiled down at me from where he was standing beside my bed.

THIRTEEN

I was so shocked, angry, and mortified at the thought that Bram was standing there the entire time I was having that horrible dream, and, worse still, that he was present to witness my *orgasm*, that I threw the covers aside and stood bolt upright. My pride had fallen somewhere around my feet and as soon as I realized I wasn't wearing anything other than my skivvies, whatever pride I might have held in reserve was suddenly nowhere to be found at all.

"I believe you were created merely to tempt me," Bram said in a soft voice, filled with desire as his gaze rested languidly on my breasts. Instantly, I crossed my arms against my chest and tried to staunch my pounding heart.

This was just so damned ... embarrassing!

"There are moments when I fear I will lose my mind if I cannot have you," he finished. His voice and words were razor sharp, but his tone was gritty, and almost earthy in its rawness.

I closed my eyes, so completely humiliated and angry, I didn't know which emotion to focus on first. My cheeks were flooded with mortification, and so hot, it wouldn't have surprised me if I spontaneously combusted right there.

I opened my eyes and fixed my gaze on Bram, who was still standing beside my bed, silhouetted by the moon. "What the hell was that?" I finally managed.

Bram's fangs were clearly elongated as he held his chin up and opened his mouth. It looked as if he were tasting the air, or catching a scent on the wind, like cats do. I wasn't sure if he was deliberately ignoring my question or if he hadn't heard it. He closed his eyes, his fangs aglow in the dim light as he continued ... mouth-breathing for lack of a better word.

"Bram!"

"Your scent is in the air," he replied, his voice low and almost painful in its delivery. "Your smell is intoxicating, so sweet, enticing like the harpy's song."

"Stop it," I responded, still so confounded by the whole situation that I didn't know whom to blame. Did Bram have something to do with the dream? Or did I simply fabricate the whole thing? One thing of which I was sure, however, was that my current state of undress wasn't helping things. Reaching behind myself for the top sheet, I gripped the satiny material and yanked as hard as I could to free it from the mattress. I wrapped it around my torso, and underneath each of my arms, tucking it back into itself. Bram was visibly disappointed.

"I'm not going to ask you again, Bram, what the hell just happened?"

Bram seemed to have gotten ahold of himself again because his fangs were back to their usual size and he no longer lapped at the air like a cat in heat. His eyes, though, still maintained a sense of otherworldliness, like he'd just taken a big bong hit or something. But, glassy eyes I could deal with. It was the elongated canines and weird breathing that weren't so easy to ignore.

"I regret to say that I can be of no assistance," he answered, still somewhat breathlessly.

I threw my hands on my hips, but thought better of it and tucked my elbows back in, afraid my bed sheet might come undone. "You don't really think I'm going to buy that?"

Bram glanced down at me and seemed to study me for a few moments. While there was still something strange in his eyes, something that told me he was still caught in passion's lustful grip, a smile began to form on his lips.

"It appeared to me, my sweet, that you quite enjoyed your brief repose," he said, his smile now a fully-fledged grin.

"Don't screw around with me, Bram," I spat out, narrowing my eyes. Feeling the resurgence of heat burning my cheeks, I remembered everything that happened, everything Bram witnessed.

He shrugged, still playing the part of the innocent. "What should cause you to think that I was in any way involved, Sweet?" He licked his lips. "Your accusations hurt me, as I was merely a bystander." The smile vanished from his lips as his canines began to lengthen again, presumably because he too was recalling what he'd seen.

I couldn't imagine ever living this one down.

I glared at him, still completely mortified that he'd seen my ... XXX-rated dream, but I wasn't dumb enough to actually believe he was "merely a bystander." No, somehow he had to be involved. He had to be. I mean, when was the last time, if ever, that I'd had a dream that felt so real, my body actually responded ... in the way it had?

Um, never.

"Why do I think you were involved?" I repeated, shaking my head. "Oh, I don't know, maybe because here you are, standing in my bedroom, watching me sleep. Plus, you're a three-hundred-year-old vampire, which means your powers could now include the ability to infiltrate other people's dreams; and, finally, vampires regularly transform themselves into fog."

"Fog, Sweet?" he asked, cocking his head to the side as if the very word confused him.

I rolled my eyes. "Yes, fog." He retained his confused expression so I figured I'd spell it out for him. "The fog was in my dream—a, uh, fog man."

He nodded as if everything now made sense. "Well, perhaps this is a good sign, after all."

"What are you talking about?"

"You dreamt of a 'fog man,' as you called him." He paused a few seconds, just smirking at me. "It pleases me to know you dream of men. There are times when it occurs to me that you might possibly be asexual."

"Really?" I asked facetiously. "We're really having this conversation right now?" Concluding very quickly that he wasn't going to answer my question, I continued. "I'm not asexual, Bram, and you already know that." I cleared my throat and tried to focus on the facts. "What did you do to me while I was sleeping?"

He crossed his arms against his chest before bringing one of his hands to his face and tapping one index finger against his lower lip while he studied me. Finally, he shrugged again and his eyebrows reached for the ceiling as if he were saying, "I don't know what you're talking about."

"I did nothing to you, Dulcie sweet," he said at last.

"Then who the hell did?"

"As we are the only people in this room, I cannot find the slightest evidence of this so-called fog man you keep referring to. As to your accusations that I was somehow involved, I believe I can accurately say that you were merely the recipient of an unfortunately realistic dream." With a shrug and a twitchy smile, he added, "Or a fortunate one, depending upon whom you ask."

But I refused to believe that no one was responsible for the dream. It felt so real. 'Course, lucid dreaming wasn't a stranger to me. Months earlier I found myself the unwilling victim of a *somnogobelinus*, a goblin that attacks people while they sleep. In order to take the perp down, I'd learned how to experience lucid dreaming. Maybe this newest dream was just my body telling me it hadn't forgotten the lucid dreaming skills I'd picked up? Maybe I had actually dreamt the whole thing completely on my own and was now falsely blaming Bram?

Either way, I didn't expect to get any answers from Tall, Dark, and Dead. "What were you doing next to my bed in the first place?"

He smiled again, his eyes roaming over my sheeted form before returning to my face again. "I was simply en route to my library, Sweet, to catch up on some of my ledgers with outstanding balances, when I heard a sound coming from your room."

"A sound?" I repeated, eyeing him skeptically.

"Yes," he continued. "However, looking back upon it now, I would better describe it as a moan."

"Holy Hades," I grumbled as I dropped my eyes, unable to watch the mirth in his any longer. He had to be eating this up—savoring every inch of my disquiet.

"Feeling concerned for your safety," the vampire continued, "I decided to poke my head in to ensure that you were, in fact, unscathed. When I found you in your ... condition, well, my dear, how could I leave?"

"If you were a gentleman, I'm sure you would have found a way," I muttered.

"I sincerely doubt that even a paragon of chivalry would have been able to avert his attention from you, Sweet. Unless, perhaps, such a gentleman preferred the company of his ... own sex."

I didn't feel like debating whether or not gay or straight gentlemen would have watched my XXX-rated dream. "So you had nothing to do with my dream?" I asked, even though I realized there was no point in asking Bram anything. He would just insist on his innocence, as he did with most things.

Bram shook his head purposefully. "I assure you, Sweet, that I had nothing to do with it at all. In fact, I swear to you."

I sighed in exasperation and tried to come to grips with the fact that the dream was my own. True, I'd never had an actual orgasm in my sleep before, but I figured there was a first time for everything. 'Course, I also wasn't a great believer in coincidence, but I knew I couldn't expect anything more from Bram, so it was basically a moot point. Yep, it was better now to just sweep the dream under the proverbial rug so I could attempt to find my pride again and move on.

Then something else occurred to me. "So why is my window open? And how were you able to get through my door when I dead bolted it last night?"

Bram shook his head again and made a big show of shrugging. "I have a master key," he said simply. "And as to the open window, perhaps it was a spirit who visited you. I have heard more than once that my home is haunted."

"It wasn't a freakin' spirit!" I yelled, but stopped once I realized what a complete and total waste of words this conversation was. "Anyway, what time is it?"

"It is nearly dawn, Sweet," the frustrating vampire responded. "I am en route to my bedchamber, but please make yourself comfortable. The manor is surrounded by guards to ensure your safety. Feel free to peruse my library, or if you prefer to watch the telly, there is one in the theater." He paused as he eyed me for a few seconds. "My home is your home," he said at last, seeming to stress each word. It was a strange thing to say, or maybe the strangeness was more in his delivery. 'Course, Bram was the epitome of the word "strange" so when it came down to it, nothing he said or did ever really surprised me.

"How long am I supposed to stay here?" I asked, sounding annoyed.

"Until your leader tells me otherwise," Bram answered, scowling. I supposed it was because my question hinted that I wasn't exactly thrilled at playing the part of Bram's hostage. "I shall bid you adieu, my sweet, until we reconvene later this evening." He paused with a lofty smile. "You shall find another gown in your wardrobe for tonight's festivities."

Before I could respond, he simply turned around, and taking long strides from the room, left me to my own defenses.

###

I took Bram up on his offer to make his home my own by deciding to engage in a little recon, yes, a little snooping. I still couldn't abandon the thought that maybe Bram wasn't as squeaky clean as he tried to make me believe.

Once he left my bedroom, I immediately got dressed in my clothes from the day before. Then I waited for the sun to saturate everything in its bright yellow rays, which meant there was no way in hell Bram could still be out and about. Well, that is, unless he had a death wish and planned to go out dramatically as a pile of ash.

I started for the door, opening it cautiously, because I expected the guard on the other side would probably quiz me about why I was venturing away from my room. I'd already planned to say that I was hungry and in search of food, but when I opened the door, there wasn't a guard in sight. Figuring that was a good sign, I started down the hallway. Bram's library was probably the best place to start my search for any clues about exactly what sort of business Bram was involved in.

Now if I could just locate the library ... I figured it was down the hallway from my bedroom, since Bram said he was en route to his library when he heard me moaning ...

Hades be damned, I didn't imagine *I'd* ever let myself live this one down.

Forcing my thoughts back to my quest, and what I was after, I wasn't really sure. I just hoped I might find something that would shed some light on whether Bram really was involved with the Netherworld and more precisely, my father. I figured if I could find his ledger books, they would be a good place to start.

I hurried down the hallway leading from my bedroom to what I hoped was the library. I passed two bedrooms along the way, both of their doors wide open. The third door, at the end of the hall, however, was closed. With my heart in my throat, I reached for the knob and turned it, only to find it locked. Dammit. 'Course, a trifling, little lock couldn't keep

160

a fairy who knew what she was doing out. I simply shook my hand until a mound of fairy dust appeared in my palm. Then I held my palm above the doorknob and opened my fingers, watching the spray of glitter dust the knob. At the same time, I imagined the locking device unlatching and the door opening. Seconds later, the door did as I commanded.

Bram's library was in one word—impressive. Every wall had floor to ceiling books and all the windows were meticulously covered by thick, damask curtains. I closed the door behind me and locked it from the inside as I started forward. The wood of the bookshelves was stained black to match the lush black carpet, for which I was incredibly thankful as it muffled the sound of my footsteps. In the middle of the room was a large desk, also stained black, with a behemoth leather chair just behind it. I hurried around the desk, quickly scanning the desktop for anything that could be of interest to me. But, it appeared Bram was a tidy vampire and there wasn't a thing out of place—not even an errant hair. I opened the first drawer of his desk and found pens and paper. The next drawer held a calculator, rolls of packing tape, boxed pencils and pens—nothing of interest to me. The next drawer down was locked. And a locked drawer meant I wanted it open.

I shook my fist until I could feel my fairy dust and dumped it hurriedly on top of the drawer, bending down until my eye was at the keyhole. I carefully blew the falling dust to make sure some of it actually entered the keyhole. Then, in the same way I imagined the library door unlocking, I envisioned an invisible key turning in the keyhole as I watched the drawer open itself. Inside was a notebook with a piece of paper folded in half on top of it. I picked up the piece of paper, unfolded it, and read:

I have chosen sides.

My heart stopped beating for about two seconds as Bram's message sunk into me.

He's already chosen sides? What? But which side did he choose?

161

The answer suddenly became abundantly evident. Bram had left the note for me, which meant he expected me to go snooping, which was also probably why he'd dropped that little hint about heading to the library to work on his ledgers. He must have figured that I would try to get to the bottom of whether or not The Resistance could trust him, and therefore, he'd, more or less, led me here. I couldn't imagine any other reason for this sudden turn of good luck. Yep, Bram was offering me the information I otherwise would have had to work for myself. And thank Hades for that because it wasn't as though time was on my side. Not when a war with the Netherworld still hung like a pendulum over all of our heads.

Knowing Bram wouldn't want his letter discovered, I folded it and wedged it into my sock before grabbing the notebook directly underneath it and sifting through the pages. What I saw made me nearly choke on my own tongue.

February 23, 2009
Hemogrophit..................................3 lbs,
$500,000..................................Sawyer Peninsula
Grondelbit....................................16 oz,
$20,000..................................Frazier St.
Ruthsbane....................................2 oz,
$75,000.....................................Holden Hall

It was a list of illegal potions, along with the weight of each potion, the money charged, and the various locations for each proposed drop off.

I had to look away from the ledger as I summed everything up in my head and tried not to gag on the information. So Bram had been involved in the illegal potions trade all along? It was a rhetorical question. The answer was as obvious as the ledger I gripped in my hands. I glanced down at the date again.

Two thousand nine! This has been going on for at least three years and I've never even realized it!

162

While I felt my whole being deflate on itself while gauging the extent of Bram's deceit, I refused to allow myself the luxury of dwelling on my own anger and shock. Nope, I couldn't—I didn't have the time. Instead, I focused on the fact that there had to be a reason Bram wanted me to find this. There had to be a reason he'd led me here, sacrificing himself in the process. Something was going on that was more of a worry to Bram than giving up his own game. And that thought scared the shit out of me.

I flipped through twenty or so pages of the notebook and found similar entries, only more recent. Flipping to the back of the notebook, I found nothing but blank pages. Backtracking, I saw the most recent entry was exactly one week ago, when Bram noted a potion delivery of *Arson Flower* to the loading docks near Splendor.

So why suddenly decide to come clean with all of this? What changed Bram's mind? I mean, he's been lying to me all along—ever since I first became involved with the ANC. Even when he accompanied me to the Netherworld, he told me he'd stopped working with my father more than one hundred years ago. So why break his silence now?

I glanced back at the drawer, but it was empty. Now on a mission, I shut it and opened the top drawer on the opposite side. There were nothing but Post-It note packs. Nothing was written on them. I closed the drawer and opened the next one down. A filing drawer. I opened a few of the first files, but found nothing more interesting than Bram's car insurance, some leather bound book club he'd signed up for, and various permits to run No Regrets. Nothing I could use.

Opening the next drawer down, I hit the jackpot. There, staring up at me proudly was Bram's cell phone. And just like the note and the ledgers, it was blatantly obvious that he'd left it for me to find. I picked it up and thought I might pass out when I clicked the power button and was greeted with a password prompt. All my hopes and dreams of solving the riddle of why Bram would lead me on this quest died with the prompt for his password.

Shit, I whispered to myself. *Shit. Shit. Shit shit shit!*

Then I realized there was no way Bram would have taken me this far just to have me come up empty-handed. He had to have left me a clue. I wracked my brain, trying to think of something.

Facing the phone, I entered "sweet," and when that failed, "Dulcie," "Dulce," and "ANC," but none of them worked. I tried "dear" and "my dear" without success. Then I re-entered each of the words again, trying with caps and without caps. Still, no go.

Then I remembered the strange way Bram had said the words "My home is your home." I figured it was worth a shot, especially since I didn't have anything else. I entered the word "home" into the phone. Nope. I entered "your home." Nada. No good. "My home" still no go. Fearing that I was soon going to lose my mind if I didn't get the damn thing unlocked, I entered: "MHIYH", the first letters of each word.

I felt my breath catch as the phone unlocked itself. Immediately, I clicked on the phone icon and discovered a short list of "numbers dialed." Grabbing Bram's folded note from my sock, I reached for a pen from the top of his desk and wrote down every number I could see: a total of four. Then I clicked on the "received calls" button and wrote down the five numbers I found there. As soon as I wrote down the last number received, the phone began to vibrate and I nearly dropped it. A text message popped up on screen that said:

Tonight. Midnight. Culligan's.

I quickly wrote "Culligan's" down next to the list of phone numbers. Then below that, I wrote the number from which the text had originated. I clicked on the icon for text messages, but noticed Bram had already cleared them out. Returning the phone to its drawer, I shut it and turned to my list of numbers.

Picking up the cordless phone on Bram's desk, I dialed the first number in the list of "numbers dialed." There were a few beeps before the operator's voice came on to tell me the number was changed or disconnected. Crossing the number off my list, I tried the next number. Same thing. Third number started to ring.

One ring. Two rings. Three rings.

"Bram?" a female voice answered.

I immediately hung up and tried to squelch the shock that fluttered from deep down within me. Why? Because Christina was the woman on the other line.

So what? I chided myself. *Bram admitted that Christina visited him on more than one occasion, so what does it matter that they exchanged phone numbers? It could be totally meaningless. In fact, it probably is totally meaningless ...*

After deciding I had a good point, I turned to the fourth number on the list and dialed it, only to find it was also disconnected. I crossed it off my list and turned to the list of phone numbers received. Four of the numbers were the same ones that were now canceled. The other two were Christina.

I sighed long and deep, trying to fight the feeling that there was something ominous about Bram and Christina being close enough to receive calls from one another. Maybe the reason the information bothered me so much was because neither Christina nor Knight ever hinted to Bram being involved in any of this Resistance related stuff. And Knight was absolutely pissed when he found out that Christina had arranged for me to stay with Bram.

Hmm, there was no use in speculation. I didn't know all the facts, and until I did, there was no point in jumping to conclusions. I turned back to my list of phone numbers and noticed the only one I hadn't checked was the number from the text. When I dialed the number, it just rang.

After five rings, I hung up. I folded my sheet of paper again, wedging it back into my sock. Then I started to leave

Bram's library, all the while wondering how Christina figured into all of this.

FOURTEEN

The gown that Bram proposed I wear this evening was just as bad as the one from the night before. While the wine-red color was slightly better than the garish gold of the first gown, little else recommended it. This dress was just as obscenely short—disabling me from bending over in the slightest, all dropped dinner utensils be damned. Not only that, but the dress was so tight, I could see the lines of every mound and valley of my body. To make matters worse, the fabric itself was beyond revealing; the intensity of the light determined whether or not you could see right through it. And I'm sure every detail of the dress was not by accident, but rather, by design. With the hem of the thing barely covering my ass, the bodice was no more than a strapless tube. And as any woman with ample, natural breasts will tell you, tube tops are "the girls'" worst nightmare.

Even now, I struggled with the top, irritated with the weight of my breasts, because they kept causing the top to roll back down again. Catching my reflection in the mirror, I heaved a sigh of quiet desperation.

"I look like a freakin' shrink-wrapped sausage," I muttered, shaking my head at the outright indecency of the whole damned thing. "Son of a bitch!"

Hearing a knock on my door, I gripped the top of the dress and re-hoisted the girls with all my might, gaining maybe three millimeters more fabric. Before I could wrestle with it any further, the door opened, revealing my vampire host. Seeing him, handsomely attired in a navy blue, three-piece-suit, indignation suddenly overcame me.

How could he have lied to me all along? How could he have been involved with my father from the get-go, but sworn he wasn't? How could I have trusted him!

That was the biggest kicker of the whole damned situation; I'd trusted Bram. I couldn't help surrendering to the tide of disappointment as well as raw anger now flowing through me. I felt my hands fisting and my fingernails digging into my palms.

Get a hold of yourself! I screamed internally. *Regardless of the past, Bram is on your side! And there must be lots more you don't know, which he wants you to discover, so don't blow that chance!*

I took a deep breath and stretched my fingers, reminding myself that as a good ANC Regulator, I had a duty to focus on the cold, hard truth without getting sidetracked by my own emotions. I'd managed as much with Quillan, so I could do it again, with Bram.

One thing you know for sure: Dulcie O'Neil is one tough chick! And what's more, she's fanfuckingtastic at her job, I reminded myself.

Yep, I was right. There was no way in hell I would miss out on whatever information still awaited me. Not when the weight of the Netherworld rode on my shoulders. Instead, I was resigned to play into Bram's game and let him lead me to the truth. I wouldn't rest until I understood exactly what was going on; and the real reason why I was being shielded under Bram's roof.

I glanced up at the vampire, who didn't make any motion to say anything. Instead, he seemed to be searching for the right words. When he opened his mouth to speak, our eyes met and the words faltered on his lips. It was as if he'd suddenly been struck dumb. Thinking more on it, he'd probably just realized the same thing I had—that things between us could and would never be the same.

I shut my eyes and ignored the sudden urge to lash out at him with words as well as my fists, but I knew that would be a mistake. I was on the brink of discovering something significant and the last thing I wanted to do was screw the whole thing up. I glanced down at myself again and tried to prioritize my thoughts. First things first, I needed a safe subject.

"This thing," I started, while shaking my head with obvious distaste over my attire, "sucks."

Bram's eyes widened in surprise only momentarily before he apparently realized there would be no long winded conversations about "why?" Then, as if reading my mind and, specifically, that I had no time for explanations or apologies, he assumed the role he always had. Doffing a devil-may-care attitude, he faced me squarely. His eyes, vapid pools of nothing, scanned my body from head to toe with undisguised appreciation.

He smirked, "It suits you, Sweet." He was back to his starring role, as both of us knew he had to be.

"I vehemently disagree," I snapped, attempting to heave the tube top up again. Finally, admitting defeat, I headed for the door, and nearly tripped over the ridiculously narrow and high stiletto-heeled boots Bram had left for me to wear. Yep, it looked like I was very successfully channeling Julia Roberts in *Pretty Woman*.

Bram didn't reply as he openly eyed me from head to toe again before stepping behind me, and repeating the process.

"I believe one of my favorite parts of your body is this line here," he whispered just above my ear. He reached down and outlined the top of my thigh, all the way up to where it met my butt. I spun around, taking a step back as outrage burned my cheeks.

"You keep your hands off me," I chided, although he didn't respond. Apparently it hadn't been a difficult feat to drop back into the role of the perverted vampire.

"The mounds of your biceps femoris, where they attach to your gluteus maximus, are something of a delicacy."

I shook my head, unable to staunch the irritability flowing through me. I still had so many questions I wanted answered, but I had the distinct feeling that Bram didn't intend to answer them. Not yet anyway.

"And your adductor magnus," he started again. This time, he traced the outline of my inner thigh until I smacked his hand and stepped away from him, fuming with indignity.

"I hope you know these cheap thrills count as the equivalent of two dinners of the four I still owe you," I grumbled. "And the only reason I even wore this ridiculous outfit in the first place is because I'm contractually obliged to do so."

Then I thought, given Bram's blatant involvement with the illegal potions industry and my subsequent anger over it, that I could renege on our agreement altogether. But after further consideration, I decided an agreement was an agreement. And, what was more, I needed to get more information from him, so I figured I'd have a better chance if I played by his rules.

So here I was, shrink-wrapped to the nines. Farmer John be damned.

Bram didn't say anything more as he offered his arm, apparently striving for gallant. I took it and we started down the hallway.

"I trust you found ways to occupy yourself while I slept?" he asked with an expression that suggested there was a double entendre in his statement.

I nodded, but the thought occurred to me that maybe we weren't quite as alone in Bram's house as it appeared. Knowing Bram was in cahoots with my father, as well as my father's general paranoia, it wouldn't have surprised me in the least to discover the whole house was bugged.

"I spent a lot of time in the library," I answered simply.

Bram didn't say anything for a few seconds, but stopped walking when we reached the stairs and turned to face me. His eyes were inscrutable as he studied me.

"Very good," he said at last, licking his lips. "And I daresay you … found something to interest you?"

Based on the way he wouldn't come out and ask me what he really wanted to know, I figured either his house had to be bugged, or maybe he was bugged. Otherwise, I couldn't imagine why he found it necessary to talk in code.

"Yes, I did," I answered, studying him meticulously. At my words, Bram's jaw tightened and I could only imagine he must've believed his plan—that I'd found not only his ledger book, but also his cell phone—had worked. I could see the epiphany in his eyes when he realized everything he'd been keeping from me for so many years was now out in the open. And, more so, that I now knew him to be a lying piece of shit.

He gave me his elbow again and after I beat down another round of anger over this whole situation, I took it with a frown and we started down the hallway, which terminated at the double doors of the dining room. The same goblin butler from last night opened the door nearest us and we entered the ornate room. I noticed an assortment of covered dishes already on the table.

"So you didn't wait for me to order this time?" I asked, my stomach growling in anticipation. I'd been so overwhelmed by everything I'd discovered earlier that I hadn't found the time, much less the interest, to eat.

"Alas, chefs live to show off their cuisine, do they not?" Bram asked. I shrugged, assuming his chef was probably less than thrilled with my order of salmon and Caesar salad from the previous night. So this time around, they'd left me out of the dinner arrangements. It didn't matter to me, really. With everything else going on in my head, I didn't have the energy to slap a dinner menu on top of it.

Bram said nothing more, but led me to the first seat just adjacent to the head of the table. He pulled my chair out and pushed me back up to the table once I sat down. The goblin followed quickly behind him and placed my unfolded napkin neatly on my lap.

Bram took the chair at the head of the table beside mine. When the goblin started to fuss over unfolding Bram's napkin and placing it in his lap, the vampire shooed him away with a wave of his hand and the expression of someone aggravated by his very existence. The goblin apparently got the message. Leaving Bram, he started removing the domes from all seven platters on the table.

The first dish was rolls of buttered bread. Without asking me, the goblin lifted my bread plate and used a pair of incredibly shiny silver tongs to place a roll on the plate. Turning to the next dish, he heaped a huge helping of what appeared to be chicken casserole onto my dinner plate. By the time he made all the rounds and returned my plate to me, it was piled over four inches high with what looked like … slop.

"Thanks," I said unconvincingly.

The goblin said nothing as he exited the room. I turned to Bram, who shook his head, sighing deeply. "Good help is not what it was two hundred years ago," he said as he eyed the smorgasbord on my plate forlornly.

"It's fine," I answered while poking around the plate with my fork, trying to find something I recognized. I settled on a grape, which I speared with the fork and brought to my lips. My stomach continued to grumble with hunger, and it seemed the more I ate of the various dishes, the hungrier I got.

After polishing off maybe a third of my plate, I pushed it away and downed my glass of water. I was eager to find out what more Bram had up his sleeve, but wasn't sure how to go about getting there. Bram still seemed to be talking in code, and I had the distinct feeling it was because we didn't have the luxury of privacy.

"Do you enjoy classical music, Sweet?" he asked after a protracted silence, during which he swirled the mouth of his water glass with his index finger lazily. Like the evening before, Bram didn't eat anything. He simply watched me curiously—as if he were trying to recall what food tasted like. He never rushed me, though, instead, seeming to enjoy the ritual of eating.

I shrugged in answer to the question of whether I enjoyed classical music. I couldn't say I did or didn't. It was one of those subjects I'd never really considered before because I always had more important subjects on my mind. "As well as anyone, I guess."

He nodded, and must've taken my response as a "yes" because he reached for a little, silver bell that sat beside his table setting. He rang the bell twice, the tinny sound echoing through the immense room and summoning the goblin instantly.

"Sir?" the squat man asked. His fleshy arms were folded neatly behind his back as he faced Bram with a pleasant grin on his round face.

"Please prepare the ballroom; we would like to enjoy some music," Bram ordered.

The goblin nodded and turned to accomplish the task when something appeared to occur to him, and he pivoted on his toes to face his vampire master again. "Any special requests, sir?"

"Hmm," Bram said while considering the question carefully. He tapped his index finger against his chin and narrowed his eyes at me. He seemed to be deciding what type of music he thought I might prefer. His lips curled into a slow smile and I figured he'd made his decision.

"Bach," he said at last, facing the goblin.

"Very good," the man said. With a hurried nod, he disappeared through the double doors.

"Shall we dance?" Bram asked, his eyes narrowing as soon as I shook my head. That was when I got his gist—there was much more to his question than he'd let on. Even though I absolutely didn't care to dance, especially to classical music because it wasn't like I had any clue what to do, I was about to have a change of heart. With a simple nod and a subdued smile, I acquiesced.

Bram rose quietly, placing his folded napkin on the table beside his empty plate. Taking my chair, he pulled it out from the table and offered me his arm. I stood to accept his arm, allowing him to lead me into the ballroom.

The ballroom was adjacent to the dining room. It was a great expanse of incredibly high ceilings, with floor to ceiling stained glass windows and the most intricate crown molding I'd ever seen. The never ending, polished hardwood floors made it look like a room bedecked for a queen. The only pieces of furniture were several ornate, antique sofas which stood against the walls and were upholstered in black chenille. There was also an enormous, black, baby grand piano in the corner. As soon as I laid my eyes on the piano, the keys began to depress and a bevy of melodious notes sounded in the once quiet room. The keys continued to play, in a flourish of sweet music.

"Fancy," I commented. "A piano that plays itself." Or maybe it was the ghost to which Bram had alluded earlier.

Bram smiled at me in response. "Yes, Sweet. At times, even I feel lazy."

I had no idea that Bram could play the piano, but I also couldn't say it surprised me. I mean, as far as he wanted everyone to believe, he was an accomplished man … er, vampire.

I didn't recognize the song playing on the piano, but assumed it was Bach, per Bram's request. Bram walked toward the center of the room, and with one arm behind his back, bowed toward me before extending his other hand, gesturing for me to join him. I took a deep breath, hoping I wouldn't regret attempting to dance, but figured there had to be a reason why Bram was so intent on us doing it in the first place. I approached him and he wrapped his right arm around me, with his hand coming to rest on the middle of my back. Then he took my right hand with his left and extended them both out, perpendicular to our bodies. I put my left hand on his shoulder and away we went!

Bram moved his left foot forward so I stepped backwards, lest my foot be trampled. Taking Bram's lead, I stepped out to the side with my left foot, mirroring his right. We continued on in this fashion, silently, of which I was grateful. I wanted to make sure I knew what I was doing before any conversations could ensue. Otherwise I didn't imagine I'd be able to concentrate on anything else. After another few minutes, during which we danced in "boxes" all around the floor, Bram leaned down and pulled me closer into him; so close, I could feel his lips against my ear.

"Speak to me very softly," he whispered. "I cannot guarantee this house has no eavesdroppers."

I nodded, having already assumed such was the case. Taking a deep breath, I tried to organize my thoughts. "What exactly is your involvement with my father?" I asked in a voice barely above a whisper. Good thing that vampires have excellent hearing …

Bram seemed taken aback by the question, and I wasn't sure why. As far as I was concerned, he should have expected it. He paused for a few seconds before finally answering.

"As you have already deduced, your father and I were involved for many years."

Even though I already knew the truth, my stomach dropped in disappointment at hearing the words on Bram's lips. Somehow, it just made it all the more real. Part of me wanted to demand the reason why he'd lied to me for so long but the more I thought about, the more I realized there was no point. Time was of the essence now and that conversation would have to wait.

"Why did you lead me to your library to find your ledger and cell phone?" I continued, now hell bent on getting as much information out of Bram as I could.

"You told me to choose sides, Sweet. I merely did as you instructed," he said, shrugging like it really wasn't a big deal at all. Then, apparently realizing his response was a lame one, he added: "And I knew the time for playing between the lines had passed."

I nodded, satisfied. "How does Christina figure into all of this?"

He was quiet for another few seconds. "That you must learn for yourself."

"How?" I interrupted, my voice coming out anxious and edgy.

"I daresay you received the text on my mobile phone?"

"Yes."

"It might behoove you to follow that clue, Sweet." His breath against my ear caused goose bumps to cover my skin as the chill reached the back of my neck.

"Culligan's at midnight?" I asked.

"Yes," he said, in what sounded like a snake's hiss. "After tonight, many of your questions will be answered."

"How far is this Culligan's place, anyway?"

"Perhaps one half hour," he responded quickly. "There is a fleet of automobiles in my garage, Sweet. I will leave the keys in the Carrera."

"What is Culligan's? I have no idea where it is or how to get there," I started, my voice sounding panicked.

"Calm yourself," Bram purred into my ear. "The address will be programmed into the navigation in the Porsche."

"Okay," I said and took a deep breath.

"After this evening, you will not return here again, as it will no longer be safe."

"Okay," I whispered, finding his words ominous. If it weren't safe for me, would it be safe for him? It was something I couldn't worry about, though, not when I had much bigger fish to fry. Besides, if Bram was good at anything, it was preserving his own neck. "Did Christina know about your connection to my father all along?" I asked, wondering how he could have been in business with my father and Christina not know about it.

"No," he crooned into my ear.

"What about Quillan?" I demanded. "He must have known you were in cahoots with Melchior all this time?"

But Bram shook his head. "No one, other than your father and a few of his henchmen, knows about me, Sweet. In all my business affairs, I have realized the valuable lesson that it is much safer to maintain one's secrecy."

"How has Trey never picked up on any of this?" I asked, amazed because there was very little that got by Trey.

"I imagine you can guess that answer to that question."

"Magic?" I asked, my jaw tight. "Were you able to deflect the truth by buffering it with magic?"

Bram simply nodded. "There are ways around every obstacle, Sweet."

Somehow that bit of information relieved me because I couldn't imagine that Quill could have known about Bram's duplicitous ways and yet not alerted me to them. "Were you responsible for the Denali explosion?" I continued with my line of interrogation, hoping and praying his answer to this question would also be a resounding negative.

"Of course not!" he said indignantly. "It wounds me to think you would even consider such a thing!"

"Really?" I asked facetiously. "It's not like you were honest with me about anything else."

"The attempt on your life was one of the paramount reasons I have exposed myself to you. " He pushed me away from him so I could see the truth in his eyes. "I would never harm you."

I wasn't sure why, but I believed him.

"After tonight, all will be revealed to you and everything that appears cloudy now will make sense," he finished with a twinge of indignation still evident in his voice.

"In choosing the side of The Resistance, you do realize what that means for your relationship with my father?" I asked, even though it was a stupid question. Obviously, he understood.

"Of course," he said simply. "The tree of liberty must be refreshed from time to time with the blood of patriots and tyrants. Thomas Jefferson."

"Nice," I answered, wondering how he came up with this stuff. "Then we can count on you?"

He paused another few seconds as he whirled me around into another box step.

"First you must identify whom, among your own, you can count on, Sweet."

FIFTEEN

Later that evening, I was overjoyed to remove the horrid red gown and wear my own clothes. Granted, I'd worn my jeans and long-sleeved T-shirt yesterday and the day before, but I'd also laundered them so it wasn't quite as gross as it might otherwise sound. And, yes, I'd already tried to create a new outfit for myself, but apparently, Bram had ensured that no magic could be conducted in his home because every time I tried my fairy dust, nothing came of it. I did recall being able to rely on magic to open the door to the library and the drawer where Bram kept his ledgers which just spoke to the fact that Bram must have really wanted me to find them, otherwise I didn't imagine I'd be able to use my magic anywhere in his house. Regardless, I couldn't really say my mind was on magic anyway, not with the nervous energy coursing through me when I thought about what was going to happen at midnight tonight.

After tonight, all will be revealed to you and everything that appears cloudy now will make sense … Bram's words echoed in my mind as I strove to understand what they could mean.

Was Christina double-crossing The Resistance? Could she have somehow maintained her ties to my father even while acting as the head of The Resistance? Bram never had indicated just what Christina's role in this whole situation was. He'd simply told me that everything would make sense after this evening. Well, I hoped he was telling the truth because right about now, I felt more than a little confused over whom to believe and whom to trust.

As I threw my sneakers on and tied my shoelaces, I heard a knock on my door. As was customary for Bram, he didn't wait for me to answer before opening it.

"Sweet," he greeted me with a grin. He was dressed in charcoal grey slacks, a black shirt, and a black jacket. With his dark hair brushed back and his devil's smile, he was the epitome of handsome. At that moment, I wondered if I might ever have developed feelings for Bram, if Knight hadn't been in the picture. But then I figured it was a waste of time to even consider because I'd never know the answer. Why? Because Knight *was* still in the picture. Despite being the most frustrating Loki I'd ever laid eyes on, I still had an incredibly difficult time whenever I tried to banish him from my mind.

"Bram?" I asked, after realizing neither of us was talking.

He smiled and his fangs gleamed in the low light. "I am leaving now for Culligan's." He stopped talking for a few seconds and I wasn't sure what to say. Luckily, he beat me to it. "Please wait ten minutes before doing the same."

I nodded, feeling suddenly dizzy as my heart began to pound. There was just so much riding on this evening, so many questions I wanted answered. Not only that, but I was also worried—both about Bram and myself. "Okay."

"When you arrive, please be very careful to disguise yourself. No one must know that you are present, do you understand?"

His lips were tight and his eyebrows creased in the middle, giving him the expression of concern. It was an expression that seemed new to him somehow. Ordinarily he was the maddeningly irritating vampire with nothing but sex or himself on his mind.

I nodded again. "Yes, I understand." I took a deep breath before facing him again. "I hope you know I … I'm putting a lot of trust in you."

His eyebrows arched as if he didn't follow, so I continued.

"I don't know where I'm going, or what to expect tonight. And after you so artfully illustrated that you've been lying to me the entire time I've known you, I'm not sure if I should trust you now."

"You have my word as a gentleman that I would never willingly put you in harm's way," he said in a steely tone.

"I better not be making a huge mistake."

Bram shook his head and dropped his gaze to the floor before looking back at me. When he did, his eyes were burning with a fire that surprised me, and his fangs started indenting his lower lip. "I know I was not honest with you regarding your father's and my … association, therefore I understand your hesitance to believe anything more from my mouth." He paused, never taking his eyes from mine. "But I will make you this promise, one which I will forever keep." He was quiet another few seconds. "I would instantly lay down my own life in order to save yours."

While I couldn't say I believed him (Bram exaggerated like nobody else), there was something in his eyes that made me want to trust him, something that told me I'd be safe with him. I didn't say anything more and the two of us just stood there in silence, both at a loss for words. It was a moment I doubt I'll ever forget—Bram's gaze was so intense, I felt as if he was staring right through me.

"Point taken," I said at last. Bram nodded, but before he could comment, I interrupted. "Are you in trouble?"

He shook his head, laughing lightly. "I have managed to remain alive these three hundred years by more than just accident, my dear." Then the laugh died on his lips. "Trouble does not frighten me."

I wasn't sure, but figured he meant "yes." But whether or not Bram was in trouble, there really wasn't anything I could do to help him, especially after he'd informed me that I couldn't return to his home after tonight. And, really, it was silly to worry about Bram—he was a vampire; survival seemed to be hard-wired into him. As to the other person who *was* absolutely in trouble, I wasn't sure where to go or what to do after tonight. But I'd have to figure it all out later. Now, I had too much on my mind.

"Be careful," I started, feeling as if a heavy weight had descended on me. I just hoped all of us, Bram included, would be able to resist my father's power, that we'd be able to beat him at his own game. Even though Bram had lied to me about being in business with my father all these years, I still considered him somewhat a victim. And, furthermore, there was something within me that insisted Bram wasn't a bad person, and I trusted that instinct. Knowing my father's affinity for imposing his own will, I could see how Bram might have been forced into a business relationship with him, just like most of us had.

Shit, maybe I was going soft.

"I will, Sweet," Bram said.

Then with a modicum of levity, I added: "Because you know, I'll have to arrest you once this shit with the Netherworld is figured out."

Bram threw his head back and laughed heartily before returning his gaze to mine. The mirth on his lips was replaced with a simple smile. "You do not know the joy you have brought me over the years, Sweet."

I was only half kidding about arresting him—I mean, part of me had absolutely decided that Bram should pay for his transgressions. But then I figured since we were basically on the brink of war and Bram had gone out on a huge limb to help me, bygones should be bygones. Who knew what our fates entailed anyway? Maybe we'd all be wiped out by my father and all of this wind up a moot point.

Just call me the harbinger of optimism.

"I'll see you in," I started, glancing at the clock before looking at him again, "forty minutes."

He nodded and we both stared at each other for another few seconds before he disappeared from the doorway. I glanced at the clock again and felt my hands go clammy as I stood impatiently, in the same spot Bram left me, just staring at the clock, watching the seconds tick by. At the end of the ten minutes, it felt like I'd been standing there for ten hours. My body switched to autopilot as I ran from my bedroom, into the hallway, and took the stairs two at a time. I glanced around to make sure no one was ready to waylay me while I was en route to Bram's garage. Not encountering anyone, I hurried to the front door and opened it a smidge, peeking outside to make sure everything was clear. It appeared to be.

I started forward, with the cold air of the dark night assaulting my face. I could see the four-car garage in the distance and jogged across the courtyard that separated the house from the garage. One of the garage doors was already up, revealing Bram's black Porsche Carrera. Seeing it now made me smile wistfully as I remembered all the times I'd gone to No Regrets in search of information. I only ever stopped in when I saw his Porsche gleaming in the parking lot, letting me know Bram was in.

Somehow those days seemed so long ago.

I reached the driver's side door and opened it, eyeing the seat and looking for the keys. They weren't there. Leaning into the car, I spotted them hanging from the ignition, so I got behind the wheel and closed the door. That was when I realized my feet were miles from the pedals. I adjusted the seat and the steering wheel before turning to the mirrors. After adjusting the rearview and both side mirrors, I turned the key in the ignition, the happy purr of the engine like music to my ears. The center console lit up, revealing a navigation screen. Even though I had no clue how to operate it, after a few minutes, I managed to find "saved destinations." There was only one destination listed as "saved" so I figured it had to be Culligan's. I hoped so anyway.

With a shrug, I clicked the start button and watched the navigation respond by bringing up a map of what I imagined was my current location. Figuring that was my cue, I started in reverse. As I was pulling out of the garage, the navigation advised me to travel west on Myrtle Street, which I presumed was the street Bram lived on.

At the end of Bram's street, the navigation was suddenly interrupted midstream when the air popped and fizzed around me. In the blink of an eye, I was deposited onto a freeway onramp, thankfully going in the proper direction. Obviously, I had to have just traveled through a portal.

"Take the 101 South for twenty-two miles," the navigation said, without missing a beat.

"Okay," I answered and stepped on the gas, more than aware I'd already lost too much time by adjusting the seat and mirrors, as well as screwing around with the navigation.

The stars twinkled at me from the safety of the sky while I remembered being in High Prison in the Netherworld with Knight. More specifically, I recalled how I'd nearly been raped by one of the two guards. Cyclops, the guard in question, was incredibly determined, not to mention strong. Just when I thought my fight was at an end, Bram intervened. But that wasn't the part that was causing my disquiet. It was the expression of the guards upon seeing Bram, how they'd both appeared to recognize him, even if they were also surprised to see him. At the time, I didn't understand how either could have recognized him, since I was still under the mistaken assumption that Bram hadn't been to the Netherworld in over one hundred years. But now the puzzle pieces were finally falling into place. No doubt, the guards recognized Bram because they'd dealt with him while in the employ of my father.

Well, shit, for all I knew, the guards could have been working for Bram! Furthermore, just how close was Bram to my father? Did Bram work for Melchior? Or were they partners, just as before, over one hundred years earlier? How much clout did Bram carry in the Netherworld?

"Take the next exit and then turn right," the navigation announced. I glanced over my shoulder to make sure no one was in the way before crossing the two lanes and finally veering onto the off-ramp. At the stop sign, I made my right and then another "pop" and "click" in the air signaled my crossing through another portal.

"Drive five hundred feet and your destination will be ahead on the left," the navigation said as I hit the brakes, not wanting my arrival to be so obvious. Looking around myself, I found I was on another empty street, this one residential. Checking the clock on the dash, it was five minutes to midnight. I pulled the Porsche over and parked as I glanced down the street again and wondered how in the hell I was going to locate Culligan's when I didn't even have an address for it. Referring to the navigation screen, I noticed there wasn't an address listed there either. Great, just great.

Remembering Bram telling me to disguise myself, I shook my hand until a mound of fairy dust appeared. Then I dumped the dust over myself, imagining my long hair suddenly short and black, with thick bangs to frame my face. Looking down at my outfit, I pictured a long-sleeved, black T-shirt and black jeans. Then, figuring I might need them, I pictured twin daggers strapped to the tops of each of my thighs. When I felt the cold metal against my skin, I grinned. Sometimes it was damned good to be a fairy. Yes, I could have tried for an *Op 6* or *7* handgun, but I wasn't convinced of my magic ability when it came to more complicated weapons. With one last look at myself in the mirror, I hoped no one would recognize me as I started for the door. Then, thinking longer on it, I imagined a ball cap, for good measure.

I secured the hat on my head and left the keys in the ignition since you never know when you're going to need a quick getaway. Then I closed the door behind me and started down the street, checking the street numbers, while still trying to figure out where I was supposed to go. There was no one anywhere to be seen, which was good because the last thing I wanted was to be noticed or recognized. After passing the second house from where I'd parked the

Porsche, I decided I was taking too big a chance by being out in the open and moved to the rear of the house.

My feet were nearly silent on the wet grass although I did come close to slipping. Hoisting myself against the rough stucco of the house, I peered around the corner and noticed a small graveyard right in front of me. It was adjacent to the house and at the end of the cul-de-sac. The graveyard was maybe twelve feet wide by fourteen feet long, and enclosed by a decrepit iron fence. There were maybe a dozen tombstones, all cracking with age.

At the sound of voices, I hung back in the shadows and watched two people walking into the graveyard to meet a third, who'd already been standing there. All three wore long, black cloaks that dragged in the dirt, their faces obscured by their hoods. If I hadn't known better, I might have thought they were a trio of monks.

Eyeing the entry to the graveyard, I noticed the wrought-iron fence stretched maybe ten feet high above the double iron gates at the entrance. It looked like cursive writing in the curlicues of the ironwork. Even though it was written in reverse, I could make out the name "Culligan" on the gate. So I *was* in the right place. Well, right place or not, I needed to get much closer, but I couldn't find anything to hide behind. After watching a fourth hooded figure enter the graveyard and join the other three waiting at the rear, I realized time was slipping through my fingers.

I shook my palm until I felt my dust, then as I dumped the particles over my head, I imagined myself shrinking to the size of a pixie (or a baby carrot) and sprouting wings in the process. I suddenly felt light-headed as my magic did its job and transformed me into Thumbelina. I felt my wings catching on my shirt, so I simply imagined the shirt ripping in order to allow for them, and the fabric complied.

Once I was Mini-Me, I tried flapping my wings and felt myself lifting into the air before fluttering to a nearby tree branch. I was still too far away from what now appeared to be giants in the center of the graveyard, so I flew to the iron fence post closest to me, concealed in the shadows. Still not able to eavesdrop adequately, I took a deep breath (flying was damned hard exercise!) and fluttered to a tombstone. Not wanting to call attention to myself, even in my mini form, I drifted down to the base of the stone and hid behind it. Poking my head out, I could still see the goings on of the four cloaked people who were now only twelve feet from me.

"Mr. S, I presume?" one of the cloaked beings began. He reached out his hand to the other man, who refused to take it.

"Yes," came Bram's succinct reply. Hmm, he must have been Mr. S. Why? I had no clue, but I prepared myself for quite a few rude awakenings where Bram's history was concerned.

"Thanks for comin'," the other man responded. I didn't recognize his voice. It was deep and sounded like he had a mild lisp.

"Where is O'Neil?" Bram asked. It was Bram's voice like I'd never heard before—there was no trace of flirtation or levity. He was all seriousness—lethal and dangerous.

"He decided it wasn't safe enough for him to come," the man with the lisp responded. "He sent us instead." He motioned to the taller of the two figures standing behind him.

Bram didn't respond right away. I had the gut feeling that he wasn't happy with this news because I guessed he was expecting my father.

"Is she with you?" Bram asked. I could tell by the way he inclined his head, that he was studying the smallest cloaked figure, who was standing just behind Mr. Lisp.

The taller figure, whom Mr. Lisp had referenced earlier, suddenly stepped forward. In the moonlight, I could only see the lower half of his face, his lips too narrow for his ample cheeks. I watched his mouth part into a smile, revealing uneven and yellowed teeth. He tugged the cloak of the smaller person who was beside him.

187

"She's right here," the man said in a raspy tone. It sounded like a voice subjected to too many years of cigarettes and alcohol.

The small woman in the cloak stumbled as she was tugged forward. The black cloak fell off her face, revealing long, dark hair and big, brown eyes that I would know anywhere. It was Christina.

Anger began gnawing at me.

Here she was, standing right in front of me, representing my father's side. She'd lied to everyone! She'd somehow managed to maintain ties to my father even while she pretended to be completely invested in our cause.

Why? I had no clue. I just couldn't understand how we'd never picked up on it, on something! As soon as the anger flared up inside of me, though, I focused on Christina's face and felt my ire begin to subside.

Something was wrong with her. She looked, for all intents and purposes, like she was in a daze. Even though she was standing on solid ground, she kept wavering as if she were drunk, and staring straight ahead, but focusing on nothing. She looked as if she were sleepwalking.

"Since we've got her right here, we should just kill her and put an end to it," the man who was standing closest to her said.

"You are a fool," Bram responded. "She has much more value to us alive."

I felt a sigh of relief hearing Bram's words. I wasn't sure what I could do if they tried to kill Christina right here and now. I'd definitely blow my cover, of that much, I was sure. Luckily, I didn't have to worry about it, at least not yet.

"There are many questions she can answer for us," Bram said as he approached Christina. He held out his hand, taking hers. As soon as their skin touched, she faced him, her eyes still hollow and nearly lifeless. She stared up at him, with no sign of recognition in her deep brown eyes, just continued to study him as if she'd never seen him before.

"How was the Netherworld informed of a war between O'Neil and The Resistance?" Bram asked her, his voice soft.

Christina didn't respond right away, but when she did, her voice was flat. "*The Netherworlder Today*," she said. "I contacted them to run the article." Her voice was almost unrecognizable. There was no inflection at all—it sounded robotic.

"Bitch!" the man closest to her yelled out as he held his hand up as if to strike her.

"Watch yourself!" Bram growled and the man dropped his hand, but the grimace on his face remained, the upper half still concealed by his hood.

"Why don't you tell Mr. S what happened with the car explosion," the man continued, obviously mocking her. "Why don't you tell him how you can't do one fucking thing right!"

At the mention of the Denali explosion, I felt myself stiffen. Was Christina responsible for it?

Christina didn't shift her almost sightless eyes from Bram. She just continued to stand there, wavering, opening her mouth and answering in a monotone. "I obeyed my orders."

Bram glanced at the man beside her. "Explain this explosion." His lips were tight, and his posture even more rigid than usual.

"O'Neil told me to get rid of Vander. So I gave this little bitch the *Maegon* and told her exactly what to do with it. 'Course the little idiot just fucked the whole thing up."

Christina didn't respond, but continued staring straight ahead. She seemed oblivious to everything going on around her.

"Why was I not informed of this?" Bram demanded, his voice suddenly furious. He frowned and his fangs lengthened, the moonlight reflecting against them.

The man shrugged but took a step back, holding his hands up in surrender. Apparently, he'd detected Bram's fangs as well. I noticed the other man also taking a step back.

"Ask O'Neil. He tells me to shit an' all I say is, 'where, boss?'"

"This is between you and O'Neil," the other man said. "We just follow orders."

"I brought the fairy to you as you instructed," Christina suddenly piped up, as though programmed to announce it. She didn't address anyone, though, so I wasn't sure who the statement was aimed at, although I imagined it must have been Bram. I also guessed she was talking about me.

"Very good," Bram said with a nod as he offered Christina a slight smile.

"You got O'Neil's daughter?" Mr. Lisp piped up.

"I do," Bram answered. "And unless O'Neil prefers I drain her lovely, little body of all its blood, he better start playing by my rules."

"I ain't gettin' in the middle o' this," Mr. Lisp responded. "All I was told ta do was get this bitch on the *Blueliss,* and tell her what the hell ta do with the *Maegon.* An' that was it! The rest is between you and O'Neil."

Suddenly, everything was crystal clear. *Blueliss* was an illegal narcotic, which I hadn't seen nor heard of in the past five years, at least. I actually thought we'd wiped it out of existence, but apparently, that wasn't the case. *Blueliss* was incredibly dangerous because it basically cleaned the user's brain of all of her memories. Victims had no idea who they were, where they lived, whom they knew, nothing. The biggest kicker, though, was that whoever provided the potion to the victim could imprint his or her will upon the victim. The effects usually took about an hour or two to wear off, allowing the victims to return to being themselves again. Except they'd have no idea they'd ever been drugged in the first place.

So somehow, Melchior was able to track Christina down, but rather than killing her, he'd decided to turn her against herself. By forcing the *Blueliss* on her, he could also force her to tell him everything The Resistance was planning. As to the Denali explosion, even though Christina had been the one responsible for attempting to kill Knight and me, she'd been drugged into doing it and, furthermore, had no memory of it. And when she'd forced all of us to take the tests which would confirm or deny our loyalty to The Resistance, the only person she hadn't tested had been herself, for obvious reasons.

I suddenly felt nauseous as I wondered how long my father had been using Christina as his puppet. It didn't seem like Bram knew anything at all about *The Netherworlder Today* running Christina's article. Maybe that meant she hadn't been under my father's influence for very long? Or maybe Bram just wasn't as much in the know as he purported to be?

As to Bram being the mastermind responsible for keeping me under his roof, he must have thought it was the safest place for me to go, after realizing that Christina had become a well-planted bomb that could go off anytime. In bringing me to his home, Bram *had* been looking out for me, just like he promised he always would. But he'd also had another purpose—to provide me with the clues that would eventually lead me here, so that I could understand exactly what was going on.

"What the hell do you want us ta do with her now?" Mr. Lisp suddenly piped up, facing Bram.

Bram approached Christina and took her by the arm, pulling her closer to him. "Leave her with me. I will inform O'Neil of our subsequent steps."

"You hopin' for a threesome or what?" the other guy spat out, laughing. "Lucky bastard's got O'Neil's hot ass daughter an' now this hot one. Maybe we should invite ourselves, Donahue."

"You will not be invited," Bram replied coolly.

Then he simply started forward, with Christina right beside him. I watched him walk through the gates of the cemetery to the sidewalk where a black limo suddenly pulled up. I wasn't sure, but I thought I recognized the goblin driver. Bram seated Christina in the back before spotting the two men who still remained in the middle of the cemetery. He said nothing to them as he removed his hood and sat down before closing the door behind him. I watched the limo as it rolled down the street, and the red taillights disappeared into the darkness.

I wasn't worried for Christina any longer. I knew Bram would keep her safe. Now, I had to worry about my own neck.

SIXTEEN

After my father's stooges left the graveyard, I super-sized myself from Mini-Me and hurried back to Bram's Porsche. Once inside, I magicked my hair from bobbed and black to its natural honey-gold. I knew I was back to myself as soon as I could feel the soft tendrils tickling my elbows. Then I turned on the engine, all the while figuring out a plan to move forward.

Shock still consumed me as I considered the fact that my father was aware of what was going on in The Resistance for Hades only knew how long. I sincerely hoped it wasn't that long. The more I thought about it, though, the more convinced I was that my father couldn't have known for very long. Why? Because I had to imagine he would've acted on whatever information he'd mind-picked from Christina much sooner than he had. For example, he never would've allowed the article in *The Netherworlder Today* to run if he'd known in advance such was her intention.

The other thing of which I was convinced was that my father would have waged an attack against us by now if he'd been in the know longer than I imagined he was. Really, with only a bit of choice information coerced from Christina, Melchior could have easily wiped out whatever threat Christina, Knight, and I might have posed, and basically shut down The Resistance, at least temporarily.

'Course, I guess, Melchior did try to off Knight and me with the detonation of the Denali; but considering how it failed, my father must have become more desperate to dispose of us. That meant things were probably about to get very ugly. Along those same lines, it would only be a matter of time before word got back to my father that Bram was AWOL and had taken Christina with him.

Recalling Bram's warning not to return to his home because it wouldn't be "safe," I could only hope he would also follow his own advice. Knowing how smart Bram was, though, I figured he probably had a secret lair somewhere in which he and Christina could lay low. Either way, I couldn't concern myself with Bram or Christina any longer. I had too much to worry about now where the entire future of The Resistance was concerned as well as The Netherworld and Melchior O'Neil.

And, yes, I was repulsed by how my father could so easily try to kill his own biological daughter without blinking an eye. But as soon as that feeling tried to rear its unwanted head, I silenced it. I refused, under any circumstances, to bemoan my father's wish that I were dead because I wouldn't so much as flutter an eyelash if the tables were turned. Just as much as he wanted me dead, I wanted *him* dead. Guess we did have something in common, after all.

Returning my thoughts to the future of The Resistance, I realized I had to come up with a plan and quickly. With Christina now out of the way (since it was too dangerous for her to participate after compromising the whole plan), Knight was now in command. First things first, I had to find Knight, whom I desperately needed. One major downside: I had no clue where I was. After traveling through two portals on my way to Culligan's, who knew if I could travel back through them to get to Knight, wherever he was? Furthermore, I had no idea what part of California I was in—Southern, Central, or Northern.

I glanced at the map on the navigation screen and tried to zoom out, hoping I might recognize some of the streets or landmarks, but I couldn't get the thing to work. After figuring it was taking too long to try to fix it, I took a deep breath and decided I had to find a phone and fast.

I checked the center consul of the Porsche, searching all the cubbies, but didn't find anything. Then I reached over to open the glove box and pulled out the owner's manual along with a folder of auto insurance and registration information. I tucked both back into the glove box and closed it, leaning over as I searched under the passenger seat, still to no avail. As I sat up, though, I caught the gleam of what appeared to be glass from a cubby in the passenger door. With my heart pounding, I stretched my fingers as far as I could, feeling my way along the cubby. When I came to something rectangular, I pulled it out and recognized Bram's cell phone.

Thank Hades! I sang to myself as my entire body became giddy with the discovery, and a wide smile curled my lips.

But, I didn't celebrate too long because now I faced a new problem: I had no clue what Knight's phone number was to his Resistance-issued cell phone. The only number I did know was his private cell phone, which probably wouldn't help me. And if Knight was anywhere near a Resistance compound, he couldn't answer anyway since personal cell phones were forbidden. But I refused to give up … not yet anyway.

Left with no other alternative, and aware that Bram's phone could be bugged, I dialed Knight's personal cell phone number anyway. I knew I was taking a chance, but I was now at the point where I had to take the chance because I needed to get in touch with Knight ASAP.

The phone rang once, then twice and I felt my stomach constricting with anxious butterflies as I hoped and prayed Knight would answer. Another ring. Then another.

"You son of a bitch!" Knight yelled into the phone, apparently thinking it was Bram calling him. "Where the fuck have you been? I've been calling you for the last two days looking for Dulcie, dammit! You better have a fucking damned good reason as to why the hell you haven't been answering your phone! And you should consider yourself lucky that I have no idea how to find you, otherwise I would've shown up a long time ago! And Dulcie better be okay or there will be absolute hell to pay!"

"Knight," I said, once he found it necessary to take a breath, and in the process, gave me the option to speak. I couldn't help grinning because I suddenly felt like everything was going to be okay. It was a ludicrous thought, really; but just hearing Knight's voice, even while yelling at me, gave me relief, in and of itself.

"Dulce?" he asked after pausing for a second or two. "Are you okay? Where are you? And why are you using Bram's phone?"

"I don't know where I am," I answered quickly as I glanced around myself. I decided I should drive away from the area, just in case anyone from the graveyard happened to still be around and, more so, happened to recognize me. I balanced the phone between my ear and my shoulder and shifted the Porsche into gear, rolling forward. When I made it to the end of the street, I took a left and tried to backtrack as far as I could remember.

"Dulce?" Knight prodded after I didn't say anything for a few seconds.

"Way too much shit just went down, so I can't explain it all to you right now," I started, thinking that I should find my way back to the freeway pretty soon. "But you need to come get me, or else tell me how to find you. The problem is that I have no idea where I am."

"I will come to you," he said immediately. "I can track Bram's phone and find you." He paused for a second. "Where is that bloodless bastard anyway?"

When I reached the freeway onramp, I figured I should get on it, if only to get as far from Culligan's as possible. "I can't explain any of it now, but Bram isn't with me."

"Are you driving?" Knight asked. "You sound like you're in a car and you seem distracted."

"Yes, I just got onto the 101, but I'm not sure where I am. I definitely went through two portals to get here, so I'm not sure how easy it'll be to find me."

"It's okay. I already have a feed on this phone line, so I should be able to pinpoint your exact location in a few more minutes."

"If *you've* got a feed on it, could anyone else have one too?" I asked, unable to conceal my concern.

"Hard to say," Knight answered quickly. "But don't take any chances. Just exit the freeway and go someplace public, or at least where there are more people around." He paused for a second and then added: "We have to end this call."

"Okay," I said, taking the next off-ramp and finding a Vons supermarket at the top of the street. "I'm pulling into a Vons and I just exited on Parker Street."

"Yep, just got the feed. We're good," he said. I could tell by the tone of his voice that he was smiling. "Just sit tight and I'll be there in a matter of minutes."

I breathed a sigh of relief as I maneuvered the Porsche into a spot just in front of the double doors to the supermarket. "Thank you."

Knight hesitated for a second or two. "At least tell me if you're okay, Dulce?"

"Yes, I'm fine," I answered quickly, watching as two men walked into the store and a woman came out. At least there were some folks milling around, considering it was so early in the morning. As soon as that thought occurred to me, I checked the time on the dash. It was nearly one a.m.

"I'm leaving now and I'll be there soon … don't worry, Dulce; everything's going to be fine."

I could only hope he was right.

Maybe thirty minutes later, I saw a black Suburban drive into the Vons parking lot. I recognized Knight in the driver's seat immediately and stepped out of the Porsche, waving to him. He smiled and nodded to let me know he saw me before parking in the spot next to the Porsche.

197

I'd been incredibly consumed with angst while I waited in the Porsche, worried that Knight wouldn't be able to find me. Or, worse yet, that someone had tapped Bram's phone line, in which case, I'd suffer a rude awakening when someone other than Knight came looking for me. At the realization that Knight had found me, though, I was overcome with relief and gratitude. My cheeks ablaze with heat, I couldn't keep the smile off my lips.

Knight left the engine running as he opened his door and jumped down from the driver's seat. He was wearing dark blue jeans and a long-sleeved, white T-shirt, which made his naturally olive complexion even sexier. His hair was in disarray, like it hadn't seen a brush for a few days. He had the overall look of someone who hadn't slept well for some time. But to me, he was just as stunningly handsome as he always was.

It was strange, but staring at him in the early morning darkness, with only the moonlight reflecting on him, made time feel like it was suddenly standing still. I was faintly aware of a car driving past with two people in a heated discussion somewhere behind Knight, but they blended into the periphery. Somehow, I couldn't unfasten my eyes from him, or find my voice, so I just stared at him. He did the same. As soon as I witnessed that charming, boyish grin that was so uniquely his, something inside me burst.

Feelings of liberation and happiness washed over me, and before I knew it, I was jogging the few steps that separated us and flinging my arms around him. The impulse to be next to him was too urgent to deny. I wanted to inhale his crisp, clean scent and languish in his arms. When I hugged him, the surprise on his face was palpable; but moments later, he wrapped his arms around me tightly. Then he lifted me up, holding me so close, I could feel his heartbeat against my cheek.

"Dulce, are you okay?" he whispered.

I nodded with fresh tears stinging my eyes. I wasn't sure why, but I seemed to be on the verge of a total breakdown. Maybe it was the fact that I'd dealt with so much lately—so much that I'd been stockpiling in my head, with the intent to deal with it all later, that I suddenly couldn't take it anymore and had to crack. Or maybe it was just the immense relief of Knight finding me and the subsequent overwhelming feelings of safety his arms promised. Or, better yet, maybe it was just because I was so damn happy to see him.

"I'm fine," I said, relishing the warmth of his strong arms. His lips grazed the top of my head as he kissed my hair.

"Let's get you in the truck so you don't freeze to death out here," he said softly, showing me to the passenger side of the Suburban. "And then you need to tell me what's going on."

"What about Bram's Porsche?"

"It'll be fine here for the time being," Knight answered dismissively.

Knight opened my door and I stepped up onto the running board before turning to face him again. Without any warning, he leaned forward and pulled me into him. Dropping his head toward me, I closed my eyes and tasted his lips on mine. The kiss was sweet and soft at first. Then I felt his tongue suddenly trying to thrust past my lips as his embrace tightened.

I closed my arms around his neck and deepened the kiss, meeting his thrusting tongue. I was overcome with the need to be close to him more than I'd ever felt it before. That was when it hit me that although Knight and I had had our differences and our miscommunications, Knight had only ever done what he thought was right and, what was more, he'd been able to see the error in his ways. Even though he'd been led down the wrong road in believing I was guilty of being in cahoots with my father, he'd also realized his mistake and repented for it.

And, what was more, Knight was really the only man I could turn to, the only man I'd ever been able to turn to.

Quillan and Bram had both disappointed me by involving themselves with the illegal potion industry and worse still, with my father. But Knight was always true to himself. Granted, we still were at odds on some subjects, and I couldn't say I condoned his keeping my father's identity from me; but now I understood that he thought he was just protecting me. And even when he'd arrested me for working under my father, it was just another example of how he refused to compromise his values and beliefs of right and wrong. He did the only thing he thought was right. Plus, he did what I would have done if I were in his shoes, and believed he was importing illegal potions.

At the end of the day, Knight was the same person now that he was when I first met him. He was just as confident, caring, and determined to see good prevail. To be honest, Knight was exactly the same person now that he was when I fell in love with him, many months ago.

I pulled away from him and smiled, even as I realized there was entirely too much on both of our shoulders at the moment for us to try and pick up the pieces of our relationship in order to put them back together again. But I supposed it was a good omen that somewhere in my over-crammed and overwhelmed head, I was sure that I wanted things between Knight and me to go back to how they were before. I wanted us to be … us again.

"We have lots to talk about," I said simply as I hoisted myself into the passenger seat. Knight nodded and closed my door. I put my seatbelt on and watched him open his door as he focused his eyes on me.

"It's about an hour's drive to get back to Compound Four, so we'll have a little time," he said. He took his seat and put the Suburban in drive, exiting the Vons parking lot.

"Knight, you're now in charge of The Resistance," I began, figuring it would take me at least an hour to tell him everything. Never mind the myriad questions Knight was sure to have.

"What?" he asked incredulously. I saw a look of worry in his eyes before he returned his attention to the road that led back to the freeway. "Christina?"

"She's fine," I said quickly, while shaking my head, realizing how awful my statement must've sounded. I explained about Christina and the *Blueliss* and told him I learned the truth at Culligan's graveyard. I finished by insisting that I believed Christina was safe with Bram.

"So, Bram's been working for your father all this time?" Knight asked, his lips drawn into a tight line.

"Yes, but that's not important now. What matters now is what we do to move forward."

"The little bastard," Knight said as he shook his head. Taking a deep breath and sighing loudly, he began to nod, saying, "You're right, we need to concentrate on our next steps." Glancing at me, he added, "And for whatever it's worth, it did mean something to know that Bram wanted to make sure you were safe. I guess, in the end, he isn't as much of a little bastard as I'd like to think."

I nodded my agreement, watching us merge onto the 101 North. Getting my thoughts in some semblance of order, I turned to face him. Our next steps were suddenly as clear as day to me. "Knight, there's no time for us to wait any longer. Where The Resistance is concerned, the time for talking is over." He eyed me and chewed his lip as he considered my statement. When he didn't say anything, I continued. "My father knows too much now and it will only be a matter of time before he learns he can't count on Bram or Christina, which means he can't discover anymore of our secrets. Then he's sure to get desperate, and things will go from bad to worse."

"So, my second in command, what do you propose we do?" Knight asked with a slight smile on his lips.

I returned the smile and nodded. I knew what our next steps should, no *had,* to be. "We need to rally our troops and invade the Netherworld … now."

Knight didn't say anything for a second or two, but just stared at the empty freeway ahead of us. Then he smiled at me.

"Melchior O'Neil, here we come."

BONUS DULCIE & KNIGHT SHORT STORY!

For all of you who couldn't find the anthology, Kiss Me, Kill Me, with the Dulcie and Knight short story, I've included it for you here!

A Ghoulish Valentine
By H.P. Mallory

It was Valentine's Day, or night, to be exact. And I actually had a date. (It's not like I'm a heinous troll who couldn't get a date if she tried, I just choose not to. Furthermore, there's nothing trollish about me—I'm a fairy.) Now, before you start telling me how great your garden is and how your lilies are in full bloom or what an awesome movie *Peter Pan* was…I'm not that kind of a fairy. I don't have wings and I'm not the size of a humming bird (i.e., I'm not a pixie). While, I'm not tall, at 5'1", I'm like a giant compared to a pixie. And rather than buzzing around with the bees from flower to flower, I work in law enforcement. I help keep the Netherworld creatures on the straight and narrow—or, at least I try.

So, tonight I'd overridden my usual indifference toward my love life and actually accepted Knight Vander's invitation to dinner and a movie. Knight Vander is a *Loki*—a creature forged from the fires of Hades. As far as I know, he's the only *Loki* in my town of Splendor, California. And as to a description of the *Loki* who happened to be my date, here goes…Knight is in one word—gorgeouscockyfrustratingsexyoverbearing and he's a detective who was sent from the Netherworld to work at our headquarters, the Association of Netherworld Creatures (ANC).

"Was it so bad?" Knight asked, peering down at me with his bright blue eyes. With his longish black hair curling over the top of his button down shirt, his tan complexion, strong jaw and Roman nose, Knight could have graced the cover of GQ.

"What?" I asked innocently, keeping my hands snug in each of my pockets so he didn't attempt to hold one. It's not that I disliked Knight—well, sometimes I did—but, it's more that I just didn't want to get involved with him. He's too cocksure, proud, demanding and argumentative. Yes, he's beautiful but that doesn't amount to much in my books. Hmm, maybe I wasn't being entirely honest—Knight was wrong for me on all levels but I couldn't help my attraction to him even against my better judgment. And that was why I wanted nothing more than to keep him at arm's length.

"Going on a date with me," he answered with that boyish smile, revealing bright white teeth that almost glowed in the moonlight.

I glanced away from him and took in the beauty of the night. We were walking down Belfry Street and there was the lightest breeze disturbing the otherwise still air. The scent of honeysuckle was thick in the air and seemed to dance through my long honey gold hair, lifting the tendrils up to caress my cheeks. Belfry Street was on the better side of Splendor—it was replete with expensive restaurants and eclectic stores. We approached the end of the street which emptied into the oldest cemetery in Splendor, Green Pastures. Course, to the locals it was known as Daiseyville.

"I guess it wasn't so bad," I responded. The date actually hadn't been bad at all. Knight had been good company, filling me in on all the adventures he'd had in Splendor since moving from the Netherworld. I knew he wasn't staying in Splendor for the long haul, but he'd be here a while, since there was lots of ANC work to keep him busy.

"I'll take that as a compliment."

I actually felt a little bit guilty about my less than thrilled response. I mean, Knight had shelled out a pretty penny on dinner and must have asked me five million times if everything met my approval. Then the movie we'd seen had been one I'd been dying to see for at least a few weeks.

"Everything was really great, Knight," I added in a small voice.

He beamed like a proud kid who'd just gotten an A on his book report. I shook my head.

Knight stopped walking once we reached the decrepit gates of Daiseyville and studied me. I felt the heat of embarrassment staining my cheeks because I knew where this would lead. A kiss. Knight wanted to kiss me and it was as obvious as the fact that I was trying to convince myself I didn't want him to kiss me. The breeze started up again and seemed to be pushing me into him, encouraging me to sample his lush and full mouth. Granted, I'd kissed Knight before but it had been solely because we had to maintain the façade of a couple hot for one another—otherwise our alibi would have been shot and our case jeopardized.

But, now there was no alibi and no case to jeopardize. It was just Knight and me—alone. I didn't actually feel myself do it, but I took a step nearer to him and he closed the remaining distance between us, never taking his eyes from mine. He bent down and held my neck between his large hands, heat searing the tender skin on the back of my neck. Yes, I was going to let him kiss me, and furthermore, I was going to enjoy it.

Just at the moment when he closed his eyes and opened his mouth to come in for the home run, I happened to glance behind him and caught the image of a skeleton lazily leaning against the fence of Daiseyville, watching us with hollow, sightless eyes.

"Son of a freaking bitch!" I seethed.

Knight jerked away from me like I'd just bitten him and apparently realizing my Tourette's Syndrome moment hadn't been aimed at him, exhaled. "What?" he asked.

"Turn around," I called to him behind my shoulder, already closing in on the ten feet separating me from the graveyard.

"You've got to be kidding," Knight said, apparently catching sight of the lounging skeleton. He jogged a few paces and caught up with me. "What do you think happened?"

I glanced at the graves, uneven with age—half had crumbled into the earth while the far side of the cemetery sported newer cement tombstones and neatly trimmed grass. But whether old or new, both were cause for alarm. I watched as the dirt of each gravesite began to bubble up as if someone were digging in reverse, from below. Skeletal fingers shot up from the ground like macabre flowers growing on fast forward—some still had flesh hanging from their appendages. I shifted my gaze from the dead who were in the process of unearthing themselves to the oily puddles of darkness that decorated each grave; slime spreading in a slow infestation of the graveyard. The puddles reflected in the moonlight, throwing prisms of color around the cemetery... something that might have been considered pretty if the spectrum of light hadn't also illuminated the rotting flesh of the recently deceased or the smooth bones belonging to the long dead.

"Some asswipe spilled *Gorm* all over the cemetery," I bit out. *Gorm* was an illegal potion. If you were alive and took it, you'd feel more alive than ever before—you'd basically be on Cloud 9 for about three hours before you suffered the worst of all come downs, starting with a migraine and ending with the feeling that the world was ending. Some creatures couldn't handle the come down and took their own lives—it had taken twelve deaths before the ANC had declared *Gorm* an illegal narcotic. If you were dead and some jerk *Gormed* you, you'd come back to life— also for about three hours. But, you'd no longer be considered human, nope—you would have passed into the realm of the ghoul.

In the three hours of *Gorm*-induced re-life, ghouls became an absolute menace to society. They sought only to escape the confines of the cemetery to basically attack the living, searching for life sustenance. Good thing for Splendor that it had Knight and me.

"Looks like our work is never done," Knight said with a sardonic smile. It was a smile that announced he was more than thrilled with the turn of events. Knight thrived on action and enjoyed nothing more than his position of detective for the Netherworld.

I was a little less enthusiastic. "I need to protect myself against their funk," I said and nodded over my shoulder towards the dead, many of whom were out of their graves and hobbling around like newly born giraffes.

As a fairy, I'm endowed with certain powers—I can create dust and then use that dust to make basically anything I want (physical or otherwise). But, I also have limitations. And one of those limitations is the fact that dead and/or rotting ghoul flesh is like acid to my skin. One drop of the nasty stuff burns a hole that never heals. Kind of like the bite of a brown recluse spider on crack. So, protecting myself against the funk of a newborn ghoul was at the top of my list.

I glanced down at my outfit and said a silent prayer of thanks that I'd worn the longest jeans I owned, protected underneath by knee high black leather boots—the kind with a square heel since I can't walk in stilettos. Thank Hades for a functioning wardrobe! I was less excited about my top. I couldn't combat ghouls with my current black leather jacket—it was just too bulky. Underneath it, though, I had on only my red halter top, exposing a landscape of unprotected skin. I reached underneath my top and fingered the Op 6 pistol which I wore strapped to my waist. Pulling it out, I eyed the dragon blood bullets loaded in the chamber.

"How many you packing?" Knight asked.

"Six. A full house."

"Not enough." He reached into the waist of his jeans and pulled out a gun I'd never seen before. It almost looked futuristic with its super short barrel and palm sized grip. Maybe it wasn't so much the shape that made it seem so foreign, but the color—neon green. It almost looked like a kid's water pistol.

"Um, what is that?" I asked, trying to shield a laugh.

Knight scoffed. "Don't laugh—this is a *KG* and the thing has major kick. It's a new toy a buddy of mine from the Netherworld sent over."

"Where's the magazine?" I asked, noting the gun didn't appear to have ammunition. The walls were see-through and it looked like it was filled with water—or something that kept sloshing against the interior sides of the gun every time Knight moved his hand.

Knight brought the *KG* into his line of sight and seemed to target a ghoul that was in the process of shaking the gates of Daiseyville, apparently hell-bent on escaping. "There isn't one. It's loaded with intestinal fluid taken from the *Kraken*."

"*KG* for *Kraken* Gun?" I asked with a smile, pleased with my stellar ability of logical deduction.

He returned my smile. "Hey, it didn't have a name and that's all I could think of."

"Real original there, Knight."

Not offended by the slight, he faintly depressed the trigger and then released it again. "You depress only halfway so the gun can take stock of how far away your target is. Then you'll see a red light. Once you see the red, pull." Just then, he must've seen the red because before he'd even finished his statement, he squeezed the trigger and what looked like a dart of bright yellow liquid shot out of the gun and hit the ghoul square between the eyes. Once the *Kraken* fluid met the ghoul, it seemed to turn from a liquid into a gel and suddenly exploded into streams of fluorescent beads, disappearing into the ghoul's eyes, nose and mouth.

"The *Kraken* fluid is engineered to enter the ghoul's body—to get back into the intestine," Knight announced. "Once it does, if there is any intestine left at all, it'll start recreating the *Kraken* which the ghoul's body won't be able to tolerate or host."

"So it'll kill the ghoul?" I finished.

"Yep."

"And if there is no intestine?" I asked, glancing at the skeletons that littered the graveyard, some so old their jaws, femurs or other large bones refused to stay intact.

"The process will just happen much more quickly."

I glanced at the recently *KG*'d ghoul and noticed it looked…confused—that's the best description I could think of for the non compos mentis thing. It had stopped attempting to escape and now just aimlessly meandered around the graveyard, taking no notice of its surroundings. It tripped over a gravestone and didn't get back up.

"Needless to say, don't get any of that *Kraken* shit on you. I have no interest in bedding a *Kraken*," Knight announced and handed me the *KG*.

"As if you'd get the chance to bed me at all, *Kraken* or not," I said with a frown. "All you think about is sex." I accepted the gun and aimed at the next ghoul in line, pressing the trigger as Knight had shown me. At the red light, I depressed it entirely and watched the line of slime make contact with the ghoul. "Ew." It was all I could manage.

Knight raised a brow. "Once you run out of dragon bullets, use the *KG*. There should be enough *Kraken* in it to last the evening."

I eyed the *KG* and suddenly had the very concerning image of the nasty intestinal fluid coming into contact with my skin and turning me into a *Kraken*. "Um, where should I put it so I don't come into contact with the fluid?"

Knight shrugged. "There are no traces of fluid on the gun. There's a one-way chamber that shoots out only so you're safe. Just put it in your holster."

I eyed him squarely. "You're sure?"

"I already told you I have no interest in bedding a *Kraken*. You're safe."

I decided to ignore that last comment and instead turned to the fact that Knight had just given me his weapon so what in the hell was he planning on defending himself with? "What are you going to use?"

He smiled. "I was going to ask you if you'd mind magicking me a sword?" He paused for a moment and narrowed his eyes. "I'm thinking something long, 100% silver with a thick blade."

I threw my hands on my hips. "Would you like fries with that?"

"Get on it, Dulce," he said and motioned toward the graveyard, as if reminding me I had better things to do than construct smart ass retorts. I shrugged and shook my palm until a mound of dust emerged. Then I opened my palm and blew the ethereal particles at Knight, closing my eyes as I imagined a sword to the specifications he'd just mentioned. When I opened my eyes, Knight was holding the impressive sword, slicing the air with it as he tried it on for size.

"Not bad."

Now, back to the problem of protecting myself against the ghoul funk to which I now added the *Kraken* funk as well. Before I had the chance to ponder creating another fistful of fairy dust, Knight was suddenly disrobing. I watched him in amazement, wondering what the hell had just gotten into him that he would start stripping. He unbuttoned his shirt, then pulled off his undershirt and handed them both to me. I tried not to focus on the ripples of muscle that echoed his movements and instead glanced at him with questioning eyes.

"Um, what the hell are you doing?"

"Put my shirts on—they'll protect you against the ghoul slime."

I started to shake my head. "I was just going to magick myself a long sleeve shirt. Thanks for the offer though." I cocked a brow. "Besides, I wouldn't want you to catch cold."

He smiled and it was a smile that overflowed with self assuredness. "I can't catch anything. Put the shirts on— they'll protect you better than anything you create for yourself."

I glanced at the shirts in my hand and tried to make sense of his statement. A light blue button down and a white tee-shirt—they looked like regular XL shirts to me, but, for all I knew, maybe they were reinforced with ghoul repellant. "What, does *Loki* sweat protect against ghoul slime?"

He nodded. "Something like that."

One more thing I forgot to mention about Knight and his being a *Loki* is that I have no idea what powers *Loki*s possess since Knight is the only one I know of. Furthermore, Knight finds it amusing to keep all the powers he does possess to himself so it's like a treasure hunt trying to discover them all. And now I had one more talent I could add to the ever growing list.

I shrugged and tore off my jacket, dropping it into a heap at the base of the Daiseyville gates. I pulled Knight's tee-shirt over my head and glanced down at myself with a frown. It looked like I was wearing a dress. Well, I wasn't going to win any fashion awards tonight but no matter, if I could manage to keep the ghoul funk off me, I'd consider it a good night.

"And the button down," Knight reminded me. "Never can be too safe."

I nodded and pushed my arms through the sleeves while Knight started rolling up the cuffs so the thing fit me better. Once I'd buttoned up the shirt and he'd rolled up both sleeves, he studied me for a moment or two, his eyes dancing.

"I like the sight of you in my clothes."

I frowned. "Yeah, well, don't get any ideas." Before he could respond, I glanced at Daiseyville which was now overrun with ghouls—all bumping into one another like a bunch of drunks. I looked back at Knight and watched him lean over and dig a fistful of dirt from the ground. He stood up and I was about to question him when he shook his head and appeared to be moving his cheeks like he was swishing mouthwash.

"What in the hell are you doing?" I demanded.

He didn't say anything but continued swishing and then finally leaned over and spit a wad into the dirt, mixing it into a nasty dirt-spit paste. That was when I realized what he intended to do with it.

"No way," I started, backing up.

"Dulce, your face is unprotected and so are your hands."

He had a point but still, a mask of mud and spit? No thanks. "I'll think of something else."

"We don't have time."

Realizing he had a point, and that I had to let him mud me, I opened my eyes again and frowned. "Hurry the hell up."

Knight laughed and began pasting me with the spit mud, until I'm sure I looked like a dirt demon. He stepped back as if admiring his handiwork and then set to dirtying up the tops of my hands. After a few more seconds, he wiped the excess on his jeans and faced me with a big smile.

"You ready to get this ghoul show on the road?"

I returned my attention to the graveyard and watched a skeleton and a ghoul attempting to climb on top of one another to make it over the fence. "Roger that. Looks like our tenants are getting restless."

Knight smiled. "After you, my incredibly sexy lady."

I swallowed down a retort and fingered the Op 6 in my palm. I wasn't nervous although adrenalin was coursing through me. I hadn't done any ANC business for a while; hopefully my skills weren't rusty. We both approached the graveyard and stopped just outside the gates.

"Might as well take these guys out first," Knight said and without further ado, he began walking along the fence, hoisting his blade above his head and repeatedly decapitating both the ghouls and skeletons alike. The bodies tumbled to the ground and the next line of undead replaced them, receiving the same treatment at the end of Knight's blade. I figured I'd just wait for him to finish up before I wasted my dragon bullets.

After the third line of ghouls and skeletons were decapitated, the remaining thirty or so had apparently gotten wise to Knight's scheme and headed for the center of the graveyard, away from us. That was our cue to go after them. Knight grabbed hold of the fence and hoisted himself over, looking like some legendary warrior going to slay the enemy, wearing only a pair of worn blue jeans and a smile. When he safely landed on the other side, he perused his surroundings and, apparently convinced there were no ghouls immediately threatening, leaned his sword against the fence and motioned for me to come.

There was no way I, with my 5'1 frame and short legs, was going to be able to leap the fence like freaking *Sea Biscuit*. So, much as I didn't want to, I accepted Knight's help. He grasped my waist and lifted me over the fence as if I weighed nothing at all, depositing me on the ground in front of him. He didn't remove his hands but, instead, pulled me close and smiled down at me.

"I'll have you know that I will still get that kiss from you."

"Oh my God, would you get over yourself?" I demanded. "You have a graveyard full of ghouls to kill or have you forgotten?"

He released me and reached for his sword. "Oh, I haven't forgotten, Dulce, but I also keep a tally on things owed me." He paused a minute and seemed to be scanning the graveyard before him. Seemingly pleased with the number of ghouls retreating to the western end of the graveyard, he started in that direction and I followed him.

"You wanted to kiss me, I could see it in your eyes," he continued.

"Don't you think it would be a good idea to focus right now?" I demanded. "I really don't want to end up a ghoul's dinner."

He glanced back at me and shook his head. "You won't be—not on my watch."

A ghoul appeared to be hiding behind a craggy oak tree just before us and Knight walked around the tree, hurling his sword in the air before bringing it down. I grimaced at the sound it made—like a hammer hitting a watermelon. The ghoul's head rolled out from behind the tree and I nearly walked into it.

"And, anyway, I'm a multitasker," Knight said with a smile, resting the enormous sword against his shoulder as he continued on like nothing out of the ordinary had just happened. "I can decapitate and engage in sexy talk at the same time."

"Well, I'm not and won't," I snapped and sensing movement near an imposing tomb just beside me, I threw my back against the tomb wall and tried to detect where the sound was coming from. Knight followed suit. The tomb was high—maybe ten feet tall by ten feet wide and the sounds of rustling in the undergrowth and the uneven hobbling of the undead interrupted the peaceful quiet of the graveyard. The cold of the cement sunk through both of Knight's shirts and chilled me to the core. I tried not to shiver but couldn't keep it at bay.

"They're at the other end," I whispered even though I didn't have to—ghouls have terrible hearing.

"You go one way and I'll go the other and we'll circle them," Knight answered and I nodded, starting forward. I crept around to the back of the tomb, trailing my hand against the cold wall. I paused momentarily as I held my Op 6 out before me, then pivoted on my toes and faced the four ghouls and one skeleton at the same time Knight did. The ghouls just stood there dumbly while the skeleton limped back and forth, holding its foot in its hand. It must have been the one that had been making the hobbling sound. Knight didn't allow the ghouls any time for reaction and hefted the sword from his shoulder, arcing it before bringing it down in a clean, fluid motion. He cleaved off two of the ghoul's heads while I fired at the other two, taking them both down. That just left the skeleton and before I had the chance to say "boo", Knight had decapitated him too.

"It's a shame about the skeletons," Knight said as he wiped the entrails of ghoul goo off on his jeans. I checked myself and was relieved to see no goo or funk had made its way near me.

"What do you mean?"

He shrugged. "They don't pose much of a risk. They don't leak toxic goo everywhere. If anything, they're just guilty of being unpleasant to look at."

I nodded. "You have a point. Anyway, they'll be dead soon enough. They have maybe another two hours of life left. So, maybe we focus on the ghouls and just ensure the skeletons don't escape."

"Sounds like a plan." He paused for a moment and appeared to be studying me. "That mud is staying nicely."

I'd forgotten about the spit mud all over my face. "Thanks for reminding me."

He didn't respond but started forward, the moonlight reflecting against his hair until it looked like it was almost blue. Knight was by far the deadliest creature in the graveyard and I was suddenly very pleased that he was on my side. With his immense height, broad stature and *Loki* abilities, he'd easily defeat me. Shaking off such thoughts, I started after him when I heard a ruckus from just behind me. I glanced around and felt my stomach drop as a shard of fear traveled through me. There were maybe twenty ghouls and skeletons standing just behind me, separated by five paces.

"Knight," I whispered, turning to face him before realizing he was nowhere to be found. "Knight!" I screamed louder and apparently awakened the ghouls because they scattered. Ghouls and skeletons aren't capable of reason but it seemed as if they were capable of reason enough to realize I was alone because they suddenly stopped their scattering and looked at me. They watched me for a few seconds, as if unsure what to do next. Then a largish ghoul who looked like he could have been a football player in life, elbowed his way to the front of the crowd and started forward, moaning and dragging his foot behind him. The others followed suit and began making their uneven way towards me, rotting flesh dripping off their bodies. It was enough to make me retch right there. The skeletons continued to wander, tripping over tree roots and gravestones in their blind migration.

I held the Op 6 up against my face and then aimed, shooting Mr. Quarterback in the chest. He fell and three others surged forward. The Op 6 took them out easily with the dragon blood bullets. Dragon's blood is lethal to any Netherworld creatures. And to the undead, Dragon's blood is even more powerful—the ghouls dropped to the ground and any life in them dissipated instantly. Good as that might have been, I was out of ammunition so the Op 6 was basically useless to me. I tossed the gun to the ground and grabbed the *KG* from my waist holster. My hands shook as I aimed it, pulling the trigger. The yellow liquid squirted angrily and missed the ghoul before me by mere inches. That was when I remembered I was supposed to hold the trigger down only partially, so I could get a read on how far away the ghouls were. Problem was, I didn't really have the space nor the time to get a read. I had to get them dead.

I backed up and held the gun out before me, aiming at two ghouls and depressed the trigger only halfway. At the sign of the red light, I depressed it fully and they both went down. Two down and a crap load more to go. It seemed as soon as their brethren fell, three or four suddenly replaced them. I needed to get to higher ground where I could take them out, one at a time.

Glancing behind me for something that might offer the benefit of height, the white of the tomb's walls stuck out like a vampire at a blood bank. But how to get up on the roof? I eyed the skeletal outline of a dead tree nearby and figured if I could climb the tree, I could jump atop the tomb and take out as many ghouls as I pleased. It sounded like a good plan but I didn't have the time necessary to run to the tree and climb it—not when I had fifteen or so ghouls closing in on me. I needed to create a diversion—something to keep them at bay and I wasn't going to be able to do that with the *KG*. Nope, I'd need some good ol' fashioned fairy dust.

I shook my palm until a mound of dust appeared then I opened my hand wide, blowing the glittering particles from left to right in front of the ghouls. The ethereal particles shimmered in the moonlight and caught the attention of the ghouls who just stared at them intently, no doubt captivated by the sparkle. Not wasting any time, I imagined a flame lighting the particles and was rewarded when a blast of light signaled the fact that the particles had caught fire, burning an arc of safety around me. The ghouls reeled back against the fire, just as I imagined they'd do. I turned around, bolting for the tomb while ramming the *KG* into my waistline. Reaching the bedraggled tree, I grabbed hold of the highest branch while hoisting myself up. My foot found purchase on the rough bark and I glanced back at the ghouls, noticing my fire was slowly dwindling and dying into reddish embers. The ghouls started forward again, making the strangest growling sound—like tires driving over rocks.

I grasped another tree branch and pulled myself up, until I was maybe another foot from the roof of the tomb. The ghouls surrounded my tree, grasping at the tree bark. Some fell down and the others appeared to use them as stepping stools, reaching their rotting flesh closer to me. One ghoul attempted to grasp my pant leg so I kicked at it, managing to knock it down. The others just stomped on it, their groans growing increasingly louder. They were nearing the end of their *Gorm* induced re-life which meant their need for life sustenance—for live flesh—was becoming more urgent.

I reached the top of the tree and pulled against the branch that would allow me to drop onto the top of the tomb. Even though the tree was long dead, the branch still seemed strong enough to support my lithe weight…or so I hoped. I took the branch in both hands and propelled myself forward until I was hanging between the tree and the tomb. There was a definite cracking sound and I glanced at the junction of the tree and my branch, noticing the bark beginning to split away. Dammit, I'd been wrong. The branch couldn't support my weight and was probably seconds from falling off and dropping me to the hungry ghouls below. I began swinging my feet, the top of the tomb so close I could feel it with my toes. I needed to get to end of the branch—that way I could just swing myself to the tomb. But, the farther I went out on the branch, the more unstable and precarious my position. I glanced down and watched the ghouls staring up at me, as if realizing their dinner was currently playing the part of monkey in a tree. Fall and I was as good as dead.

I edged myself down the tree branch, my legs flailing in the air. Hearing the unmistakable sound of tree branches cracking, I swung myself again and my knees struck the top of the tomb just as the tree branch gave way and landed on the ghouls below. I felt my cheek smack against the top of the tomb and was momentarily stunned, bright lights dancing before my eyes. I shook my head, hoping the damage wasn't permanent. Able to shake the stars out of my vision, I reached inside my holster and grasped the *KG*. I aimed at the ghouls below, depressed, caught the red light and fired. One went down. I repeated the process and another went down. Followed by another and another until every last one was down.

I leaned back against the roof and breathed a sigh of relief. That had been a close call. A large shadow making its way underneath a nearby tree caught my attention and I felt my heartbeat starting to race. It slowed once I recognized Knight.

"Where the hell have you been?" I demanded, glaring down at him, the beginnings of a headache pounding through my temples.

"Fighting ghouls—nice of you to hide up there!" he yelled back at me, leaning his sword against the tree that had very nearly failed me.

I shook my head and turned to the task of getting myself down from the tomb. "I wasn't hiding."

Knight glanced down at the heap of recently undead before looking back up at me with an appreciative smile. "Nicely done."

"Yeah, no help from you," I muttered before reaching the conclusion that there was no way I was going to be able to get down. "How about helping me down from here?"

"Drop your legs off the edge and I'll grab you."

I dropped to my stomach and tried to grab onto the sides of the tomb but there really wasn't anything to hold onto. Instead, I maintained my balance with my waist against the tomb's roof and dangled my legs over the side.

"Gotta drop lower."

"I can't," I yelled. "There's nothing to hold onto."

"Just trust me. I'll catch you."

Famous last words. I muttered something unintelligible even to my own ears and pushed away from the tomb, hoping this little stunt wouldn't result in catastrophe. The headache coursing through my head was pain enough. I dropped for maybe a second before I felt his large hands around my waist as he caught me and hoisted me down to my feet.

"We make a good team," he started, his hands still encircling my waist.

I gave myself a second or two to catch my breath. This had been a long ass night. "Let me guess…"

"I still want that Valentine's Day kiss you owe me," Knight finished, the smile gone from his lips.

I laughed. "As if I owe you anything."

He shrugged. "You say potato; I say I want my kiss."

I could feel mirth welling up inside me. Oh, he was going to get his kiss alright, a kiss that just happened to be from someone covered in mud and spit. I grabbed his head and stood up on my tip toes as he bent down. His mouth was warm and his lips so incredibly soft as they touched mine. I opened my mouth and his tongue was hot, demanding in the way it mated with mine.

I pulled away and smiled up at him. "Consider that payment in full."

Then I tapped him on the chest and walked away, leaving him in the middle of the graveyard, covered with ghoul slime while a skeleton limped toward him and tripped over his foot.

To Be Continued In:

FOR WHOM THE SPELL TOLLS

NEW YORK TIMES
BESTSELLING AUTHOR

book **6** of the dulcie o'neil series
from bestselling author

H.P. MALLORY

Available Now!

Also Available From HP Mallory:

Turn the page for chapter one!

"Midway upon the journey of our life, I found myself within a forest dark, For the straight foreward pathway had been lost." --Dante's Inferno

ONE

The rain pelted the windshield relentlessly. Drops like little daggers assaulted the glass, only to be swept away by the frantic motion of the wipers. The scenery outside my window melted into dripping blobs of color through a screen of gray. I took my foot off the accelerator and slowed to forty miles an hour, focusing on the blurry yellow lines in the road.

Lightning stabbed the gray skies. A roar of thunder followed and the rain came down heavier, as if having been reprimanded for not falling hard enough.

"This rain is gonna keep on comin', folks," the radio meteorologist announced. Annoyed, I changed the station and resettled myself into my seat to the sound of Vivaldi's "Four Seasons, Summer." *Ha, Summer...*

The rain morphed into hail. The visibility was slightly better, but now I was under a barrage of machine-gunned ice. I took a deep breath and tried to imagine myself on a sunny beach, sipping a strawberry margarita with a well-endowed man wearing nothing but a banana hammock and a smile.

In reality, I was as far from a cocktail on a sunny beach with Sven, the lust god, as possible. Nope, I was trapped in Colorado Springs in the middle of winter. If that weren't bad enough, I was late to work. Today was not only my yearly review but I also had to give a presentation to the CEO, defending my decision to move forward with a risky and expensive marketing campaign. So, yes, being late didn't exactly figure into my plans.

With a sigh, I turned on my seat heater and tried to enact the presentation in my head, tried to remember the slides from my PowerPoint and each of the points I needed to make. I held my chin up high and cleared my throat, reminding myself to look the CEO and the board of directors in the eyes and not to say "um."

"Choc-o-late cake," I said out loud, opening my mouth wide and then bringing my teeth together again in an exaggerated way. "Choc-o-late cake." It was a good way to warm up my voice and to remind myself to pronounce every syllable of every word. And, perhaps the most important point to keep in mind—not to rush.

This whole being late thing wasn't exactly good timing, considering I was going to ask for a raise. With my heart rate increasing, I remembered the words of Jack Canfield, one of the many motivational speakers whose advice I followed like the Bible.

"'When you've figured out what you want to ask for', Lily, 'do it with certainty, boldness and confidence'," I quoted, taking a deep breath and holding it for a count of three before I released it for another count of three. "Certainty, boldness and confidence," I repeated to myself. "Choc-o-late cake."

Feeling my heart rate decreasing, I focused on counting the stacks of chicken coops in the truck ahead of me—five up and four across. Each coop was maybe a foot by a foot, barely enough room for the chickens to breathe. White feathers decorated the wire and contrasted against the bright blue of a plastic tarp that covered the top layer of coops. The tarp was held in place by a brown rope that wove in and around the coops like spaghetti. I couldn't help but feel guilty about the chicken salad sandwich currently residing in my lunch sack but then I remembered I had more important things to think about.

"Choc-o-late cake."

The truck's brake lights suddenly flashed red. The coops rattled against one another as the truck lurched to a stop. A vindictive gust of wind caught the edge of the blue tarp and tore it halfway off the coops. As if heading for certain slaughter wasn't bad enough, the chickens now had to freeze en route. My concern for the birds was suddenly interrupted by another flash of the truck's brake lights.

Then I heard the sound of my cell phone ringing from my purse, which happened to be behind my seat. I reached behind myself, while still trying to pay attention to the road, and felt around for my purse. I only ended up ramming my hand into the cardboard box which held my velvet and brocade gown. The dress had taken me two months to make and was as historically accurate to the gothic period of the middle ages as was possible.

I finally reached my purse and then fingered my cell phone, pulling it out as I noticed Miranda's name on the caller ID.

"Hi," I said.

"I'm just calling to make sure you didn't forget your dress," Miranda said in her high pitch, nasally voice which sounded like a five year old girl with a cold.

"Forget it?" I scoffed, shaking my head at the very idea. "Are you kidding? This is only one of the most important evenings of our lives!" Yes, tonight would mark the night that, if successful, Miranda and I would be allowed to move up the hierarchical chain of our medieval reenactment club. We'd started as lowly peasants and had worked our way up to the merchant class and now we sought to be allowed entrance into the world of the knights.

"Can you imagine us finally being able to enter the class of the knights?" Miranda continued. Even though I obviously couldn't see her, I could just imagine her pushing her coke bottle glasses back up to the bridge of her nose as she gazed longingly at the empire-waisted, fur trimmed gown (also historically accurate!) that I'd made for her birthday present.

"Yeah, instead of burlap, we can wear silk!" I said as I nodded and thought about how expensive it was going to be to costume ourselves if we actually did get admitted into the class of the knights.

"And maybe Albert will finally want to talk to me," Miranda continued, again in that dreamy voice.

I didn't think becoming a knight's lady would make Albert any more likely to talk to Miranda but I didn't say anything. If the truth be told, Albert was far more interested in the knights than he ever was in their ladies.

"Okay, Miranda, I gotta go. I'm almost at work," I said and then heard the beep on the other line which meant someone else was trying to call me. I pulled the phone away from my ear and after quickly glancing at the road, I tried to answer my other call. That was when I heard the sound of brakes screeching.

I felt like I was swimming through the images that met me next—my phone landing on my lap as I dropped it, my hands gripping the wheel until my knuckles turned white, the pull of the car skidding on the slick asphalt, and the tail end of the truck in front of me, up close and personal. I braced myself for the inevitable impact.

Even though I had my seatbelt on, the jolt was immense. I was suddenly thrown forward only to be wrenched backwards again, as if by the invisible hands of some monstrous Titan. Tiny threads of anguish weaved up my spine until they became an aching symphony that spanned the back of my neck.

The sound of my windshield shattering pulled my thoughts from the pain. I opened my right eye—since the left appeared to be sealed shut—to find my face buried against the steering wheel.

I couldn't feel anything. The searing pain in my neck was soon a fading memory and nothing, but the void of numbness reigned over the rest of my body. As if someone had turned on a switch in my ears, a sudden screeching met me like an enemy. The more I listened, the louder it got—a high-pitched wailing. It took me a second to realize it was the horn of my car.

My vision grew cloudy as I focused on the white of the feathers that danced through the air like winter fairies, only to land against the shattered windshield and drown in a deluge of red. Sunlight suddenly filtered through the car until it was so bright, I had to close my good eye.

And then there was nothing at all.

~

"Number three million, seven hundred fifty thousand and forty-five."

I shook my head as I opened my eyes, blinking a few times as the scratchy voice droned in my ears. Not knowing where I was, or what was happening, I glanced around nervously, absorbing the nondescript beige of the walls. Plastic, multicolored chairs littered the room like discarded toys. What seemed like hundreds of people dotted the landscape of chairs in the stadium sized room. Next to me, though, was only an old man. Glancing at me, he frowned. I fixed my attention on the snarly looking employees trapped inside multiple rows of cubicles. Choosing not to focus on them, I honed in on an electric board above me that read: *Number 3,750,045.*

The fluorescent green of the board flashed and twittered as if it had just zapped an unfortunate insect. I shook my head again, hoping to remember how the heck I'd gotten here. My last memory was in my car, driving in the rain as I chatted with Miranda. Then there was that truck with all the chickens. *An accident—I'd gotten into an accident.* After that, my thoughts blurred into each other. But nothing could explain why I was suddenly at the DMV.

Maybe I was dreaming. And it just happened to be the most lucid, real dream I'd ever had and the only time I'd ever realized I was dreaming while dreaming. *Hey, stranger things have happened, right?*

I glanced around again, taking in the low ceiling. There weren't any windows in the dreary room. Instead, posters with vibrant colors decorated the walls, looking like circus banners. The one closest to me read: *Smoking kills.* A picture of a skeleton in cowboy gear, atop an Appaloosa further emphasized the point. Someone had scribbled "ha ha" in the lower corner.

"Three million, seven hundred fifty thousand and forty-five!"

Turning toward the voice, I realized it belonged to an old woman with orange hair, and 1950's style rhinestone glasses on a string. A line of twelve or so porcelain cat statues, playing various instruments, decorated the ledge of her cubicle. What was it about old women and cats?

The cat lady scanned the room, peering over the ridiculous glasses and tapping her outlandishly long, red fingernails against the ledge. Her mouth was so tight, it swallowed her lips. As her narrowed gaze met mine, I flushed and averted my eyes to my lap, where I noticed a white piece of paper clutched in my right hand. I stared at the black numbers before the realization dawned on me.

3,750,045. She was calling my number! Without hesitation, I jumped up.

"That's me!" I announced, feeling embarrassed as the old man glared at me. "Sorry."

"Come on then," the woman interrupted. "I don't have all day."

Approaching her desk, I thought this dream couldn't get much weirder—I mean, I was number three million or something and yet there were only a few hundred people in the room? I handed the woman my ticket. She scowled at me, her scarlet lips so raw and wet that her mouth looked like a piece of talking sushi. She rolled the ticket into a little ball and flung it behind her. It landed squarely in her wastebasket, vanishing amid a sea of other white, scrunched paper balls.

"Name?" she asked as she worked a huge wad of pink gum between her clicking jaws.

"Um, Lily," I said with a pause, feigning interest in a cat playing a violin. It wore an obscene smile and appeared to be dancing, one chubby little leg lifted in the semblance of a jig. I touched the cold statue and ran the pad of my index finger along the ridges of his fur. I was beginning to think this might not be a dream, because I could clearly touch and feel things. But if this weren't a dream, how did I get here? It was like I'd just popped up out of nowhere.

"Last name?"

I faced the woman again. "Um, Harper."

The woman simply nodded, continuing to chomp on her gum like a cow chewing its cud. "Harper… Harper… Harper," she said as she stared at the computer screen in front of her.

"Um, could you, uh, tell me why I'm here?" My voice sounded weak and thin. I had to remind myself that I was the master of my own destiny and needed to act like it. And that was when I remembered my presentation. A feeling of complete panic overwhelmed me as I searched the wall for a clock so I could figure out how much time remained before I was due to sway a panel of mostly unenlightened penny-pinchers on why we needed to invest nearly a quarter of a million in advertising. "What time is it?" I demanded.

"Time?" the woman repeated and then frowned at me. "Not my concern."

I felt my eyebrows knot in the middle as I glanced behind me, wondering if there was a clock to be found anywhere. The blank of the walls was answer enough. I faced forward again, now more nervous than before and still at a complete loss as to where I was or why. "Um, what am I doing here?" I repeated, not meaning to sound so…stupid.

The woman's wrinkled mouth stretched into a smile, which looked even scarier than all the grimaces she'd given me earlier. She turned to the computer and typed something, her talon-like fingernails covering the keyboard with exaggerated flourishes. She hit "enter" and turned the screen to face me.

"You're here because you're dead."

"What?" It was all I could say as I felt the bottom of my stomach give way, my figurative guts spilling all over my feet. "You're joking."

She wasn't laughing though. Instead, she sighed like I was taking up too much of her time. She flicked her computer screen with the long, scarlet fingernail of her index finger. The tap against the screen reverberated through my head like the blade of a dull axe.

"Watch."

With my heart pounding in my chest, I glanced at the screen, and saw what looked like the opening of a low-budget film. Rain spattered the camera lens, making it difficult to decipher the scene beyond. One thing I could make out was the bumper-to-bumper traffic. It appeared to be a traffic cam in real time.

"I don't know what this has to do…"

She chomped louder, her jaw clicking with the effort, sounding like it was mere seconds from breaking. "Just watch it."

I crossed my arms against my chest and stared at the screen again. An old, Chevy truck came rumbling down the freeway, stopping and starting as the traffic dictated. The camera angle panned toward the back of the truck. I recognized the load of chicken coops piled atop one another. Like déjà vu, the camera lens zoomed in on the blue tarp covering the chickens. It was just a matter of time before the wind would yank the tarp up and over the coops, leaving the chickens exposed to the elements.

Realization stirred in my gut like acid reflux. I dropped my arms and leaned closer to the screen, still wishing this was a dream, but somehow knowing it wasn't. The camera was now leaving the rear of the truck and it started panning behind the truck, to a white Volvo S40. *My white Volvo.*

I braced myself against the idea that this could be happening—that I was about to see my car accident. Who the heck was filming? And moreover, where in the heck were they? This looked like it'd been filmed by more than one cameraman, with multiple angles, impossible for just one photographer.

I heard the sound of wheels squealing, knowing only too well what would happen next. I forced my attention back to the strange woman who was now curling her hair around her index finger, making the Cheeto-colored lock look edible.

"So someone videotaped my accident, what does that have to do with why I'm here?" I asked in an unsteady voice, afraid for her answer. "And you should also know that I'm incredibly late to work and I'm due to give a presentation not only to the CEO but also the board of directors."

She shook her head. "You really don't get it, do you?"

"I don't think *you* get it," I snapped as reminded myself more than once that I was the master of my own destiny. The woman grumbled something unintelligible and turned the computer monitor back towards her, then opened a manila file sitting on her desk. She rummaged through the papers until she found what she was looking for and started scanning the sheet, using her fingernail to guide her.

"Ah, no wonder," she said snapping her wad of gum. She sighed as her triangular eyebrows reached for the ceiling. "He is not going to be happy."

I leaned on the counter, wishing I knew what was going on so I could get the heck out of here and on with my life. "No wonder what?"

She shook her head. "Not for me to explain. Gotta get a manager."

Picking up the phone, she punched in an extension, then turned around and spoke in a muffled tone. The fact that I wasn't privy to whatever she was discussing even though it involved me was annoying, to say the least. A few minutes later, she ended her cocooned conversation and pointed to the pastel chairs behind me.

"Have a seat. A manager will be with you in a minute."

"I don't have time for this," I said gruffly, trying to act out a charade of the fact that I *was* the master of my own destiny. "Didn't you hear me? I have to give a presentation!"

"A manager will be with you in a minute," she repeated and then faced her screen again as if to say our conversation was over.

With hollow resignation, I threw my hands up in the air, but returned to the seat I'd hoped to vacate permanently. The plastic felt cold and unwelcoming. It creaked and groaned as if taunting me about my weight. I didn't need a stupid chair to remind me I was fat. I melted into the L-shaped seat and stretched my short legs out before me, trying to relax, and not to cry. I closed my eyes and breathed in for three seconds and out for three seconds.

Lily, stress is nothing more than a socially acceptable form of mental illness, I told myself, quoting one of my favorite self-help gurus, Richard Carlson. *And you aren't mentally ill, are you?*

No, but I might be dead! I railed back at myself. *But if you really were dead, why don't you feel like it?* I reached down to pinch myself, just to check if it would hurt and, what-do-you-know? It did… *So, really, I couldn't be dead.*

And furthermore, if I were dead, where in the heck was I now? I couldn't imagine the DMV existed anywhere near Heaven. If I'd gone South instead... oh jeez...

Don't be ridiculous, Lily Harper! This is nothing more than some sort of bad dream, courtesy of your subconscious because you're nervous about your presentation and your review.

I closed my eyes and willed myself to stop thinking about the what ifs. I wasn't dead. It was a joke or something. Heck, the woman was weird—anyone with musician cat statues couldn't be all there. And once I met with this manager of hers, I'd be sure to express my dissatisfaction. That woman deserved to be fired for freaking me out like this.

You are the master of your own destiny, I told myself again.

I opened my eyes and watched the woman click her fingernails against the keyboard. The sound of a door opening caught my attention and I glanced up to find a very tall, thin man coming toward the orange-haired demon. He glanced at me, then headed toward the woman, who leaned in and whispered something in his ear. His eyes went wide; then his eyebrows knitted in the middle.

It didn't look good.

He nodded three, four times then cleared his throat, ran his hands down his suit jacket and approached me.

"Ms. Harper," he started and I raised my head. "Will you please come with me?"

I stood up and the chair underneath me sighed with relief. I ignored it and followed the man through the maze of cubicles into his office.

"Please have a seat," he said, peering down his long nose at me. He closed the door behind us, and in two brief strides, reached his desk and took a seat.

I didn't say anything, but sat across from him. He reached a long, spindly finger toward his business card holder and produced a white, nondescript card. It read:

Jason Streethorn
Manager
Afterlife Enterprises

"We need to make this quick," I started. "I'm late to work and I have to give a presentation. Can we discuss whatever damages you want to collect from the insurance companies of the other vehicles involved in the accidents over the phone?" I paused for a second as I recalled the accident. "I think I was at fault."

"I see," he said and then sighed.

I didn't know what to say, so I just looked at him dumbly, ramming the sharp corners of the business card into the fleshy part of my index finger until it left a purple indentation in my skin.

The man cleared his throat. He looked like a skeleton.

"Ms. Harper, it seems we're in a bit of a pickle."

"A pickle?"

Jason nodded and diverted his eyes. That's when I knew I wasn't going to like whatever came out of his mouth next. It's never good when people refuse to make eye contact with you.

"Yes, as I learned from my secretary, Hilda, you don't know why you're here."

"Right. And just so you know, Hilda wasn't very helpful," I said purposefully.

"Yes, she preferred I handle this."

"Handle this?" I repeated, my voice cracking. "What's going on?"

He nodded again and then took a deep breath. "Well, you see, Ms. Harper, you died in a car accident this afternoon. But the problem is: you weren't supposed to."

I was quiet for exactly four seconds. "Is this some sort of joke?" I sputtered finally while still trying to regain my composure.

Jason shook his head and glanced at me. "I'm afraid not."

His shoulders slumped as another deep sigh escaped his lips. He seemed defeated, more exhausted than sad. Even though my inner soul was starting to believe him—that didn't mean my intellect was prepared to accept it. Then something occurred to me and I glanced up at him, irritated.

"If I'm going to be on some stupid reality show, and this whole thing is a set-up, you better tell me now because

I've had enough," I said, scouring the small office for some telltale sign of A/V equipment. Or failing that, Ashton Kutcher. "And, furthermore, my boss and the board of directors aren't going to react well at all." I took a deep breath.

"Ms. Harper, I know you're confused, but I assure you, this isn't a joke." He paused and inhaled just as deeply as I just had. "I'm sure this is hard for you to conceptualize. Usually, when it's a person's time to go, their guardian angel walks them through the process and accompanies them toward the light. Sometimes a relative or two might even attend." His voice trailed until the air swallowed it entirely.

Somehow, the last hour of my life, which made no sense, was now making sense. I guess dying was a confusing experience.

He jumped up, as if the proverbial light bulb had gone off over his head. Then, throwing himself back into his chair, he spun around, faced his computer and began to type. Sighing, I glanced around, taking in his office for the first time.

Like the waiting room, there weren't any windows, just white walls without a mark on them. The air was still and although there wasn't anything offensive about the odor, it was stagnant, like it wouldn't know what to do if it met fresh air. The furniture consisted of Jason's desk, his chair and the two chairs across from him, one of which I occupied. All the furniture appeared to be made of cheap pine, like what you'd find at IKEA. Other than the nondescript furniture, there was a computer and beside that, a long, plastic tube about nine inches in diameter, that disappeared into the ceiling. It looked like some sort of suction device.

With a self-satisfied smile, he faced me again. "We have your whole life in our database."

He pointed toward the computer screen. "My whole life in his database" amounted to a word document with a humble blue border and my name scrawled across the top in Monotype Corsiva. It looked like a fifth grader's book report.

He eyed the document and moved his head from right to left with such vigor, he reminded me of a cartoon character eating corn. Then I realized he was scanning through the Lily Harper book report. With an enthusiastic nod, he turned toward me.

"Looks like you lost your first tooth at age six. Um... In school, you were a year younger than everyone else, but smarter than the majority of your class. You double majored in English and Political Science. You were a Director of Marketing for a prestigious bank."

"'Were' is a fitting word because after this, I'm sure I'll be fired," I grumbled.

The man paused, his eyes still on his computer. "When you were eighteen, you had a crush on your best friend and when you tried to kiss him, he pushed you away and told you he was gay."

I stood up so fast, my chair bucked. "Okay, I've heard enough."

The part about Matt rebuffing my kiss was something I'd never told anyone. I'd been too mortified. Guess the Word document was better than I thought.

"It's all there," Jason said as he turned to regard me with something that resembled sympathy.

"I don't understand..." I started.

He nodded, as though satisfied we'd moved beyond the "you're dead" conversation and into the "why you're dead" conversation. He pulled open his top desk drawer and produced a spongy stress ball—the kind you work in your palm. The ball flattened and popped back into shape under the tensile strength of his skeletal fingers.

"I'm afraid your guardian angel wasn't doing his job. This was supposed to be a minor accident—just to teach you not to text and drive, especially in the rain."

"I wasn't texting," I ground out.

Jason shrugged as if whatever I *was* doing was trivial. "Unfortunately, your angel was MIA and now here you are."

I leaned forward, not quite believing my ears. "I have an angel?"

Jason nodded. "Everyone does. Some are just a little better than others."

I shook my head, wondering if there was a limit to how much information my small brain could process before it went on overload. "So, let me understand this, not only do I have a guardian angel, but mine isn't a very good one?"

"That about sums it up. Your angel…" He paused. "His name is Bill, by the way."

"Bill?"

"He's been on probation for… failing to do his duties for you and a few others."

My hands tightened on the arms of my chair as I wondered at what point my non-comprehending brain would simply implode with all this ridiculousness. "Probation?"

He nodded. "Yes, it seems he's had a bit of trouble with alcohol recently."

"My angel is an alcoholic?" I slouched into my chair, the words "angel" and "alcoholic" swimming through the air as I began to doubt my sanity.

"Yes, I'm afraid so."

Jason parted his thin lips, but that exhausted look resurrected itself on his face. I was quick to interrupt, shock and anger suddenly warring within me until I couldn't contain them any longer. "This is the most ridiculous thing I've ever heard! Alcoholic angels? I didn't even know they could drink!"

"They can do everything humans can," he said in an affronted tone, like he was annoyed with my outburst.

I sat back into my chair, not feeling any better with the situation, but also figuring my outbursts were finished for the immediate future. Well, until I could come to terms with what was really going on. But flipping out wasn't going to do me any good. I needed to stay in control of myself and in control of my emotions. Wayne Dyer's words, "it makes no sense to worry about things you have no control over because there's nothing you can do about them," floated through my head as I tried to prepare myself for whatever I had coming.

Jason Streethorn, the office manager of death, folded his hands in his lap and leaned forward. "Since your angel, our employee, failed you, we do have an offer of restitution."

Apparently, this was where the business side of our conversation began. "Restitution?"

"Yes, because this oversight is our fault, I'd like to offer you the chance to live again."

I had to suspend my disbelief of being dead in the first place and just play along with him, figuring at some point I'd wake up and Jason Streethorn, the orange-haired woman and this DMV-like place would be nothing more than the aftermath of a cheese pizza and Coke eaten too close to bedtime. "Okay, that sounds good. What do I…"

He rebuffed me with his raised hand. "However, if you accept this offer, you'll have to be employed by Afterlife Enterprises."

I sank back into my chair, suddenly wanting nothing more than to pull my hair out. I had a sinking feeling I probably wouldn't be able to resume my title of Director. "What does that mean?"

He sighed, as though the explanation would take a while. "Unfortunately, Afterlife Enterprises is a bit on the unorganized side of late. When the computer system switched from 1999 to 2000, we weren't prepared, and a computer glitch resulted in thousands of souls getting misplaced."

The fact that death relied on a computer system which wasn't even as good as Windows XP was too much. "The Y2K bug didn't affect anyone."

Jason worked the stress ball between his emaciated fingers, making multiple knuckles crack, the sound imbedding itself in my psyche. "On Earth, it didn't affect anything, but such was not the case with the Afterlife." He exhaled like he was trying to expel all the air from his lungs. "Unfortunately, we were affected and it's a problem we've been trying to sort out ever since." He paused and shook his head like it was a great, big shame. Then he apparently remembered he had the recently dead to contend with and faced me again. "As I said before, due to this glitch, we've had souls sent to the Kingdom who should've gone to the Underground City. And vice versa." He paused. "And some souls are locked on the earthly plane as well. It's been a big nightmare, to say the least."

My mouth was still hanging open. "The Kingdom and the Underground City? Is that like Heaven and Hell?" Why did I have the sudden feeling he was going to start the Dungeons and Dragons lingo?

"Similar."

I rubbed my tired eyes and let it all sink in. So, not only were there bad dead people in Heaven, aka the Kingdom, but there were good dead people in Hell, aka the Underground City? And to make things even more complicated, there were bad and good dead people stuck on Earth? "Is that still happening now? Or did you fix the computer glitch?" I asked, wondering if maybe I'd been sent to the wrong place. I thought this place seemed like Hell from the get-go. And though I was never a church-goer, I definitely wasn't destined for the South Pole.

"We fixed the glitch, but that doesn't change the fact that there are still thousands of misplaced souls. And the longer those souls who should be in the Kingdom are left in the Underground City, or on the earthly plain, the bigger the chances of lawsuits against Afterlife Enterprises. We've already had a host of them and we can't afford anymore."

I didn't have the wherewithal to contemplate afterlife lawsuits, so I focused on the other details. "So how are you going to get all those people, er souls, back where they belong?"

"That's where you would come in, should you accept this job offer."

"I would bring the spirits back?" I asked, aghast. "I'd be a ghost hunter or something?"

He laughed; it was the first time he seemed warm and, well, alive. Funny what a laugh will do for you.

"Yes, your title would be "Retriever" and we have thousands who, like you, are currently retrieving souls."

An image of the Ghostbusters jumped into my mind and I had to shake it free. Whatever this job entailed, I doubted it included slaying Slimer. "And if I don't agree?"

Jason shrugged and turned to the computer again. After a few clicks, he faced me with a frown. "Looks like you'll be on the waiting list for the Kingdom."

"The waiting list?" I said, shocked. "I think I've led a pretty decent life!"

He shook his head and faced the computer again. "I show three accounts of thievery—when you were six, nine and eleven."

"I was just a kid!"

He cleared his throat and returned his attention to the Word doc. "I also show multiple accounts of cheating when you were in university."

Affronted, I launched myself from the chair. "I've never cheated in my life!"

He frowned, looking anything but amused. "No, but you aided a certain Jordan Summers by giving him the answers in your Biology class and I show that happened over the course of the semester."

I sat back down and folded my arms against my chest. "I would think helping someone wouldn't slate me for a waiting list!"

"Cheating takes more than one form." He glanced at the screen again. "Shall I go on?"

"No." I frowned. "So how long will I be on the waiting list?"

He leaned back in his chair and resumed working the stress ball. "You're fairly close to the top of the list since your offenses are only minor. I'd say about one hundred years."

"One hundred years!" I bit my lip to keep it from quivering. When I felt I could rationally conduct myself again, I faced Jason. "So where would I be for the next one hundred years?"

"In Shade."

I frowned. "And what is that? Like Limbo?"

"Yes, close to it."

"What would I do there?"

He shrugged. "Nothing, really. Shade exists merely as a loading dock for those who are awaiting the Kingdom… or the Underground City."

I didn't like the sound of that. "What's it like?"

"There is neither light nor dark, everything exists in gray. There's nothing good to look forward to, nor anything bad. You just exist."

"But if those people who are going to Hell," I started.

"The Underground City," he corrected me. "Those destined for the Underground are kept separate from those destined for the Kingdom," he finished, answering my question before I even asked it.

I felt tears stinging my eyes. "Shade sounds like my idea of hell."

Jason shook his head while a wry chuckle escaped him. "Oh, no. The Underground City is much worse." He paused. "The good news is that if you do become a Retriever and you relocate ten souls, you can then go directly to the Kingdom and bypass Shade altogether."

"So I wouldn't have to go to Shade at all?"

"As long as you relocate ten souls, you bypass Shade," he repeated, nodding as if to make it obvious that this was the choice I should make.

"What does retrieving these people mean?"

He started rolling the stress ball against his desk. "We'd start you with one assignment, or one soul. With the help of a guide, you'd go after that soul and retrieve it." He paused. "Are you interested?"

I exhaled. Did I want to die and live the next century in Shade? The short answer was no. Did I want to be a soul retriever? Not really, but I guessed it was better than dying.

"Okay, I guess so."

"We could start you out and see how you do. You can always decide not to do it."

"But then I'd die?"

"I'm afraid that's the alternative."

"Why can't you let me go back to my old life?"

He shook his head. "It's not possible. Your soul has already left your body. Once the soul departs, the body goes bad within three seconds. Unfortunately, you are way past your three seconds. That and the coroners have already pronounced you dead and the newspapers are preparing your obituary. Your mother was notified, as well."

Mom has been notified... Something hollow and dreadful stirred in my gut and started climbing up my throat. I gulped it down, hell-bent on not getting hysterical. Tears welled up in my eyes and I furiously batted them away.

"I never got to say goodbye," I managed as I tried to wrack my brain to remember the last conversation I'd had with my mother, the only person (besides Miranda) with whom I was close. Truly, my mother and Miranda were my best friends. And right about now, both of them had to be traumatized.

Jason nodded, but it wasn't a nod that said he was sympathizing. It was a hurried nod. "I'm sorry; but you need to make a decision soon. Time is of the essence and Shade will be calling soon to find out if you're joining them."

I forced my tears aside and focused on his angular face, trying to ignore my grief so I could come to a decision which would completely change the course of my life… or afterlife. "So, if I take this job and choose to live, I can't do so in my own body?"

It wasn't like I was thrilled with my appearance: I was short, overweight and plain. I was the woman who no one ever noticed—the one always behind the scenes. I'd had one major boyfriend in my life and that had lasted all of two months. Yep, anyway I looked at it, I was basically hopeless—a twenty-two year old workaholic virgin with nothing but the redundancy of a stress-inducing job to force me to wake up each morning. But, I was me, and the idea of coming back in another body left me cold. No pun intended.

"You would not be able to come back as yourself," Jason said. "You'd have to come back in another body."

I glanced down at myself. As far as I could tell, I still looked the same. "But, I'm in my body now."

"You're here in spirit only."

The phone on his desk rang and he faced me with impatience etched in his eyes and mouth. "That's probably Shade calling."

He picked up the phone. "Jason Streethorn, Afterlife Enterprises, how can I help you?"   After a few nods, he glanced at me. "Yes, she's here. She's just deciding what she wants to do. Yes, I understand it's been over an hour."

He muffled the end of the phone with his palm and faced me again. "You need to decide now." He faced the phone again. "Yes, I've informed her. You're going to send someone over within the hour?"

"Wait," I said. "Tell them I'll take the job. I want to live."

Available Now!

Also Available From HP Mallory:

Turn the page for chapter one!

ONE

It's not every day you see a ghost.

On this particular day, I'd been minding my own business, tidying up the shop for the night while listening to *Girls Just Wanna Have Fun* (guilty as charged). It was late—maybe 9:00 p.m. A light bulb had burnt out in my tarot reading room a few days ago, and I still hadn't changed it. I have a tendency to overlook the menial details of life. Now, a small red bulb fought against the otherwise pitch darkness of the room, lending it a certain macabre feel.

In search of a replacement bulb, I attempted to sort through my "if it doesn't have a home, put it in here" box when I heard the front door open. Odd—I could've sworn I'd locked it.

"We're closed," I yelled.

I didn't hear the door closing, so I put Cyndi Lauper on mute and strolled out to inquire. The streetlamps reflected through the shop windows, the glare so intense, I had to remind myself they were just lights and not some alien spacecraft come to whisk me away.

The room was empty.

Considering the possibility that someone might be hiding, I swallowed the dread climbing up my throat. Glancing around, I searched for something to protect myself with in case said breaker-and-enterer decided to attack. My eyes rested on a solitary broom standing in the corner of the Spartan room. The broom was maybe two steps from me. That might not sound like much, but my fear had me by the ankles and wouldn't let go.

Jolie, get the damned broom.

Thank God for that little internal voice of sensibility that always seems to visit at just the right time.

Freeing my feet from the fear tar, I grabbed the broom and neared my desk. It was a good place for someone to hide—well, really, the only place to hide. When it comes to furnishings, I'm a minimalist.

I jammed the broom under the desk and swept vigorously.

Nothing. The hairs on my neck stood to attention as a shiver of unease coursed through me. I couldn't shake the feeling and after deciding no one was in the room, I persuaded myself it must've been kids. But kids or not, I would've heard the door close.

I didn't discard the broom.

Like a breath from the arctic, a chill crept up the back of my neck.

I glanced up and there he was, floating a foot or so above me. Stunned, I took a step back, my heart beating like a frantic bird in a small cage.

"Holy crap."

The ghost drifted toward me until he and I were eye level. My mind was such a muddle, I wasn't sure if I wanted to run or bat at him with the broom. Fear cemented me in place, and I did neither, just stood gaping at him.

Thinking the Mexican standoff couldn't last forever, I replayed every fact I'd ever learned about ghosts: they have unfinished business, they're stuck on a different plane of existence, they're here to tell us something, and most importantly, they're just energy.

Energy couldn't hurt me.

My heartbeat started regulating, and I returned my gaze to the ectoplasm before me. There was no emotion on his face; he just watched me as if waiting for me to come to my senses.

"Hello," I said, thinking how stupid I sounded—treating him like every Tom, Dick, or Harry who ventured through my door. Then I felt stupid that I felt stupid—what was wrong with greeting a ghost? Even the dead deserve standard propriety.

He wavered a bit, as if someone had turned a blow dryer on him, but didn't say anything. He was young, maybe in his twenties. His double-breasted suit looked like it was right out of *The Untouchables*, from the 1930s if I had to guess.

His hair was on the blond side, sort of an ash blond. It was hard to tell because he was standing, er floating, in front of a wooden door that showed through him. Wooden door or not, his face was broad and he had a crooked nose—maybe it'd been broken in a fight. He was a good-looking ghost as ghosts go.

"Can you speak?" I asked, still in disbelief that I was attempting to converse with the dead. Well, I'd never thought I could, and I guess the day had come to prove me wrong. Still he said nothing, so I decided to continue my line of questioning.

"Do you have a message from someone?"

He shook his head. "No."

His voice sounded like someone talking underwater.

Hmm. Well, I imagined he wasn't here to get his future told—seeing as how he didn't have a future. Maybe he was passing through? Going toward the light? Come to haunt my shop?

"Are you on your way somewhere?" I had so many questions for this spirit but didn't know where to start, so all the stupid ones came out first.

"I was sent here," he managed, and in his ghostly way, I think he smiled. Yeah, not a bad looking ghost.

"Who sent you?" It seemed the logical thing to ask.

He said nothing and like that, vanished, leaving me to wonder if I'd had something bad to eat at lunch.

Indigestion can be a bitch.

~

"So no more encounters?" Christa, my best friend and only employee, asked while leaning against the desk in our front office.

I shook my head and pooled into a chair by the door. "Maybe if you hadn't left early to go on your date, I wouldn't have had a visit at all."

"Well, one of us needs to be dating," she said, knowing full well I hadn't had any dates for the past six months. An image of my last date fell into my head like a bomb. Let's just say I'd never try the Internet dating route again. It wasn't that the guy had been bad looking—he'd looked like his photo, but what I hadn't been betting on was that he'd get wasted and proceed to tell me how he was separated from his wife and had three kids. Not even divorced! Yeah, that hadn't been on his *match.com* profile.

"Let's not get into this again …"

"Jolie, you need to get out. You're almost thirty …"

"Two years from it, thank you very much."

"Whatever … you're going to end up old and alone. You're way too pretty, and you have such a great personality, you can't end up like that. Don't let one bad date ruin it." Her voice reached a crescendo. Christa has a tendency towards the dramatic.

"I've had a string of bad dates, Chris." I didn't know what else to say—I was terminally single. It came down to the fact that I'd rather spend time with my cat or Christa rather than face another stream of losers.

As for being attractive, Christa insisted I was pretty, but I wasn't convinced. It's one thing when your best friend says you're pretty, but it's entirely different when a man says it.

And I couldn't remember the last time a man had said it.

I caught my reflection in the glass of the desk and studied myself while Christa rambled on about all the reasons I should be dating. I supposed my face was pleasant enough—a pert nose, cornflower blue eyes and plump lips. A spattering of freckles across the bridge of my nose interrupts an otherwise pale landscape of skin, and my shoulder length blond hair always finds itself drawn into a ponytail.

Head-turning doubtful, girl-next-door probable.

As for Christa, she doesn't look like me at all. For one thing, she's pretty tall and leggy, about five-eight, and four inches taller than I am. She has dark hair the color of mahogany, green eyes, and pinkish cheeks. She's classically pretty—like cameo pretty. She's rail skinny and has no boobs. I have a tendency to gain weight if I eat too much, I have a definite butt, and the twins are pretty ample as well.

Maybe that made me sound like I'm fat—I'm not fat, but I could stand to lose five pounds.

"Are you even listening to me?" Christa asked.

Shaking my head, I entered the reading room, thinking I'd left my glasses there.

I heard the door open.

"Well, hello to you," Christa said in a high-pitched, sickening-sweet and non-Christa voice.

"Afternoon." The deep timbre of his voice echoed through the room, my ears mistaking his baritone for music.

"I'm here for a reading, but I don't have an appointment ..."

"Oh, that's cool," Christa interrupted and from the saccharin tone of her voice, it was pretty apparent this guy had to be eye candy.

Giving up on finding my reading glasses, I headed out in order to introduce myself to our stranger. Upon seeing him, I couldn't contain the gasp that escaped my throat. It wasn't his Greek God, Sean-Connery-would-be-envious good looks that grabbed me first or his considerable height.

It was his aura.

I've been able to see auras since before I can remember, but I'd never seen anything like his. It radiated out of him as if it had a life of its own and the color! Usually auras are pinkish or violet in healthy people, yellowish or orange in those unhealthy. His was the most vibrant blue I've ever seen—the color of the sky after a storm when the sun's rays bask everything in glory.

It emanated out of him like electricity.

"Hi, I'm Jolie," I said, remembering myself.

"How do you do?" And to make me drool even more than I already was, he had an accent, a British one. Ergh.

I glanced at Christa as I invited him into the reading room. Her mouth dropped open like a fish.

My sentiments exactly.

His navy blue sweater stretched to its capacity while attempting to span a pair of broad shoulders and a wide chest. The broad shoulders and spacious chest in question tapered to a trim waist and finished in a finale of long legs. The white shirt peeking from underneath his sweater contrasted against his tanned complexion and made me consider my own fair skin with dismay.

The stillness of the room did nothing to allay my nerves. I took a seat, shuffled the tarot cards, and handed him the deck. "Please choose five cards and lay them face up on the table."

He took a seat across from me, stretching his legs and rested his hands on his thighs. I chanced a look at him and took in his chocolate hair and darker eyes. His face was angular, and his Roman nose lent him a certain Paul Newman-esque quality. The beginnings of shadow did nothing to hide the definite cleft in his strong chin.

He didn't take the cards and instead, just smiled, revealing pearly whites and a set of grade A dimples.

"You did come for a reading?" I asked.

He nodded and covered my hand with his own. What felt like lightning ricocheted up my arm, and I swear my heart stopped for a second. The lone red bulb blinked a few times then continued to grow brighter until I thought it might explode. My gaze moved from his hand, up his arm and settled on his dark brown eyes. With the red light reflecting against him, he looked like the devil come to barter for my soul.

"I came for a reading, yes, but not with the cards. I'd like you to read … me." His rumbling baritone was hypnotic, and I fought the need to pull my hand from his warm grip.

I set the stack of cards aside, focusing on him again. I was so nervous I doubted if any of my visions would come. They were about as reliable as the weather anchors you see on TV.

After several long uncomfortable moments, I gave up. "I can't read you, I'm sorry," I said, my voice breaking. I shifted the eucalyptus-scented incense I'd lit to the farthest corner of the table, and waved my hands in front of my face, dispersing the smoke that seemed intent on wafting directly into my eyes. It swirled and danced in the air, as if indifferent to the fact that I couldn't help this stranger.

He removed his hand but stayed seated. I thought he'd leave, but he made no motion to do anything of the sort.

"Take your time."

Take my time? I was a nervous wreck and had no visions whatsoever. I just wanted this handsome stranger to leave, so my habitual life could return to normal.

But it appeared that was not in the cards.

The silence pounded against the walls, echoing the pulse of blood in my veins. Still, my companion said nothing. I'd had enough. "I don't know what to tell you."

He smiled again. "What do you see when you look at me?"

Adonis.

No, I couldn't say that. Maybe he'd like to hear about his aura? I didn't have any other cards up my sleeve ... "I can see your aura," I almost whispered, fearing his ridicule.

His brows drew together. "What does it look like?"

"It isn't like anyone's I've ever seen before. It's bright blue, and it flares out of you … almost like electricity."

His smile disappeared, and he leaned forward. "Can you see everyone's auras?"

The incense dared to assault my eyes again, so I put it out and dumped it in the trashcan.

"Yes. Most people have much fainter glows to them—more often than not in the pink or orange family. I've never seen blue."

He chewed on that for a moment. "What do you suppose it is you're looking at—someone's soul?"

I shook my head. "I don't know. I do know, though, if someone's ailing, I can see it. Their aura goes a bit yellow." He nodded, and I added, "You're healthy."

He laughed, and I felt silly for saying it. He stood up, his imposing height making me feel all of three inches tall. Not enjoying the feel of him staring down at me, I stood and watched him pull out his wallet. I guess he'd heard enough and thought I was full of it. He set a one hundred dollar bill on the table in front of me. My hourly rate was fifty dollars, and we'd been maybe twenty minutes.

"I'd like to come see you for the next three Tuesdays at 4:00 p.m. Please don't schedule anyone after me. I'll compensate you for the entire afternoon."

I was shocked—what in the world would he want to come back for?

"Jolie, it was a pleasure meeting you, and I look forward to our next session." He turned to walk out of the room when I remembered myself.

"Wait, what name should I put in the appointment book?"

He turned and faced me. "Rand."

Then he walked out of the shop.

~

By the time Tuesday rolled around, I hadn't had much of a busy week. No more visits from ghosts, spirits, or whatever the PC term is for them. I'd had a few walk-ins, but that was about it. It was strange. October in Los Angeles was normally a busy time.

"Ten minutes to four," Christa said with a smile, leaning against the front desk and looking up from a stack of photos—her latest bout into photography.

"I wonder if he'll come," I mumbled.

Taking the top four photos off the stack, she arranged them against the desk as if they were puzzle pieces. I walked up behind her, only too pleased to find an outlet for my anxiety, my nerves skittish with the pending arrival of one very handsome man.

The photo in the middle caught my attention first. It was a landscape of the Malibu coastline, the intense blue of the ocean mirrored by the sky and interrupted only by the green of the hillside.

"Wow, that's a great one, Chris." I picked the photo up. "Can you frame it? I'd love to hang it in the store."

"Sure." She nodded and continued inspecting her photos, as if trying to find a fault in the angle or maybe the subject. Christa had aspirations of being a photographer and she had the eye for it. I admired her artistic ability—I, myself, hadn't been in line when God was handing out creativity.

She glanced at the clock again. "Five minutes to four."

I shrugged, feigning an indifference I didn't feel. "I'm just glad you're here. Rand strikes me as weird. Something's off ..."

She laughed. "Oh, Jules, you don't trust your own mother."

I snorted at the comment and collapsed into the chair behind her, propping my feet on the corner of our mesh waste bin. So I didn't trust people—I think I had a better understanding of the human condition than most people did. That reminded me, I hadn't called my mom in at least a week. Note to self: be a better daughter.

The cuckoo clock on the wall announced it was 4:00 p.m. with a tinny rendition of Edelweiss while the two resident wooden figures did a polka. I'd never much liked the clock, but Christa wouldn't let me get rid of it.

The door opened, and I jumped to my feet, my heart jack hammering. I wasn't sure why I was so flustered, but as soon as I met the heat of Rand's dark eyes, it all made sense. He was here again even though I couldn't tell him anything important last time, and did I fail to mention he was gorgeous? His looks were enough to play with any girl's heartstrings.

"Good afternoon," he said, giving me a brisk nod.

He was dressed in black—black slacks, black collared shirt, and a black suit jacket. He looked like he'd just come from a funeral, but somehow I didn't think such was the case.

"Hi, Rand," Christa said, her gaze raking his statuesque body.

"How has your day been?" he answered as his eyes rested on me.

"Sorta slow," Christa responded before I could. He didn't even turn to notice her, and she frowned, obviously miffed. I smiled to myself and headed for the reading room, Rand on my heels.

I closed the door, and by the time I turned around, he'd already seated himself at the table. As I took my seat across from him, a heady scent of something unfamiliar hit me. It had notes of mint and cinnamon or maybe cardamom. The foreign scent was so captivating, I fought to refocus my attention.

"You fixed the light," he said with a smirk. "Much better."

I nodded and focused on my lap. "I didn't get a chance last time to ask you why you wanted to come back." I figured it was best to get it out in the open. I didn't think I'd do any better reading him this time.

"Well, I'm here for the same reason anyone else is."

I lifted my gaze and watched him lean back in the chair. He regarded me with amusement—raised eyebrows and a slight smirk pulling at his full lips.

I shook my head. "You aren't interested in a card reading, and I couldn't tell you anything … substantial in our last meeting …"

His throaty chuckle interrupted me. "You aren't much of a businesswoman, Jolie; it sounds like you're trying to get rid of me and my cold, hard cash."

Enough was enough. I'm not the type of person to beat around the bush, and he owed me an explanation. "So are you here to get a date with Christa?" I forced my gaze to hold his. He seemed taken aback, cocking his head while his shoulders bounced with surprise.

"Lovely though you both are, I'm afraid my visit leans more toward business than pleasure."

"I don't understand." I hoped my cheeks weren't as red as I imagined them. I guess I deserved it for being so bold.

He leaned forward, and I pulled back. "All in good time. Now, why don't you try to read me again?"

I motioned for his hands—sometimes touching the person in question helps generate my visions. As it had last time, his touch sent a jolt of electricity through me, and I had to fight not to lose my composure. There was something odd about this man.

I closed my eyes and exhaled, trying to focus while millions of bees warred with each other in my stomach. After driving my thoughts from all the questions I had regarding Rand, I was more comfortable.

At first nothing came.

I opened my eyes to find Rand staring at me. Just as I closed them again, a vision came—one that was piecemeal and none too clear.

"A man," I said, and my voice sounded like a foghorn in the quiet room. "He has dark hair and blue eyes, and there's something different about him. I can't quite pinpoint it … it seems he's hired you for something …"

My voice started to trail as the vision grew blurry. I tried to weave through the images, but they were too inconsistent. Once I got a hold of one, it wafted out of my grasp, and another indistinct one took its place.

"Go on," Rand prodded.

The vision was gone at this point, but I was still receiving emotional feedback. Sometimes I'll just get a vision and other times a vision with feelings. "The job's dangerous. I don't think you should take it."

And just like that, the feeling disappeared. I knew it was all I was going to get and I was frustrated, as it hadn't been my best work. Most of the time my feelings and visions are much clearer, but these were more like fragments— almost like short dream vignettes you can't interpret.

I let go of Rand's hands, and my own felt cold. I put them in my lap, hoping to warm them up again, but somehow my warmth didn't quite compare to his.

Rand seemed to be weighing what I'd told him—he strummed his fingers against his chin and chewed on his lip. "Can you tell me more about this man?"

"I couldn't see him in comparison to anyone else, so as far as height goes, I don't know. Dark hair and blue eyes, the hair was a little bit longish, maybe not a stylish haircut. He's white with no facial hair. That's about all I could see. He had something otherworldly about him. Maybe he was a psychic? I'm not sure."

"Dark hair and blue eyes you say?"

"Yes. He's a handsome man. I feel as if he's very old though he looked young. Maybe in his early thirties." I shrugged. "Sometimes my visions don't make much sense." Hey, I was just the middleman. It was up to him to interpret the message.

"You like the tall, dark, and handsome types then?"

Taken aback, I didn't know how to respond. "He had a nice face."

"You aren't receiving anything else?"

I shook my head. "I'm afraid not."

He stood. "Very good. I'm content with our meeting today. Do you have me scheduled for next week?"

I nodded and stood. The silence in the room pounded against me, and I fought to find something to say, but Rand beat me to it.

"Jolie, you need to have more confidence."

The closeness of the comment irritated me—who was this man who thought he could waltz into my shop and tell me I needed more confidence? Granted, he had a point, but damn it all if I were to tell him that!

Now, I was even more embarrassed, and I'm sure my face was the color of a bad sunburn. "I don't think you're here to discuss me."

"As a matter of fact, that's precisely the reason I'm …"

Rand didn't get a chance to finish when Christa came bounding through the door.

Christa hasn't quite grasped the whole customer service thing.

"Sorry to interrupt, but there was a car accident right outside the shop! This one car totally just plowed into the other one. I think everyone's alright, but how crazy is that?"

My attention found Rand's as Christa continued to describe the accident in minute detail. I couldn't help but wonder what he'd been about to say. It had sounded like he was here to discuss me … something that settled in my stomach like a big rock.

When Christa finished her accident report, Rand made his way to the door. I was on the verge of demanding he finish what he'd been about to say, but I couldn't summon the nerve.

"Cheers," he said and walked out.

AVAILABLE NOW!

H. P. Mallory is the author of the Jolie Wilkins series as well as the Dulcie O'Neil series.

She began her writing career as a self-published author and after reaching a tremendous amount of success, decided to become a traditionally published author and hasn't looked back since.

H. P. Mallory lives in Southern California with her husband and son, where she is at work on her next book.

If you are interested in receiving emails when she releases new books, please sign up for her email distribution list by visiting her website and clicking the "contact" tab:

www.hpmallory.com

Be sure to join HP's online Facebook community where you will find pictures of the characters from both series and lots of other fun stuff including an online book club!

Facebook: https://www.facebook.com/hpmallory

Find H.P. Mallory Online:

www.hpmallory.com

http://twitter.com/hpmallory

https://www.facebook.com/hpmallory

THE JOLIE WILKINS SERIES:

Fire Burn and Cauldron Bubble
Toil and Trouble
Be Witched (Novella)
Witchful Thinking
The Witch Is Back
Something Witchy This Way Comes

Stay Tuned for the Jolie Wilkins Spinoff Series!

THE DULCIE O'NEIL SERIES:

To Kill A Warlock
A Tale Of Two Goblins
Great Hexpectations
Wuthering Frights
Malice In Wonderland
For Whom The Spell Tolls

THE LILY HARPER SERIES:

Better Off Dead

CPSIA information can be obtained at www.ICGtesting.com
Printed in the USA
LVOW01s2246170814

399617LV00009B/75/P